The Archivists

The Archivists

Stories

Daphne Kalotay

TriQuarterly Books / Northwestern University Press

Evanston, Illinois

Northwestern University Press
www.nupress.northwestern.edu

This is a work of fiction. Names, characters, places, and incidents either are the
product of the author's imagination or are used fictitiously, and any resemblance
to actual persons, living or dead, business establishments, events, or locales is
entirely coincidental.

Printed in the United States of America

10   9   8   7   6   5   4   3   2   1

ISBN 978-0-8101-4608-2 (paper)
ISBN 978-0-8101-4609-9 (ebook)

Cataloging-in-Publication Data are available from the Library of Congress.

For Julie Rold

Was it a vision, or a waking dream?
Fled is that music: —Do I wake or sleep?

—John Keats

Contents

Relativity

According to the notes in her file, Rozsa Fischer, aged ninety-nine, of 124 Babcock Street, was dying. Her heart and kidneys were on the verge of failure, not to mention the raw sore on her foot, from one of those new antibiotic-resistant infections. Yet hospice had trundled her home and abandoned her, after she insisted she wanted no more to do with them.

Robert, who had overseen Rozsa Fischer's case for the past four years, sat uneasily beside the hospital-issued bed. "We provide a contract lawyer free of charge," he explained, part of the dour conversation that was among his duties. He would also, again, be coordinating Rozsa Fischer's remaining doctor's visits, food delivery, hygiene services, and the aides who came to run errands and see that she took her pills—though the doctor, a fellow by the name of Turley, hadn't seemed particularly insistent about the pills.

"For any legal documents you may need," Robert continued, though it felt wrong to him, now. "Our services include—"

"Bring me the grocery flyer."

Rozsa Fischer's voice, with its sharply trilled *r*'s, sounded to Robert as strong as ever. Though instructed to perform only tasks within his purview, he found the Sunday *Globe* where the weekend aide had tossed it and searched for the slippery pages of the Star Market circular. Bright images of sliced cantaloupe, grilled salmon, water-spritzed green grapes. He handed the insert to Rozsa Fischer.

Slowly—so slowly—she pointed a long forefinger. In the past year, her bones seemed to have lengthened, flattened. Her chest was concave, her knobby shoulders and elbows like the joints of a marionette. "Melon is on special. If they look good, buy two."

Robert tried not to squirm on the hard wooden chair. "I'm sure your afternoon aide will be happy to—"

"Also some ground beef. Eighty percent okay, nothing leaner."

"Mrs. Fischer, I've restarted Meals on Wheels for you." He had done so despite her habit of preserving certain dishes, sometimes for weeks, to display on his monthly visits in order to prove their unappetizing nature.

"Two dollars for grapefruit—is *criminal!*"

"Please, Mrs. Fischer! Dr. Turley says your heart—"

"Robert." Rozsa Fischer lay back and let the pages rest atop the knit blanket. "Dr. Turley is very nice, but he is not so smart."

Robert hoped no reaction showed on his face. Dr. Turley was the agency's go-to doctor because he made house calls. That appeared to be his main talent.

"I want to tell you something, Robert." Rozsa Fischer looked surprisingly regal for someone propped in a mechanized bed. Her hair was gray and only slightly thinned, her milky eyes alert. "I see that your wife is not feeding you."

Normally he would have laughed. It was true he had lost weight in the months since the baby was born. "I appreciate your concern, Mrs. Fischer, but I'm here today to discuss your—plans. We provide a lawyer and other services—"

"I have done my will, thank you."

"Ah, good." There was also the matter of the funeral, outstanding bills, and whom she would want contacted at her death; Robert had been trained to discuss these preparations. Indeed, he had navigated such conversations many times over the past years, proceeding calmly, point by point, through the brochure the agency provided. Now, though, the very notion of such planning seemed to him obscene.

He placed the brochure—*Timely Decisions*—on the bedside table, within her reach. "You might find this helpful. Why don't I come again on Friday, when you've had time to read it?"

Not that it had ever seemed to him right to discuss death as a simple business matter. Some clients responded with affront. Others, like Rozsa Fischer, appeared generally unfazed. Perhaps at such a great age, death no longer frightened. Or perhaps, when you have survived Auschwitz, Buchenwald, and the surgical replacement of two hips, death seems something you might cheat indefinitely.

*

Outside, it had begun to rain. Thick, icy drops; April in New England. The trolley, packed to capacity, was rounding Packard's Corner, wheels slowly screeching against the tracks. Robert could see the students pressed up against the windows, staring impassively at their cellphones. He took out his phone to check on Katie but when her voicemail answered, hung up.

He tucked his scarf into the collar of his coat and tried to avoid the cold puddles of grit and dirt. This stretch of Commonwealth Avenue was always gray. In the window of the chicken wings takeout place, a handwritten sign advertised HOT JOB OPPORTUNITIES.

He had stopped telling people, when asked about his work, precisely whom his organization aided. "Senior services," he made a point of saying, after years of the same jokes. *You do realize pretty soon you're gonna be out of a job, right?*

It was true that in the past year, the number of "expired" clients had doubled. Back when he applied for the position, the year he received his MSW, he did not yet know that one-fifth of the world's

Holocaust survivors lived in the United States. Among the benefits Robert's clients received were home visits, transportation services, psychological counseling, and a $3,000 restitution payment from the German government. Nearly $80 billion paid out since 1952. And yet, among the many survivors residing outside Germany, fifty thousand had yet to submit a claim.

Of course, doing so meant exhuming the past, in order to prove having been interned in a ghetto, or deported to a camp, or hidden from the Nazis for at least six months. Still, the restitution money continued to bring survivors out of the woodwork. Such as Abe Linder, Robert's next case of the day, Survivor Services' youngest client. Seventy-six years old.

A retired mathematician, Abe lived just over in Brighton. He was not really Jewish, he always made a point of reminding Robert, though the papers in his file told otherwise. In the accent of a Transylvanian count, he would explain, "I am Swiss."

That said, he wanted his three grand, plus the twenty hours per week of home care. Stick it to the Germans, as he put it. He seemed to really like that it was the German government ponying up the money. He disliked Germans as much as he disliked Jews.

Robert (half-Jewish, non-practicing) felt it was not his place to judge. Abe was certainly not the first client to hold special contempt for anything related to the cataclysm that had shaped his life. According to his file, Abe had spent over a year hidden with seven other Jewish children in the crawl space of a physics laboratory somewhere in Poland. In his twenties he had emigrated to Zurich, married, and raised a daughter who in turn wed an American and brought Abe over when his wife died. Now, the daughter had divorced and joined a commune in New Mexico. Abe was again on his own.

He lived on the first floor of a big brown-shingled house off Washington Street. The door knocker was a lion's head holding an iron ring in its mouth. Inside, the apartment smelled of curry from the unseen kitchen of a family on the second floor. Robert joined his client at the heavy wooden desk laden with obsolete things: a leather desk blotter with wide sheets of paper tucked into its corners, a neat round pencil sharpener and white rectangular eraser, a Rolodex thick with yellowing note cards. With Abe at his side, Robert set to filling out the paperwork that would bring in the money from the Germans.

Abe was all business, not the sort to prolong visits. No idle chit-chat or stories of long ago. Other clients fell into reminiscence at a mere turn of phrase. So many stories! Robert filed them away in his mind like grizzly fairy tales.

Magda Blum at the Danube: *They lined us up along the river. I was at the end of the line. The officer across from me was young, and I had always been pretty. He looked left and right and moved his head, like "Go." He was letting me leave! He did not shoot when I walked away. But I could hear the shots at the others.*

Hans Aaldenberg on Liberation Day: *So we went to see what the trouble was, where was our soup? But the guards were no longer there—they had run away!*

Yvette Klinger's baby: *I was starving when my son was born. I had no milk, I could not feed him. I ground some beans and gave him that. His stomach was in such pain, I thought I would die.*

That was always where Yvette Klinger started crying. No matter that she had been dead two years now: even if he chose to, Robert would not know how to discard her memories. Or the others. Scraps of history that, frankly, served mainly to slow things down for the aides trying to get to their next clients. Hans Aaldenberg would stand, one foot on the ottoman, clear his throat, and in a booming voice launch into a reminiscence like a professor at a lectern, while the aides shifted uncomfortably and stole glances at their cellphones. Magda Blum had once talked at the rep from Blue Cross Blue Shield for forty-five minutes. Neither Robert nor the rep dared interrupt her.

Not that Robert faulted them for these interludes. Often such recollections were unavoidable, potholes along any path of conversation. One could not help but slip into them.

There were those who used their dark histories combatively, lobbed like grenades at any perceived slight. Some even ranked their woes competitively: *She* was never in a *camp*—I was in a *camp*. Or, *So she was in a camp—I was sent away and never saw my parents again*. Or, *He still has his brother—my entire family was murdered!* The indifferent lumping together of so many tragedies became yet another offense.

Until three months ago, Robert had found these rankings merely curious. He had not understood the need to search for order and reason in things that would never make sense.

As for clients like Rozsa Fischer, who never mentioned their past trials, Robert used to believe there was dignity in silence. Now he was not so sure. Why should it be any less noble to cry out at the world for having been cruel to you? Robert's clients had lost their families, their childhoods, their treasures. Some had lost their names.

Just a number, they would say, and show him the tattoo on their forearm. Or, *I used to be a Baum, but we changed it to Bolgar*. Even when they did not tell him, Robert saw their documents. Stern had become Sterling. Blau had become Bonner. Kohn had become Kalotai.

"I do not know why it says that," Abe Linder said now, of the consonant-laden name on his restitution documents. "It is incorrect. I am Swiss."

*

"We must give her a name," Katie had said on their second day at Mass General. In her arms she held their daughter, a tiny being with a perfect face—sweet mouth, tiny ears, nose, even minuscule nostrils that flared with each breath.

6

A name. For months they had collected favorites on a notepad on the fridge, like some whimsical grocery list. It had become a game. Fanciful ones: Moxie, Bebe. Old-fashioned: Delia, Mavis. Sleek power broker: Sloane, Blake. But this tiny creature, what name would not overwhelm her? What name would not seem a cruel joke?

Still, they would have to name her. It had been explained to them why.

None of the names on their list would do; Robert knew Katie felt the same way. Perhaps it was the New Englander in him that conjured a new list: those prim, humorless abstract nouns the Puritans invoked to steel children against hardship. *Patience. Honor. Prudence.* He wondered if he dared suggest them to Katie, or if that would just upset her more.

It seemed an impossible task. But they had to come up with something. You could not bury a child in Massachusetts without a name.

*

His last case of the day, Emma Mueller, was eighty-nine years old. She lived with her husband in Roslindale in a house where all the doors squeaked. Her memory was failing; according to the aides, she had taken to addressing them in her native tongue. Her husband insisted all was well, but that was common. Robert had arranged for an assessment.

The specialist was to have arrived fifteen minutes ago. Waiting with his client, Robert sipped hot tea and listened to the windows jitter at each breeze. When the husband opened the side door to let the dog out, Emma Mueller called out, her words rushed, hissing under her breath. Though she spoke in German, Robert—hired in part because of his rudimentary skills in that language— understood. He would have to tell the specialist.

He told Katie that night, while they ate the microwaved palak paneer from Trader Joe's. They used to make two packages at once, but tonight they shared one between them and drank frothy beer from glass mugs Robert had chilled in the freezer. "She was warning him that if he wasn't careful, they might catch him. The SS."

Katie shook her head. "As if once wasn't enough."

"She started sweating and shaking. I think she thought I was one, too. I didn't know how to reassure her. Luckily the psychologist showed up."

"Yeah, to interrogate her!" Katie gave a small, sad laugh.

It was good to see her laugh. Even just to talk this way, casually, about people other than themselves. Each day it seemed they were inching back toward the couple they had been.

They had agreed not to shut the episode away like some shameful tragedy. Sometimes, asked if he had children, Robert took a moment to explain—and then felt bad to have thrust his story on some unsuspecting innocent. Often he would simply give a small shake of the head. Friends and acquaintances, when they learned what had happened, said things that never seemed to him quite right: that surely it was a blessing for a child not to lead a severely compromised life; that she was an angel in Heaven now; that she would never know life's disappointments.

The thawing beer mug, no longer frosty, had a goofy insignia on the side, from an Oktoberfest celebration that now seemed, like so many things, somehow ridiculous—residue from some naïve, frivolous former life. Robert said, "What if we took a trip? Even just a long weekend, somewhere warm, Bermuda, the Bahamas." He had been wanting to suggest it but worried it might sound flippant. Also his salary wasn't enough for anything lavish. But he wanted—needed—to do something to mark a break between the past and their future.

Katie took his hand in hers. She was the one who liked beach vacations; Robert tended to become restless. "So you can get sunburned and antsy?" She squeezed his hand. "Thanks, bub. I'll think about it."

*

She had done everything the books and websites said—drank protein shakes, swam three times a week. Robert had watched her practice the prescribed breathing exercises; she even listened to music said to be nourishing for a developing fetus. Everything seemed to be going fine, and nothing strange had shown up in the tests. She was young enough that after five months they stopped doing tests altogether. But when she went into labor (a full two months early, yet even that had seemed feasible), the tiny being to whom she gave birth weighed just four pounds and had no hands or feet—nor, they soon discovered, sufficiently developed vital organs.

In an age of digital readings, of blood analysis and ultrasounds, the surprise of it was the part that no one, when Robert later confessed the news, seemed able to believe. As if it were some craziness on Robert and Katie's part that had prevented any clue from revealing itself. But the doctors assured them it was no one's fault. Whatever had gone wrong had happened after those ultrasounds and exams. They could not have known, nothing to be done. Their daughter simply did not possess what was necessary to survive.

And yet they would have to wait five days, it turned out, for her to stop trying.

*

When, on Friday, Robert returned to see Rozsa Fischer, he was alarmed to find her upright and out of bed, leaning on her four-wheeled walker. Her head bobbed on the thin, loose-skinned neck, her marionette limbs lanky and strange as she persisted toward him. The scent of something roasting wafted from the kitchen.

9

Robert hung his coat on the wooden rack and eyed Rozsa Fischer's swollen, bandaged foot wedged into its terry-cloth slipper. Dr. Turley had said more than once that if the infection did not subside, they would have to amputate.

"Did the nurse say you could stand on that leg?"

"These nurses of yours. Each one fatter than the next."

There was even some color in her cheeks. Now that he was closer, Robert also noted—with curiosity more than concern—that the precancerous mole they had made sure to have surgically removed was already growing back.

Rozsa Fischer said, "I have baked you a meatloaf."

"Mrs. Fischer—"

"I did not even take the ibuprofen today, Robert. I woke up and was not in pain. I thought, Wow, maybe they are right and I am dead."

She certainly did seem in better form than in the past few months, perhaps even the past year. An odd moment, Robert supposed, to bring up *Timely Decisions*.

"Robert." With her wheelie walker, Rozsa Fischer was making her slow progress toward the drawing room. "You must *eat*."

That was when the doorbell rang. Rozsa Fischer's eyes opened wide. "I must hurry." She began the slow, awkward trek down the hall.

"Would you like me to answer that?"

She was heading doggedly for the bedroom and did not reply.

The bell rang again. "One minute," Robert called out. But he took his time returning to the foyer. Dr. Turley had already let himself in and was replacing the key in the lockbox.

"Robert, hello!" Dr. Turley strolled over to shake his hand. Quick strong pump-pump. He was exceedingly fit and not balding at all, which always made Robert feel inferior.

Robert said, "I was just about to leave, actually."

From the bedroom, Rozsa Fischer called, "Take your meatloaf!"

Dr. Turley raised his eyebrows and in a booming stage voice said, "Is that you, young lady?" He was already slipping past Robert, calling out pleasantries.

Robert headed to the kitchen, where the meatloaf, wrapped in aluminum foil, sat atop the stove. She must have taken it out just before he arrived. How had she managed it? The aide had to have helped her. In Robert's hands the loaf was warm and yielding.

He could hear Dr. Turley—jocular, loud—as he returned to the hall. Robert poked his head into the bedroom, to thank Rozsa Fischer and let her know that he was leaving.

"Now, listen, young lady," Dr. Turley was saying, as Robert caught Rozsa Fischer's eye and waved the meatloaf, "you'd better follow your doctor's orders!"

Robert left quickly. If he stayed, he might say something rude.

*

The doctor at the hospital had worn her hair in a thick gray braid. Her face showed no emotion when, explaining the path their daughter's life would take, she said quietly, "I'm so sorry."

That was on the first day, in the room where Katie was still recovering. The doctor sounded sincere enough, though her poise, or perhaps it was New England manners, allowed her to appear unmoved. It was the hospital chaplain, a fellow who looked much too young for the job, whom Robert still thought of sometimes.

They had not asked for him. They were sitting silently, watching their daughter sleep. It was the fourth day, their hundredth hour at her side. The doctors were baffled that it could take this long. When the chaplain stopped at the door to inquire if he might be of help—lightly, in a relaxed tone that made him sound like he might be from California—Katie had surprised Robert by nodding.

She said, "Come see our daughter."

They still had not named her. It was too morbid, too futile a task. Although in his head Robert added to his list (Amity, Faith, Mercy), no name seemed right.

The chaplain looked to be in his late twenties, with an unlined face and a shaggy haircut that curled at the tips. Robert sensed an air of leisure about him, as if he had just come in from a round of volleyball. Probably it was his faith that gave him that untroubled look. Robert could not help but envy such people, envy their conviction, which he did not share and could not draw on to render this disaster somehow meaningful. He had glimpsed that certitude on a visit he and Katie had made, early in their romance, to Emily Dickinson's house, had never forgotten the simple words on her tombstone: CALLED BACK.

Like a sign on an office door: called away on urgent business. What a reassuring sense of self, of industry, of necessity. In that room in the hospital, Robert felt a surge of something close to jealousy as the chaplain approached their sleeping daughter. He looked so young and unruffled, divinely armored against death's whimsy.

The chaplain stood easily over the bassinet and gazed down at her—their imperfect child with the perfect face.

The chaplain's face did something then. A small twitch. Not of alarm; more like surprise. Perhaps even amazement. What had he expected? Not this tiny slumbering thing. He looked at her and it seemed he was no longer simply performing a ritual, nor the automatic motions of his day, but seeing, taking in, their child.

Then the chaplain began to blink—an effort, Robert realized, not to cry. Robert watched him pressing his lips together as if to stop his mouth from quivering. Even when he had regained his composure, the chaplain looked somehow bewildered.

He turned to them, then, and said in a tone of astonishment, "She's like a little jewel."

12

When Robert thought about those days in the hospital, this was the moment he often arrived at. This stranger's appreciation of their child and of their private calamity. For those few moments, this other person held some portion of their grief.

*

Over the next weeks, the weather improved, the sun warming the car during case visits. Robert realized he had been dreading the change of season. The short winter days had left less time to get through, the gray puddles of snow matching his mood. Now, there was sunshine and the palpable relief of an entire city having made it through the final throes of winter.

After a visit to Hans Aaldenberg one bright afternoon, Robert stepped outside to find Coolidge Corner bustling, a nip of a breeze in the air. The trolley rang its little bell and shoved slowly ahead.

Rozsa Fischer lived not far from here. Robert pictured the *Timely Decisions* brochure on the table by her bed. Though Dr. Turley maintained she ought to have died by now, Robert had heard no such news. Her street, Babcock, was on the way to his last visit of the day.

At her building, he removed his cap and typed her number into the intercom. He waited a long time for her to answer. Hearing her voice, thick and slow, he felt guilty to have woken her.

"No, you come up—I want to see you."

Robert took the stairs rather than the elevator, to allow her more time. He opened the key box and let himself into the apartment. The foyer was quiet as he removed his jacket and called out, "It's me."

"Come here." Her voice came from the bedroom. She lay atop the bedcovers, wearing a yellow sweater, gray pants, and one white sock. The other, infected, foot was greatly swollen and wrapped in gauze, propped on a thickly folded blanket. At the opposite side of the bed stood the nurse's cart with its cotton swabs, bandages, iodine, and a big bottle of Cipro.

Rozsa Fischer frowned at him. "Sit down." She spoke as if a wad of cloth were caught beneath her tongue. "The nurse tells me you are going on holiday."

"Indeed I am." Robert eyed her swollen foot. "That looks painful."

"You go somewhere warm?"

"Bahamas, five days. Has Dr. Turley seen that foot?"

"Robert, I want to tell you something." Rozsa Fischer reached slowly for her mug of water. The afternoon aide was known for leaving full glasses of water on every possible surface so that one was always within reach. Robert watched Rozsa Fischer drink, a simple act that took much effort. Very slowly she placed the mug back down. She began to speak.

"In the camp we were very hungry. I had sores all over my body. One day, an onion rolled off a cart. Before I could pick it up, another girl grabbed it. She, too, was starving; she could have eaten one hundred onions. But Robert, she shared it with me. And the sores on my body, they *healed*."

She seemed to wince.

"Mrs. Fischer, are you in pain?"

"Do you see, Robert, why you must eat?"

Robert searched her face to see if this were an explanation or a simple declaration, that a person could heal. Or did she mean this story for *him?* He supposed some other "provider" might have mentioned something to her. Told her what had happened with the baby. Or perhaps she had simply noticed that he had lost weight.

Robert looked at her mug of water, at the nurse's cart laden with supplies. His pulse, he realized, was racing. He heard himself speak. "Four and a half months ago, our daughter was born. She was very ill. They told us she wouldn't survive. But it took five days."

14

At the end of those five days he had felt an exhaustion unlike any he had known. Not just his heart but his face, his bones, even the backs of his eyes, ached. Yet with each day spent in that room at the hospital, something else had been happening, growing. A sense of himself as a father and of that tiny creature as his daughter.

Rozsa Fischer said, "I am sorry for you, Robert."

He immediately felt ashamed. For having wrenched out his pain and laid it before a dying woman. But something kept him standing there beside the bed, kneading his cap in his hands.

He felt his face turning hot. "Her name was Ruby."

Sometimes when he found Katie crying, and held her, and whispered useless sentiments, he would think this name to himself, how it seemed to have been handed to them, and the warm way it held their child inside it. That for much of that fourth day, and all of the fifth, their child had been Ruby, alive. And that even borne away from life, she remained Ruby, missed and longed for. Sometimes, that helped.

"Ruby." Rozsa Fischer gave a heavy nod. "Beautiful."

Robert watched the heavy head, the marionette shoulders. He wondered if he would see her again, or if he would return from vacation to find another name checked off his list, added to that other column of names, the public ones and the secret, private ones he had been allowed to know.

He said, "I didn't mean to talk about myself. I just thought I'd check in on you. I should be leaving now."

"Me too, Robert." A slow, nearly silent laugh. But she was still here.

Heart-Scalded

Twilight's hazy glow, the world covered in gray lint. Viv hailed a ride and set out toward the crumbling edge of town.

Though it was nearly November, leaves still clung to branches, some in the blazing colors of life, most a parched brown. Odd how warm it is, her driver said, as they rose over the bridge that just months ago she would have crossed on her bike. A cluster of figures slipped toward them along the walkway, dressed strangely, like characters in a play. She turned to look but they were already past.

Fun plans for the evening? her driver asked. The streetlamps weren't yet lit, and the fading sky looked thick enough to touch.

I'm going to a pig roast.

Parties at Len's always began early and went into the wee hours. Viv told herself she was just stopping by, didn't have to stay long, though she'd taken time on her makeup—smoky eyeliner, and a thin feathery pencil for her brows. She had even considered false lashes, since they seemed to be in fashion even for women in their thirties like her. Slid silver hoops through her earlobes, draped her favorite twisty cotton scarf around her neck, found her silver cuff bracelet and pushed it up to her bicep like a sort of amulet.

It's here on the right, she said. A house like a wilting wedding cake, where Len rented rooms to a few former grad school friends who, like him, had yet to convert to more standard arrangements. She thanked her driver and stepped out into the gloaming.

Voices wafted from the backyard, where winking orange bulbs dipped along the fence and the pig smoldered in its box. The company called it *a Chinese box*, Len had told her, while Viv held back any commentary on corporate opportunism or Len's naiveté, tried not to be so *Viv*; no one liked being forced to see the truth. A dozen or so thirty-somethings looked vaguely her way. There was something odd about them, or maybe it was just her nerves.

Hey, stranger! Len came to envelop her in one of his hugs. He was wearing a chain-mail getup, like a knight in armor. His embrace was awkward.

Viv didn't find it odd that he was wearing chain mail; Len ordered a new limited-edition LEGO set each year and still liked to play dress-up. The orange bulbs reflected in the lenses of his glasses. On-off, on-off. He said, I love your look. You've got the heroin chic thing *down*.

She laughed, though she'd used bronzer and lip tint, had even purchased a sparkly body cream. Probably she should pull her sweatshirt on. She was wearing loose crepe pants because they were the baggiest she had, with a silvery tee shirt and black canvas sneakers with the anklet she still wore even though it was from Aziz and she had rid herself of most things he had given her. The anklet had a small silver starfish that had once seemed to her to be good luck. The past two years had not caused her to remove it.

Around her, the air was sticky, smoky. She said, How long until you think it's ready?

Should be done about now. Can I get you a drink?

I'll get it, she said, already searching warily, though Aziz often arrived later to these things. A head taller than most, he was usually easy to spot. She wondered if he would look the same or if, like Len, he would have gone thicker in the face.

At a table crowded with bottles and stacked plastic cups and a bowl of melting ice cubes, she poured herself a lukewarm soda water, squeezed a tight wedge of lime. Up close she saw the fence was covered in a thin fuzz of the vivid green mold-like moss that had overtaken everything after a summer of too much rain. Despite its dire warning, a stunning color. Even in the dusk, it glowed, bright with rejuvenation. A few times, she had tried mixing her paints to match it, but always ended up with neon yellow.

Hullo, said a frowning man plucking a can of beer from the plastic cooler. Cyrus, he said. I work with Len.

Their parent corporation had been caught falsifying data concerning waste disposal at their factories, Viv knew from texting with Len the other night. Len said he just had to pay off his student loans and then could look for a new job.

I'm Viv. The bubbles in her glass sped upward, exploding at the surface.

Cyrus moved to take a sip of beer but had to pull down a long white beard strapped to his chin. Viv realized he was in costume, too—some sort of wizard. She said, Is this a costume party?

He laughed. A Halloween party!

But—Halloween isn't until—

Wednesday!

Oh! She had lost track of time. Except for her friend Laurel, who worked in New York but still hadn't fully moved there, she had mainly spent these past months alone in her apartment, painting watercolors when she wasn't woozy, or watching movies sideways on the sofa. The institute where she wrote educational pamphlets and other communications had hired a freelancer to cover the hours she missed.

Not big on Halloween, eh? Do you know anyone here?

She nodded. She used to come here all the time when she and Aziz were together. I actually met you before, she said. I came with Len to a Christmas party a couple of years ago, up in Prudential Center.

He looked at her more closely. Ah, right, you're the artist. You've cut your hair.

She said, I remember you telling me how your wife used to be a competitive ice skater.

The man shook his head mournfully, his artificial beard swaying from his neck. He said, Viv, I have the worst marriage in Massachusetts.

He had an explanation for what had gone wrong, something to do with his wife being a descendant of *Mayflower* Pilgrims. Viv glanced up when she could, to see if Aziz had arrived.

She had been warned that the fiancée would be with him. Though Viv had known about her for a year already, it mattered to have to see her for the first time. Just as it had mattered when, after Len broke the news, he had added, perhaps thinking it would make her feel better, *She's not as pretty as you.* That was when Viv's heart shredded to bits, because it meant the fiancée was real. That even if Viv could have her old prettiness back, it wouldn't matter, because Aziz loved someone else now.

They had taken the pig from the Chinese box and laid it out on the picnic table. A few vegetarians appeared briefly repulsed.

Will you look at that, the man said. A mosquito. In October. He flicked it from the back of his hand.

Perhaps sensing she was toxic, the insect avoided her. The man said, The apocalypse really is coming, if mosquitos are out this late.

But she could tell from the way he said it that he didn't believe it.

Viv! It was Joe and Jerry, Aziz's and Len's soccer friends. They were at least a decade older but never missed Len's parties. She wasn't sure if they were in costume or not. Joe liked to cross-dress and tonight wore a slender black dress awink with sequins, while Jerry wore a dark suit over a white shirt. Viv began to make introductions, but everyone had already met.

Viv, Joe said, I was just saying to Jerry the other day—I swear—I wondered what ever happened with that garden plot you'd been on the waitlist for forever—

I got it.

She got it! What are you growing? You always had such a green thumb with Aziz's poor dejected plants . . .

It was true she had resuscitated the houseplants Aziz's mother had bought to brighten the affectless bachelor pad, with Viv feeding and pruning them until some even needed to be repotted. After Viv moved in, an entire wall of the apartment became jungle-like, plants practically climbing out of their pots, the air in the apartment fresh, moist.

Well, she said, this wasn't the best growing season, actually, with so much rain.

Of course, of course. God, I mean, look at this thing. Joe gestured toward the cement planter beside him, which held the stubby remains of a bare, clearly dead plant. Or maybe he meant the cement tub itself. It was covered in a light fuzz of that alarmingly bright green moss that seemed to be growing on so much else, giving an eerie glow to the decorative pattern embossed on the planter: a circle of figures dancing. Perhaps because the original cement mold was cheap, the figures' faces were blank. The thing somehow struck Viv as sinister.

Exactly, she said, rather than add that there had been stretches where she could not make it to her plot at all. She saw the way everyone was looking at her, realizing. As if to compensate, Jerry said, Your hair looks fantastic!

Viv wished she hadn't left her sweatshirt on the folding chair by the picnic table. People were tearing into the pig now, stripping off

20

the meat and piling it onto big oval platters. Yearning to hide, Viv lowered her gaze. There was the cement planter, the neon fuzz. It really was eerie, the way the faceless dancers glowed beneath those spores or lichen or whatever that green fuzz was, while inside the planter lay nothing but the finality of death. Desperate, trying to think of some diversion, she said, Are you in costume?

We're that Bryan Ferry video, the one with the models! At Viv's reaction, Jerry turned to Joe. I told you they're too young to know it.

She saw them then. Aziz and the fiancée. They must have just arrived, because Aziz was carrying a six-pack of the hard cider he liked. He and the fiancée were dressed as Daddy Warbucks and Little Orphan Annie. Even as a joke, it still seemed to Viv repulsive; everyone knew Aziz had sold out to Len's corporation and now had a corner office in Kendall Square. Len said it was one of those new constructions, sky-high, with lunch ordered in daily, delivered by unseen couriers at a back entryway.

Just seeing them made her feel briefly dizzy. She had to remove her scarf. Jerry said, Come on, let's eat!

Along with the oval platters of meat, there were broad aluminum trays of sticky yellow cornbread and dusty buttermilk biscuits, vats of barbecue sauce and gravy, of coleslaw and gooey baked beans. Viv scooped clumps of the food onto a paper plate. It was tricky because she was trying to keep her arms folded, to hide the bruises where the nurse struggled to insert the tube into her veins. For a long time now the nurses, beleaguered, had been urging her to get a port.

Well look who's here. A warm hand touched her arm.

Oh—hi, Aziz. She let herself be kissed on the cheek, Aziz bending down to her. His lips were warm.

Cute haircut! Annoyingly handsome in his crisp black suit and bow tie, Aziz did not look very disturbed to see her transformed. Len had probably told him what to expect. Hey, meet Stacy.

21

So good to meet you, Viv, I've heard so much about you! She seemed genuinely pleased. As much as Viv wanted to appear composed, she had to place her plate down. The fiancée shook her hand, her palm—like Aziz's—much warmer than Viv's. And Viv felt herself smiling, heard herself speaking, thought, *I am chatting with Aziz's fiancée,* and later on, when the air had cooled and she had found her sweatshirt, as they sat in chairs around the woodstove on the patio and ate from the paper plates on their laps, *I like Aziz's fiancée, she's pleasant.*

The drugs made the food taste strange. The compostable utensils seemed to be decomposing in her hands. She wondered if it was the toxins, glanced around her to see if others were having trouble. Len was at least right that the fiancée wasn't as pretty as Viv. Well, how could she be, in an orange Orphan Annie wig.

Aziz told Viv she looked fetching with her eyes all circled in black like a raccoon.

That wasn't the look I was going for, Slim, but thanks. The humidity must have smudged her makeup. She used her paper napkin to dab the skin below her eyes, secretly grateful for Aziz's teasing, as if nothing had changed.

You called him Slim, Stacy said.

Oh—I call him that sometimes.

It gave Viv a small pleasure to know this was something Aziz hadn't shared, that he also would have kept to himself his pet name for Viv. Sometimes she ached to hear him call her Beep again.

Hmm, now I've smeared it. I'll be back. Viv stood to make her way to the bathroom, passing a woman dressed in scrubs, with gloves, protective goggles, and elastic booties, like a nurse in a toxic emergency. Or maybe that really was her job, and she had simply worn her work clothes as her costume.

There was a line for the bathroom. Viv leaned against the wall, unzipped her sweatshirt. She had avoided these gatherings for a long time, but Len must have known that telling her the fiancée would be here would dare her to come. And, he had added, I miss you.

He was the only one among them to whom she still spoke. Gave updates. But she knew he told the others. There were emails from a mutual acquaintance who practiced acupuncture, enclosing a diet she suggested Viv follow, along with a mantra: *You can choose bliss!* Though Viv never responded, the messages continued to arrive in her inbox.

She listened to the conversation ahead of her, whispers about Len's corporation and its ties to one of the candidates in next year's election.

Elections don't matter—

What do you mean, don't you vote?

No, I don't vote! The voice sounded offended. But the bathroom door had opened, and the speaker disappeared inside. The interlocutor turned in bafflement to Viv. Can you believe it?

It was one of Len's renters, or former renters. Viv tried to recall her name. She was dressed, it seemed, as a sexy witch, an excuse, Viv supposed, to wear—along with the pointy black hat and green face paint—fishnet stockings, thigh-high boots, and nothing across her midriff, which (this Viv *did* remember) she had always spent a lot of time on at Pilates classes. She said, Viv, wow, hi! I love your hair!

It wasn't *her* hair, but it was true it looked better than her real hair ever had. Same bronze color, but short and flirty, with a little curl at the ends. The witch said, It looks *French.*

Her face paint was not the usual witch green, more like the color of the worrisome mold outside. Viv asked if she still lived in the house.

I moved to Atlanta for work, can you believe it? I'm just here for the weekend, I have to go to a memorial service tomorrow. She shrugged. I still have that drawing you did, of the blue jay. I love it.

Viv said, I like the color of your face paint.

Thanks—it was actually a darker green, but I use this serum and it made it turn this color. Oh, my turn. The bathroom was free again.

Viv waited, voices reverberating off the walls.

. . . teaches this like adult ed class it's called Time for Terrariums and like people actually take it.

We made a pact, next year we'll go to the DR if this year he comes with me to Iceland.

Len said she has some rare kind of cancer, there's no real treatment, they just try whatever until it stops working, then try something else . . .

Viv tried not to listen. Tried not to think of Stacy in her red dress with the white collar. The costume said it all, Viv supposed. Deep down Aziz must have longed for someone like that, who could be ironic and fully participate in the rituals of the masses. Unlike Viv, who on the night they met had bonded with him over having grown up in the suburbs without any sense of fitting in. As much as Aziz said he liked how Viv looked at the world askance, clearly what he had needed was a Stacy.

Stacy wouldn't chide him for taking start-up money from a developer who opposed the bill to stop illegal fishing off the Cape. Wouldn't dare ask if *smart* technology was always necessarily *smart* (knowing full well his company was based on the premise). Wouldn't have set off their worst fight by calling his approach to business *remorseless*.

How you holding up? It was a mutual friend of Viv and Aziz, dressed as Mary Poppins. For a moment it seemed she knew how hard it had been for Viv to come here tonight, to see Stacy in the flesh, and to be seen herself, looking like this.

The truth was, in order to come here, Viv had actually allowed herself to think of the party as perversely restorative: a trial-by-fire cure. Because if she could live through this—seeing Aziz and his fiancée together, and all the while being witnessed, by everyone else, seeing them—then surely she could survive anything.

I'm fine, how about you? She said it by rote.

Mary Poppins said, I didn't realize Stacy was pregnant. I'm always the last to hear these things. Still, I imagine it kind of sucks.

The floor dropped from under Viv's feet. Viv looked for the bathroom door to open, managed to stammer something. Oh, yeah, well. She thought of the gentle confidence she had noted in Stacy, reassessing it as a pleased smugness.

Thank god, here was the witch. Viv escaped into the bathroom, leaned against the sink. In the mirror, her face shocked her. She didn't look ugly. But with the dark eyeliner and circles of fatigue, she looked skinny and strung out.

Stupid, stupid.

There was a phrase Laurel had taught her, back when Viv and Aziz first split up and Viv, alone in the attic studio she had found, felt a despair she hadn't known possible. When each night her thoughts followed the same looping circle—that as much as Aziz had loved her, she had not been what he thought he wanted, that she should never have expressed the thoughts that had hurt him. When her mother, trying to be helpful, said, *It's not the end of the world.*

You're heart-scalded, Laurel had explained. A term from the British side of her family. An anguished, active grief. Viv's dictionary said it meant *tormented by bitter disappointment, sorrow, or remorse.*

Not just grief at the loss, but the ongoing torment of her regret. The sense that if she could have been different, could have tamped down her horror at human obduracy, Aziz would have loved her as she had loved him: wholly, unstintingly, enough to have endured.

She went to use the toilet, telling herself not to dwell on what she had just heard. What did it matter. She would be gone, she already knew, before any baby arrived.

Someone knocked on the bathroom door.

Be right out! Viv flushed her toxic pee into the sewers. Washed her hands. Did not look in the mirror. Time to leave. There was nothing left for her here.

*

She was still making her way through the narrow echoing hallway when someone stopped her. Like Viv, he did not appear to be in costume, just dark jeans, black tee shirt, and sneakers. And while he seemed to know Viv, she could not quite remember him. How are you feeling? he asked, and the pity in his voice made her want to slug him.

He swallowed his swig of beer, not waiting for a response, said, Seeing her with him, must be hard. Aziz doesn't deserve her *or* you. That guy just gets things handed to him.

It wasn't true. Aziz had worked late every night to get his company going. Plus lunches and dinners with investors who made him feel that all he did was beg, a nonstop cycle of schmoozing. He had even confessed to Viv that he couldn't stand a good half of those guys, whom he suspected wouldn't deign to speak to him if they didn't think he was worth something to them. And now that he had partnered with Len's corporation, he was basically trapped.

Anyway, I put a spell on him for you.

Viv would have raised her eyebrows if she had any. What's that supposed to mean?

A curse. On Aziz.

Um, that was actually unnecessary. I don't harbor any ill will toward Aziz. In fact—

Sure you don't. He gave a closemouthed smile.

No, really—

But the guy tilted his head and said, Be honest with yourself, Viv. It's okay to want it.

But she didn't want it. At least, she didn't think so. Whenever she glimpsed the starfish anklet around her bony ankle, she still thought of how Aziz had noticed her admiring it in the shop at Wellfleet and gone back for it while she was napping on the beach. He called her Beep from early in their relationship, when he came out dancing with her, which he had pretended to enjoy, but Viv could tell he didn't like bumping up against other sweaty bodies. She kept trying to carve out a space for just the two of them, to discreetly elbow away all the others. *Beep beep!* he had said when he noticed what she was doing, to which she had countered, *Mister open-source communal tech guy needs his personal patch of dance floor!* And he had danced with her until late, because he saw she was happy.

God, I was awful, she thought now. Shaking her head, she asked this guy who so clearly envied Aziz, What do you know about spells?

I took a class! Looking insulted, he added, I've been practicing.

In that case, how about a cure, huh? Instead of a curse?

An interesting premise, he said. If you had a choice of being cured but no longer having Aziz in your life, versus no cure but getting Aziz back, which would you choose?

Well that's a ridiculous question. Obviously—

Is it really?

She nearly added that it was obnoxious, too. Instead, she just said, Look, I don't need your help.

But he just winked and said, It's already taken care of.

Viv did not thank him. I've got to go now, bye. She looked around the room as if someone were waiting to escort her out. There was the *You can choose bliss* woman, in some sort of superhero attire. Viv quickly turned toward the kitchen, to make a beeline out the back door.

*

Outside, the woodstove spat sparks at the circle of guests in chairs, still digging into their soggy plates of food. On the ground around them were half-empty bottles of alcohol. The pig carcass lay on the picnic table. Viv meant to slip away—she would text Len tomorrow to thank him—but someone tapped her arm.

Have you seen Aziz?

It was Stacy. She had removed the orange wig, exposing a short hairdo not unlike Viv's: pixie bangs and little commas in front of her ears. She said, I can't find him anywhere.

Hi, no, I haven't seen him. He must have gone to use one of the upstairs bathrooms.

I already asked . . . Frustration showed on her face, but she went over to try someone else. Viv heard Len's voice sifting through an upstairs window, Aziz, hey, you up here?

She was glad people were huddled around the woodstove, that they wouldn't see her slinking away and not helping to look for Aziz. Starting down the slate path, she reached up to loop her scarf.

It took a moment to remember where she had discarded it. Back at the drinks table, there were now just empty bottles and used plastic cups. Ah, there was the scarf, under the winking orange lights. She snatched it up, relieved to have remembered.

A sound startled her. She felt herself tense; she knew there were rats around. There it was again. A kitten? Not quite a squeak, not quite a mew. A small, weak sound.

She moved nearer to the winking lights and heard it again, the muffled sound of some tiny being. Less a cry than a hum. The sound seemed to be coming from within the cheap cement planter.

She bent to examine it—difficult with just the light from the porch. But she must have frightened the tiny creature. There was only silence. The porchlight illuminated the side of the planter, so that even in the dark, Viv noticed something in the raised pattern. One dancer whose shape did not match the others.

Taller and thinner. The pattern of the cement mold must have been cut off halfway. Viv took out her phone to turn on the flashlight, shone it on the pattern. Unlike the other dancers, covered in mossy green, this figure had a face.

A nose protruded from the cement, creases where the corners of lips met. And the edge of an eye. Viv touched the lips—quickly drew back her hand. The lips were warm.

She hurried away, out to the street. Did not linger to hire a car. She had stayed too late; her scalp prickled hot with sweat. Removing the wig, she decided to walk the three blocks to the bus stop. She would call a car there, or just take the bus.

With each footfall on the cracked pavement, the thought became clearer. That sound she had heard. It had sounded an awful lot like *Beep*.

Just one more hypersensitivity. A side effect, like the thrush and the fevers and nausea—some hearing mirage, with warping of vision. He was on her mind, after all. That must be why she had heard it.

Felt that heat burn her fingertips.

But such things simply weren't possible.

She thought of Aziz's choices. The perpetual dance he had entered into, caught in his devil's bargain each day simply by going to work. Wasn't any so-called curse one he had brought on himself? Well, who hadn't, really, so many daily pacts and *just this onces*. Little excuses on the collective march toward the end of the world—even if no one seemed to realize it.

The other week she had heard a conversation not meant for her. As she sat in the chair with the tube in her arm, behind the curtain that separated her from the man who had come to take his seat in the next bay, an oncologist, with the aid of a social worker, told the man that his time on earth had come to an end—the treatment was no longer working, there were no more remedies, it was time to go

29

home and plan for the "next step." Something about the young doctor's voice made it absolutely clear that she had never once paused to contemplate her own mortality. And though Viv knew from other overheard conversations that the man had been sick for years, it was evident even through the curtain that only now did he understand that all this was to end. His voice shook awfully when he asked the social worker how to best break the news to his children.

At the bus stop, under the streetlamp, Viv took a seat on the bench to wait. She wondered if Stacy had found Aziz yet. A few meters away, two punk-looking kids, or maybe addicts, skinny in their worn-out hoodies, turned to observe her. They seemed about to approach her, maybe thinking her one of them: a lanky teen with her head shaved and needle marks in her arm. But after a moment they seemed to see more clearly and turned away.

Awake

He had lived in that town for over a year when he decided, on a July morning thick with the chant of cicadas, to take care of an errand he had put off for too long.

All winter and throughout the spring he hadn't ventured farther than the Price Chopper or Agway, spending much of each day feeding logs to the woodstove in the house he rented. An instructor of online writing courses, he had plenty of time at home. Now he got the pickup going and rolled the windows open to the cicadas' ruckus. Shake-shake-shake, a million tiny maracas. To get to the highway (two lanes, view of the Catskill Mountains) he would take the bypass, avoiding Main Street with its decrepit brick storefronts and sagging Victorians and the rowdy, luckless bunch who hung around the bus stop not because they were going anywhere but because there was a bench to sit on.

It was a town of three restaurants, an ice cream stand, and a jail. Houses with neon yellow For Sale signs that meant the bank owned them. The movie theater, with its big white marquee, had seemed promising, until Peter understood that it hadn't opened its doors in years.

Other once-grand towns along the Hudson had sprouted a café here, a Pilates studio there. He had seen their lights and banners on the other side of the river, where the train from New York deposited exiles like himself, people with degrees from art departments, film schools, music programs—diplomas no one bothered to frame, because no diploma could change the fact of having to move to a place like this to survive.

Over there, near the station, where buildings were bought cheap and spruced up, and weekend visitors browsed antiques and bought éclairs at Manhattan prices, you could tell yourself you were a mere two-hour trip from the city, that this was just a stop along a continuum. Convince yourself you, too, were on your way out of a slump. But on Peter's side, west of the river, the buildings were smaller and sadder. The For Sale signs slowly faded until a storm or vandals knocked them down.

It had been Andrea's idea to move here. She was a copy editor, in her late thirties like Peter. When he met her, he was teaching at three different schools and had been working on a novel for probably too long. Briefly they shared a diminutive apartment in Fort Greene, with plants that seemed to bloom at Andrea's touch. And then a married couple Andrea knew bought a house online for $12,000. Property owners! Landed gentry! Lots of creative types were trickling in, ones who couldn't afford the other, resuscitated riverbank and instead crossed the bridge to come here.

A bridge named after a fairy tale. "Rip Van Winkle" made the place sound quaint, enchanted. "We're pioneers!" Andrea said. But it was hard to feel like a pioneer when the natives were right there, jobless, sitting on a busted front porch, or hanging around the creek in the center of town, shouting at a boyfriend in front of little kids who probably should have been at school. Then came the brutal winter, during which Andrea decided she was not in love, nor a pioneer, and moved to San Francisco.

She was tired of making decisions for both of them. Didn't he see that life was passing him by?

It was true he often felt time slipped past him. There were those alarming Christmas cards from friends whose infants appeared to have been replaced, overnight, by prepubescent children, and the online acquaintances who posted photographs of weddings and honeymoons when it seemed mere seconds, at most minutes, since they had announced having just met someone, or divorced.

"You're passive," was how Andrea put it. But wasn't patience a virtue? Peter was used to waiting. He sent work to literary journals and waited forever to hear back. For over a year one of his stories had been slated for a glossy monthly people actually *read*—but it kept being held back until the next issue.

His friend Dez said he wasn't passive; he was depressed. To which Peter said: Well, who *isn't?*

Now, he told himself he didn't need either of them and steered the pickup past rolling hills and farmland. Here was the turn, onto the seasonally treacherous dirt road where a traffic sign warned travelers not to attempt passage between December and April. Up he drove, to the crest of a hill thick with ancient trees, where a wooden board on a post read DON'S SEW-N-VAC.

Don's was a one-man operation, with a host of near-obsolete services. Don could fix your radio, your camera, and the leather on your armchair. A large, wheezy fellow with fingernails permanently caked in black. Peter had never met anyone that hairy.

The trees throbbed with a rattling so intense, it was deafening. Stepping from the truck, Peter crushed more of those cicada carapaces that had been littering the ground all over town. Apparently these were the thirteen-year kind. Thirteen years buried underground, feeding on the sap of tree roots, and then mere weeks in the treetops to court, mate, and live out their destiny.

Thirteen years ago Peter's life hadn't been so different from now. He just weighed less and wasn't yet disabused of the notion that the world wanted what he had to offer.

A frantic barking started up, and a tiny furious dog came scrambling at him, growling, seemingly unaware of having only three legs. The dog snapped at Peter's jeans, and now Don lumbered out of the slumped barn that housed his business. "That's right, Eleanor, you show him who's in charge."

Peter swatted lightly at Eleanor and said he had come to pick up his chair.

"That's enough, Eleanor." Don scooped up Eleanor and tossed her aside. He was sweating in the heat, the dark hairs of his forearms glistening. Peter reached out to shake his hand, an attempt to make himself welcome. Don professed a great, loud disdain for city transplants like Peter, just as he did for the indigenous unfortunates all along this corridor of the Hudson: the dropouts, the meth addicts, the pregnant teens. Don hated the white ones, the black ones, and their tea-colored babies, too. He had made sure to let Peter know—but by then Peter had relinquished the chair and it seemed too late to boycott the business.

"A teak armchair," he reminded Don now. "Mid-century modern? The back needed caning."

He had spotted it on the street last autumn in front of one of the foreclosed houses. Beat up, the wicker back torn, the wood tacky with grime—but a classic Danish-modern design. A rare hopefulness had coursed through him. He and Andrea schlepped the chair home, where he scrubbed it clean, the suds turning an opaque gray, and then used some foul-smelling, noxious liquid to remove what was left of the varnish before sanding, first with low-grit paper, for the nicks and scratches, and then gradually higher, with a super-fine garnet sandpaper for final smoothing. Andrea said he was using the chair as a distraction, to avoid real work. But to Peter the chair was proof of possibility, of transformation. Carefully he chose the shade of stain and a pricey natural bristle brush for the application. Two coats, with drying time in between, and then two more of varnish. Just the caning needed to be replaced.

"Waited for you to come pick it up. Ain't heard from you. Sold it."

"Sold it!"

"Had my handiwork, and no one to claim it." Don wiped his thick hands on the canvas apron covered with stains. Even the pads of his fingertips sprouted dark hairs. Like an ogre living on the outskirts of town in a little stone house—Peter could see it from here—built into a slope of hill.

"I couldn't come for it because it was winter." Peter knew it was a lame excuse. "And then I was going through a tough time, and—"

"Chair was here all along."

Doing nothing becomes its own action, Andrea had said. *Not deciding is a decision itself.*

"That chair was mine," Peter said. "I found it and fixed it up."

Don said nothing, just crossed his big hairy forearms over his thick abdomen.

Peter shook his head. But he couldn't help wondering. "Who'd you sell it to?"

"NYC pothead wuss come out here in his porkpie hat."

Peter pictured the teak chair in a weekend home on the other side of the river. "Maybe you should pay me back. With what you made on the chair."

Don gave a big, wheezy snort. The heat was heavy around them, the air vibrating with the cicadas. Even the mountains and their dark shadows seemed to shimmer. A thick shelf of black clouds hung low where minutes ago there had been sun.

"All right, you win." Peter walked back to the truck. Probably there was something else he should do, or ask for, or demand. That's what Andrea would have said. But even finding the will to

35

get himself here to retrieve the chair—retrieve his old hope, his sense of potential—had wearied him.

He slammed the truck door just as a thunderclap shook the trees. And though he knew that, in the scheme of things, a chair wasn't worth crying over, he was overcome by a deep, unnamable sadness.

When he pulled back onto the mountain pass, the rain was coming in sheets. Already the road was a rushing gully. Peter turned the truck around to loop back the other way, where the incline was milder, the terrain less rocky.

But now the rain was slapping his windshield like those mops in the drive-through car wash. For a brief, terrifying moment, Peter felt the truck skidding, but he managed to right it in time. Shaking, he pulled over to the shallow ditch where the roadside met the woods. He set the hazard lights winking and turned off the engine, to wait this one out.

*

A sound from the back of his throat took him by surprise. For a moment he was startled to find himself there in the truck on the mountain pass, and had to shake his head until he felt fully awake. The sun was out, the air no longer heavy. Peter continued down along the less steep part of the loop, which he was pleased to discover had been paved.

The smooth drive made the fiasco with the chair seem not so bad. Peter thought he might pick up some empanadas at the scrappy outdoor market that had sprung up down by the creek, and pop over to see Grant and Chloe.

They were the ones who had bought the house for $12,000. What they hadn't mentioned, at the time, was that the house had no electricity, plumbing, or doors. Every free evening and weekend (Chloe worked as a massage therapist on the other side of the river, and Grant was a photographer) was spent slowly adding these amenities. And though they now had running water and plenty of outlets, the "bathroom"—a toilet and tub hidden by a plywood wall—still lacked a door.

Peter usually managed to park right next to the farmers' market, but today he had to leave the truck near the ice cream stand and cross back to the booths. There was a strange ache in his back. He hadn't been by in a few weeks and noticed that there was now also a food truck, with a long line of people waiting. "What are they selling?" he asked a young woman in the queue holding a Chihuahua.

"Vietnamese sandwiches. They're amazing."

Maybe he should pick up some of those, instead of the empanadas. He looked around for Velma's booth. "Velma not here?"

"Velma?"

"The empanada stand." Actually, Velma was a sculptor who made her living as a freelance publicist, but she also did swift business with the empanadas.

"Oh, right, I've heard about her," the girl said. "They say she made so much money, she bought a place in Santa Fe."

"Acapulco," said a man in front of her in line. Peter didn't know him, either. "Sort of an urban legend," the man said. "Took in thousands of dollars cash each weekend, saved up, and moved away."

Not that they'd been friends, really, but Peter was surprised she hadn't mentioned it. He looked at the line for the food truck. Too long. Instead he went over to a booth he'd never seen before, peddling baklava, and bought some of that, to shake off the sense of having been thwarted.

His lower back twinged again, and he walked back to the pickup, noting that it looked battered, rusty around the wheel wells. How had he let it get so bad? At least it was a different sort of beat-up from the dented cars that roared around town with missing mufflers or something dragging underneath, scraping the road—cars that didn't signal when they turned, not necessarily because they lacked a tail-light but because petty infractions were the least of their drivers' worries.

He drove to Grant and Chloe's, though it was close enough to have walked. A small house from the early 1800s, with a grubby swatch of lawn in front. It was looking spiffy, though, Peter saw as he parked the truck. The lawn had grown in. Walking up, he heard voices and laughter coming from behind the house. They must be having a cookout.

Well, they'd been Andrea's friends, after all. ("Andrea the Opportunist" was how Dez referred to her.) Understanding, now, why there were so many cars parked along the street, Peter turned to hurry back to the truck.

"That who I think it is?" Chloe was calling from the side yard, holding a badminton birdie. Peter stopped, feeling awkward with the little bag of baklava.

"Well now look at that!" Chloe said, rushing up to him. "It is! Hey, everyone, look who's here!"

Peter gave her a hug, said, "You're looking lovely." She had cut her hair very short, which showed off her cheekbones.

Grant came over now. "Hey, man, long time no see."

"Nice whiskers," Peter said, nodding at the new beard and mustache. "I was down at the market and picked up some baklava . . ." He felt ridiculous with the heady smoke of grilled meat wafting over. Fifteen, twenty people milled about under the shade of the big oak tree, not to mention the children and toddlers running around.

"Friends of ours are in from California," Chloe said, "and we thought we'd have a party. In fact, Pete, you should meet Nick. He's a writer, too." She called to their friend, "Nick, come meet our friend the novelist."

Well now, that wasn't very nice. But Chloe wasn't a writer and probably didn't understand the particular, acute shame of being unpublished.

The visitors from California were a tan, fit couple, mid-forties. Chloe told them, "Peter used to live here in town."

Peter turned to stare at her.

Grant said, "Still wish you'd bought when that prick landlord of yours said he was selling. You know that place sat on the market a year and a half? Guy who bought it totally lowballed him. Anyone could've got it at that price."

Why would they tease him this way? Was it for the benefit of these friends from California? One of them, the wife, asked, "Where did you move to?"

Peter wondered if he should play along. "Oh, I bought a luxury apartment on Park Avenue." He gave a laugh.

But Grant and Chloe looked uncomfortable. Chloe chewed on her lip, and Grant reached over to give Peter a sort of sympathetic pat on the back. Chloe said, "Peter had to go hide away to do his writing."

"That's right." Grant nodded. "No distractions."

"He has a story in that book—you know, with the year's best short stories!" Chloe turned to Peter. "We bought a copy as soon as it came out."

Had he done something to make them want to poke at him like this? Hurt, confused, not knowing what to say, Peter looked at the ground.

The cicada carapaces. Peter's heart gave a quick, hard thump and his eyes searched the yard. He looked up at the big oak tree, then next door, at those other thick-limbed trees. After all, cicadas moved around. But there was no sign of them. The thrumming sound he had taken for granted, and those shed outer casings everywhere— they were gone.

The little bag of baklava trembled in his hand. "I actually have to go, but please take these." He thrust the bag at Grant.

"You really can't stay?" Chloe looked genuinely disappointed. "Here, let us at least walk you to your car."

They followed him out to the truck, where Chloe gently took Peter's hand in hers. "Next time stay and visit, okay?"

Peter nodded and let himself back into the driver's seat. He turned the key and revved the engine until it caught.

Grant reached in through the open window to give him another pat on the shoulder. "I loved your story, man." He stepped aside to let Peter pull out from the curb.

"Me too!" Chloe said. She was waving, now, and as he drove away called after him, "I cried at the end!"

*

He was still shaking as he turned the corner, toward his house. It seemed he might have suffered some sort of stroke. Or maybe this was one of those waking dreams, he told himself as he headed down the hill toward the dell.

But the breeze licking at him through the window felt real enough. He turned onto his street and pulled up in front of his house, already aware that it was not the same one he had left that morning. A bay window had been built in front, and the small yard had been landscaped—too pretty. Butterflies bobbed at thickly clustered flowers, while bumblebees thumped about a bush of bright purple blossoms. In the stub of driveway sat a white van.

Probably he should get himself to the ER. But what if they locked him up in some sort of loony bin? A cousin of his once underwent electroconvulsive therapy, and the idea had frightened Peter ever since (though his cousin claimed the treatment had saved his life).

Peter closed his eyes. When he looked out again, the butterflies and bumblebees were still dipping clumsily at flowers that had not, that morning, existed.

His entire body felt weak. But he stepped down from the truck and walked up the front path. He wondered if the doorbell had been fixed. Yes, a dull chiming. He waited, then stepped over to the bay window and peered inside. The woodstove was still there, and next to it a wrought-iron contraption holding split logs. In the spot where he had imagined the teak armchair would go, there was a metal-framed seat of thick brown rough-edged leather that stretched over the frame like a sling. Facing it were a matching metal-and-leather love seat and footstool.

"Sorry, dude, he's out of town."

Peter turned to see a lanky guy, early twenties at most, shirt and jeans splattered with paint. He was holding a weed-trimmer. "I'm, like, taking care of the place, if you need something." He looked surprisingly proprietary, considering that he reeked of marijuana.

"Oh, I'm just. Stopping by." When the kid gave him a quizzical look, Peter added, "I know—knew—the guy who . . . used to live here."

"The writer dude?"

Peter's eyes widened. "Yes."

"Yeah, my lady read a story of his and saw he was local and wanted to, like, interview him for the paper. But I guess he was in a funk or something."

"A funk?"

"Like, checked himself in somewhere, maybe?" The kid squinted at the sky as if some key bit of information were hiding there. "Or maybe just, you know, shut down for a while?"

There was a terrible lump in Peter's throat. "Maybe you'd better get your story straight."

"Sorry, man, just telling you what I heard." But the kid narrowed his eyes as if having caught on to something.

Peter took a deep breath. Dez had called his mood after Andrea left "emotional freefall"—but he had never had a breakdown. Had never been "in crisis" like his cousin (who after the electroconvulsive therapy had gone on to do quite well for himself, actually). Peter dared to ask, "Well, so then . . . who lives here now?"

41

"Composer. Like, you know, orchestra music." The kid nodded slowly, almost proudly. "He's famous, travels a lot. Abroad. Like, you know, Europe."

Peter exhaled loudly. It still seemed faintly possible that this was all a joke, that someone had replaced his own scant furniture with that ugly metal-and-leather stuff, and landscaped the yard, and even parked this stoner kid here, as some elaborate prank. But his gaze lingered at the fulsome flowerbeds and perfectly pruned hedges. They were much too full to have been recently planted.

His mouth had gone dry. "I'm sorry, I've got to get going." He turned to hurry back to the truck.

"If you're free later," the kid called after him, "me and my lady are going down to the river. I know she'd want to meet you."

Peter clambered back into the driver's seat and slammed the door. And though it scared him to do it, he reached up for the rear-view mirror. Angled it to catch his reflection.

He still had his hair, if markedly less of it. Heavier cheeks, and a sagging around his eyes. Lines on his face where he hadn't had so many before. Not to mention that dull aching in his back.

He shifted the mirror back in place. Then he turned the ignition key and did the only thing he could think of. Headed down to the river, to find Dez.

Dez was the friend Peter had begun sleeping with after Andrea left. He liked her an awful lot, actually, but her ex, a guy named Derek, still showed up every so often, and Peter had never had it in him to make more of a play for her. In fact, he'd tried to convince himself it was best to stay away. And though in their best moments it seemed Dez had fallen for Peter, too, other times he suspected she was annoyed with him.

She was a freelance illustrator who lived in the riverfront neighborhood she called "Arkansas" because of the shack-like homes with torn screen doors, and tarps raised as canopies over old automobiles propped on cinder blocks, and nasty dogs barking indiscriminately, and occasional out-of-season gunshots in the woods. Really, many of the little houses down there were perfectly well kept, some with window boxes and built-on porches. Others had been sold to developers, who were replacing them with multi-story homes.

The road here was narrow, the river just visible through the leafy trees. Already Peter could see that more houses had been built. He wasn't surprised when, arriving at the one where Dez lived, he saw, with dismay, a demolition permit pasted across the door.

He turned the engine off and for a moment just sat there. Then he got out and began walking along the road, to see if someone might know where Dez had gone.

A few doors down, on the other side of the street, at one of the new multi-story homes, an in-ground pool was being built. A big yellow construction vehicle sat in front, making the place next door—a prefab house with a little porch tacked on—look that much smaller.

There was some sort of yard sale in front of the smaller house. Junk on tables and in boxes. No one around. Peter crossed over to the little onion-grass yard. On the tables were yoga DVDs, paperbacks with Harlequin covers, two pillowcases that said *forty winks*, and an extensive collection of puppy figurines—one dollar each or the entire collection for fifteen dollars. On a clothes rack hung a closet's worth of dresses, shirts, jeans, and skimpy shorts and skirts.

An extremely large woman was squeezing herself out the front door. "Feel free to take your time."

"I'm looking for a friend," Peter said, in a rush. "She used to live here. Dez." He pointed across the street.

"Oh, yeah, she bought one of them lofts."

"Lofts?"

"Down near the landing. That old warehouse. Some guy from Google turned it into condos."

43

Peter realized he was shaking his head. "Okay, thanks." He turned to leave, but something made him stop. He grabbed one of the dog figurines and handed over a dollar—not as payment for information so much as acknowledgment of the girl whose things these had been. Then he ran back to the truck, to head to the other side of town.

Lofts! Near the landing! He was still shaking his head as he wound his way down the road, past the duck pond and the cemetery and the empty stretch of land that he was relieved to see remained untamed. Some guy from Google! He turned off at a curving road that led not to the expanse of cracked asphalt and disused warehouse he recalled but to a neat parking lot and wide patio bordered by troughs of geraniums. He parked and ran up to the brick archway, where a shiny panel of buttons listed the names of residents.

Dez's name was there. He pressed the buzzer, held his breath.

There was a clicking sound, and then Dez's voice. Never had Peter been so happy to hear it.

"It's me, Peter."

"Peter!"

The door buzzed open and Peter rushed inside, up the wide, handsome staircase, two steps at a time. He quickly became winded, and realized he didn't know which apartment Dez lived in. But it didn't matter, he could hear her calling from above: "I'm up here, come see!"

She was standing on the third-floor landing, wearing a kimono he hadn't seen before. Peter bounded up the staircase, nearly out of breath. And now here was Dez's dog, Henry, a Labrador mix, greeting him joyously, if more slowly than he used to.

Peter rustled the dog's head, too hard, he realized, overzealous.

"Well, now, look at you," Dez was saying. Her hair was wet, and a deeper red than before. "Sorry, I just got out of the shower. Here, come in." She reached over, a bit awkwardly, to embrace him. Feeling her wet hair against his neck, Peter clung to her, until he realized she had let go.

44

"I'm so glad I found you." He was still out of breath, and there was a gulping sound to his voice. Henry was panting at his feet. The condo was one big room, sun washed, the ceiling high, the west-facing windows enormous. There was the orange sofa he remembered from her old place, and two lime-green bar stools at the kitchen counter. On a small round mat by the door were a few pairs of shoes. Some were large, a man's.

Dez was looking at him expectantly. Peter realized he ought to compliment the apartment. "It's fantastic," he said. "Wow. Great windows." But he heard how his voice sounded.

Dez must have noticed. The lines around her mouth tugged down at the corners, and she seemed to be searching Peter's face, warily or hopefully, he wasn't sure. "Here, it's cooler out here." She slid open a glass door, and Peter followed her out to a small balcony.

Beautiful view of the river, and of the fairy-tale bridge, its steel piers glinting in the sun. Below, one of those party boats was chugging by—a squat thing, pulsing with music and the bright rebound of voices bouncing off the water.

"It's beautiful, Dez." She, too, was beautiful. Peter decided, despite those man's shoes in the corner of his vision, to say so.

But Dez was offering him something to drink. "And then, I don't mean to be rude"—she said it gently—"but I need to get ready. I'm meeting a client for dinner." She slipped back inside.

Peter rested his sweaty hands on the railing, hoping his heartbeat would slow. He watched the party boat putt along, and looked out at the bridge. He had always found it encouraging: built in the midst of the Great Depression, a five-thousand-foot stretch of cantilevered girders arching over the water. Yes, the traffic was audible from here, but that couldn't be helped. Refracting off the moving cars, the late-afternoon light skipped like shiny coins.

"Here, I put a wedge of lemon in it." Dez stepped back onto the balcony and handed him a glass of soda water. The dog followed her, tail slapping the chair and little glass-topped table. Dez said, "Pete, are you okay? What's going on?"

He wanted to tell her about hairy-fingertipped Don, and the rainstorm, and Grant and Chloe, and his house with the awful furniture, and the sad junk sale down by the river. But all it seemed to add up to was that he had been through something hard and baffling, and was still making his way to the other side of it.

"I guess that's what I'm trying to figure out."

Dez gave a small, barely audible huff—of concern, or annoyance? But then she cocked her head and in a soft, hopeful voice said, "I heard things were looking up."

"Really?"

"Well, I mean, I know your story's in that anthology, and that you were saving up, and—Oh, don't tell me your cousin kicked you out."

His cousin! Peter had vowed never to ask him for help.

Dez bowed her head and said, softly, "I heard the therapy was a success."

Peter stood there, bewildered.

She seemed to be looking at him through her eyelashes. "Did it hurt?"

Peter wondered. "I guess I don't recall."

"Yeah," Dez nodded. "I hear it can sometimes affect your memory—but not for long, right? Just temporarily."

Peter nodded back. Because it seemed she had been right all along—about him, about what the trouble was.

And if she were right, that meant Andrea was wrong. Peter stood up straighter, while next to Dez the dog thwacked the chair with his tail.

A teak chair. Like the one Peter had found so long ago. Same shade of stain. The wicker back in perfect condition. "Wait," Peter said, "where'd you get that chair?"

"Oh, Steve—the guy I'm seeing—found it in one of those annoying antique stores I always said I'd never shop at." She gave a little pleased shrug. As if to prove a point, Henry, panting, labored up onto the chair, the cane creaking beneath him.

Peter watched the dog settle into the seat, and began to laugh.

Dez looked perplexed. "What?"

Peter laughed harder, though really it wasn't funny. "The chair still managed to get here."

"Oh, please, I know I shouldn't have it outdoors. Don't tease. I always take it back in."

"No, no—the chair is exactly where it was meant to be."

Dez was watching him curiously. "Look, I have to go get dressed. And then, I really do hate to kick you out, but I have that dinner to get to."

The dog's tail thumped against the wicker caning. Peter felt his own heart thumping. "I actually might go meet some folks over by the river."

Dez had stepped back inside, was heading to the bedroom. "Maybe I can find you there later."

Down on the river, the party boat was already farther away, the tinkling voices fading. On the balcony, the dog, Henry, sat ensconced in his chair. Peter reached into his jeans pocket for that other dog, the cheap figurine. Some kind of terrier, he saw, turning it over in his hand.

Though it wasn't much, he set it on the ledge, proof of where he had been.

The Archivists

Ottawa, March 28. At the teak desk in her living room, the grand-mother writes to her granddaughter:

My Darling!

Thank you for the flowers! The petals are the <u>exact</u> color blue. I will have Sable take a picture. For dinner we are having roast duck. Also soup, potatoes, asparagus, and the chocolate cake. Don't worry, we have two ducks!

Love,
Bunica

The flowers, blue hydrangeas, are a gift for her birthday. Big plump periwinkle clusters, like outrageous pompoms. The vase arrived with a shiny pink ribbon tied round in a bow, but the grand-mother found it inelegant and removed it.

Her daughter, Lea, is already in the kitchen. There are the two ducks to roast, plus the vat of soup to start simmering, not to mention the side dishes for Sable, her grandson's wife. A vegetarian.

The grandmother pushes herself up from the desk. With the aid of a cane fashioned after a stalk of bamboo, she makes her way to the narrow, fluorescent-lit kitchen, where Lea is arranging the ducks side by side on the enormous roasting pan. No heads or feet, just the cold plump bodies, firm and slick. The grandmother stands at the kitchen doorway to watch her daughter truss the stubby legs with twine. She likes to make certain everything is prepared the right way.

*

In an under-heated dance studio in New York City, a retired ballerina stretches her leg from passé into développé. Over her thin leotard she wears loose sweatpants and a little bolero-style knit sweater tied in a knot at her breastbone. "Not quite so high," she explains, her leg fully outstretched, toes pointing at the air in their tight leather slippers. It feels good, the strong reach of her leg, the arch of her foot, muscles extended in a single, focused intention.

The young star she is coaching, a dancer with her hair in a high blond ponytail, repeats the movement. Too eager. Her effort is visible, beads of sweat crowning her forehead, her leg jabbing the air rather than piercing it. The combination she is learning—choreographed a quarter century before her birth and intensely difficult—has not been danced in three decades.

The retired ballerina's name is Brynn. She is sixty-eight years old and works in Houston as a consultant to the Ballet. *Off to NYC, and into distant memory*, she wrote last night to registered fans on her blog, while waiting for her flight to New York.

She has promised her doctor to do nothing that will in any way strain her bad knee.

*

The two trussed ducks are slid into the oven. The grandmother secretly worries two won't be enough. She has this same worry every year. The fact that there are always leftovers in no way eradicates the residual hunger cautioning her to worry once again.

Clinging to her cane, she tugs open the refrigerator door and peers at the crowded shelves, searching for the turkey scraps for the soup. Wings (just the tips, less expensive) and a neck.

Lea says, "Let me get those," and lifts the Styrofoam trays, shuttles them to the sink, rinses the cold, slippery turkey parts under the faucet. In the stock pot, wedges of parsnip and carrot sizzle against sweating layers of a quartered onion. With a wooden spoon, the grandmother nudges the vegetables to the edges of the pot, to make room for the turkey parts. Lea drops the neck and wings in and lets them splutter for a bit, then covers everything with water and sets the lid partially across the top. The grandmother turns the flame higher.

*

In a laboratory a few miles northeast of Los Angeles, two research associates are beginning the day's work. It's 9:30 a.m. The study is at an early stage, data collection, simple, repetitive.

The first subject to arrive is a twenty-seven-year-old girl. "Woman," the first researcher—also a woman—grumbles to her colleague, a man, who sees nothing demeaning in referring to women as girls.

"It's infantilizing," the female researcher explains.

Her colleague explains that he would never use the word *girl* for anyone who isn't actually young. For women too old to be girls, he prefers the term *ladies*.

Practicing the deep, full breaths she has been advised to engage in at such moments, the female researcher heads down the hallway to the room where she will collect the *girl's* data. Before entering, she taps a quip into her smartphone, about men who call women *girls*. As much as her Twitter account is a diversion, it is also a record of her daily thoughts and activities. To not record something would mean, she believes, to lose it.

*

The solo the young blond star is to learn was choreographed in 1969, in protest against the Vietnam War. All wars, the choreographer later clarified, and told of his mother's beloved blue-eyed brother, who died in a labor camp.

The dance, *Forced March*, was first performed on a sweltering July evening at the Jacob's Pillow Festival in Massachusetts. In the *Times* the next day, a critic wrote of Brynn's "dignified carriage giving way to fury and heartbreak" and of the way she "seemed to radiate perseverance in the face of infinite pain."

Photographs from that date show a young, round-cheeked Brynn in a black leotard with a thin white belt at her waist, the expression on her unlined face resolute. Though brief, the dance required prodigious strength; by the end, the floor of the stage was wet from her perspiration. For the entire fourteen minutes that she was dancing, she could feel her pancake makeup melting.

From that night forward, each time she performed it, she told herself it was her very last dance. She felt it her duty to use up everything she had, sweat pasting her leotard to her skin, veins pulsing, bruises emerging on her knees where she sometimes fell too hard. Just a limp wet rag, that was how she felt by the end. It was a wonderfully satisfying feeling.

"I looked online," says the young star. They are taking a break, drinking water from big plastic bottles emblazoned with the company's logo. "I guess it's true no one ever filmed it. I wonder why. I found lots of recordings of you, but none of this one."

*

The grandmother's other guests have begun to arrive. First her son, Benjie, and now her grandson Dave, his six-month-old baby, and his wife, Sable, the vegetarian.

Everyone is cooing at the baby—an oblivious creature packed into a car basket. It's thanks to the baby that Dave and Sable have moved back to Kingston, to be closer to family. As the grandmother is embraced by Sable, her cheeks soft and cool, Dave sets down the manifold bags that accompany the baby on even the shortest of travels.

Already Sable is complimenting the grandmother's fine color, how lovely she looks. Somehow her flattery always seems genuine. In fact, the grandmother has always found herself fascinated by Sable—her easy manner, calm and untroubled, that air of steady contentment. Even now, a new mother, Sable appears relaxed about the baby and seems to have gotten enough sleep (which Lea always claims to find suspicious but the grandmother secretly admires).

"Happy birthday," Benjie is saying, holding out the gift he has brought: a glazed ceramic pot containing a bright blue hydrangea.

*

The research associates are collecting data concerning a gene connected to the regulation of stress hormones.

That is all they have been told. They do not yet know that their subjects have come to this study via archives begun twenty years ago. They do not know that the archives, founded by a famous film director, are video testimonies collected from around the world, recorded for an institute now located here at the university. The testimonies describe starvation, brutality, and death. They speak of life in ghettos, in hiding, in camps—in forests, in alleys, on the run.

Instead of watching archived videos, the laboratory researchers read swabs of DNA. The institute began collecting samples over a decade ago, in an effort to reconnect dispersed families and identify bodily remains. But the researchers have been employing the samples toward a different end: an ongoing study of intergenerational effects of extreme trauma. Specifically, how the stresses of the Holocaust may have altered the DNA not only of Holocaust survivors but also of their descendants.

Epigenetic inheritance is the term. Environmentally caused modifications of genetic material, via chemical tags that attach themselves to DNA. In previous studies, Jewish Holocaust survivors and their offspring were shown to share the same epigenetic tags, while the control group (Jewish families living outside of Europe during the war) did not.

This new study will test the theory that epigenetic tags are passed not only to children but to grandchildren.

*

The blue of the second hydrangea (the one from her son) is very close to that of the first—but slightly more violet. The petals, bright and absurdly healthy, could be leaves from some oversized blue clover, or the wings of a strange blue butterfly.

The grandmother has her son set the planter on the teak desk. Meanwhile, atop the round glass coffee table, the bouquet from her granddaughter in California makes a sort of altered reflection, periwinkle blossoms spilling over the lip of the vase.

The plant from her son has a small white tag dangling over the edge of the ceramic pot: *Hydrangea* written in looping script. The grandmother leans closer to read the tag.

> *Hydrangeas require plenty of light and daily watering.*
> *A hydrangea is a symbolic way to say*
> *"Thank you for understanding."*

She looks over to the coffee table, at the vase bursting with hydrangea blossoms. Those periwinkle ones, from her granddaughter, are the right ones.

*

53

Brynn massages the area around her bad knee. So far, so good. She just needs to remember to ice it when she gets back to the hotel.

For a few years, the *Forced March* solo was her signature piece, created for her when she was not yet twenty. Danced for the first minutes in silence, with live drumming gradually layered in, the piece begins slowly, meditatively, building to a frenzy and then ultimately calming itself. Among the photographs on her website is one of a young, fearless Brynn hurtling herself across the stage while a stern-faced drummer plays impassively behind her.

It was flattering, an honor, to have a dance made for her, even if she had also been fending off the choreographer's advances for some time. After she left the company for a troupe in San Francisco, the dance was retired from the repertoire and never performed again. When the choreographer died, a few years ago, Brynn spoke lovingly, if with carefully chosen words, at his memorial service.

Her work with this new star is part of a project to archive "lost" dances. It began as an internet campaign and has since received national attention. Brynn finds the online platform—GoFundMe—crass. It seems these days anyone can ask for money for anything and, astonishingly, receive it.

Once revived, Brynn's piece will be publicly performed, recorded, and added to an electronic archive. *Dances long forgotten*, the funding page explains, *will exist once again, recalled, performed, and shared in perpetuity.*

*

"I will explain," the grandmother tells Sable, who has not yet heard the story. Leaning closer on the sofa, she tells her about her first love, whom she last saw in 1939.

Mihail, brother of her friend Ana. He had the most beautiful eyes! But it was not until she was sixteen, she tells Sable, that he finally took notice of her. It happened at a dance. There were weekend dances back then, everyone would go. A favorite song had started up, and out of a sense of duty—it seemed—Mihail asked her to join him. Moving together, their bodies warm and full of life, she glimpsed a change in his face, some new softness, or perhaps simply attention. He was, she realized, seeing her anew. After that, he was always walking her home, loping along beside her, carrying her books, and, in the dark of the cinema, warming her hands between his, trembling when he dared lean in to kiss her.

When the war came, the grandmother and her family fled to the countryside, while Mihail and Ana and their parents hid in town. It made no difference; in the end, all of them were sent to the camps—but the grandmother escaped!

On the run, hiding in safe houses, in abandoned homes, miserable places she has blocked from memory. Entire weeks, months, erased from mental record.

Even when she gave her testimony to the institute, she found she could not account for great swaths of time. This troubled her. As if those painful stretches never existed.

She tells Sable some of what she remembers—far away, now, perhaps, from what she meant to explain. There was a courtyard where she found herself alone, a searing hunger in her stomach. No strength left, no last surge of energy to move forward, to make a decision, to save her own life by shoving one raw inflamed foot in front of the other.

Looking at the rusted gate to the courtyard, thinking that if she looked long enough, her father would appear and tell her what to do.

The hunger, she tells Sable, is what she has never forgotten. That was something she tried to convey during her testimony—how even after many decades, the hunger has never gone away.

*

. . . causing physiological mutations, including increased chances of stress disorders such as anxiety, anorexia, and addiction. In this manner, it seems the epigenetic effects of history are passed intergenerationally through the body . . .

*

In the kitchen, the two ducks are roasting, grease dripping into the pan. The salad has been assembled but not dressed. The potatoes await mashing, and the asparagus still needs to be sautéed. For Sable there is also a lentil burger slowly shriveling in the toaster oven.

Lea adds a ladle of broth to a small saucepot of simmering water. Next comes a dusting of her mother's signature ingredient, which the grandmother considers a spice though really it is MSG. Lea cracks an egg into a bowl, shakes some salt at it, and briskly scrambles the egg with a fork. She sifts a tablespoon of farina into the bowl and stirs. Too runny. She adds more farina, stirs again. The trick is not to add too much, or the dumplings won't hold together.

When the mixture looks about right—a sticky yellow paste—Lea lightly drags the tines of the fork across the top. The indented lines remain briefly visible, then start to fill in.

That's how you know it's the right consistency, her mother taught her many years ago, in this very same kitchen, when Lea was a little girl. Guiding her hand, dragging the fork.

The motion of another hand, of another girl, in a drafty kitchen in Brașov. Ana, sister of Mihail, showing her friend how to test the găluşcă: "Just pull the fork through, until it leaves a mark, like this."

*

"Like this," Brynn tells the young dancer. She lowers herself into a wide plié—slowly, careful with her knee—while her arms push above her head, palms flat and wide, as if trying to push away the sky.

56

Fascia stretching, ligaments tightening. "Muscle memory"—though for Brynn the emotions, too, return, how it felt to be young, knowing her choreographer was in love with her, knowing that she did not need to love him back, that it was enough to dance for him, to follow his direction with her body.

No matter that she had not yet lost a loved one, had not, yet, known what it was to be bereft. Her body seemed to know, and carried her to those bleak places.

There are no recordings of the dance because the choreographer forbade it—no one seems to remember this. To Brynn, this lapse is just one more reminder that what once seemed to matter greatly can be so quickly forgotten. The very point of the piece, the choreographer told her, was its brief flicker amid the indifference of war. Like the brevity of life, Brynn always thought. Ephemeral. Lost.

Now, though, its loss seems a mistake. She is here to bring it back.

*

We could not risk looking as if we were going on a journey, the survivor says on the videotape from 1997. *That is why I have no photographs or family keepsakes. We had to leave everything behind.*

For the institute, this same survivor left behind a buccal swab of her DNA. Which is how, nearly two decades later, subject 1207B—the "girl"—came to be asked to participate in the study here at the university, and why she has stopped by this air-conditioned room, missing her morning tae kwon do class, to answer a detailed questionnaire and open her healthy, strong jaw for the research associate, who leans forward and rubs a sterile swab inside the girl's cheek.

*

"So you see, I have no pictures of him," the grandmother explains to Sable, nudging herself toward the edge of the sofa to pose for her photo. "But to this day, I never have met anyone with such beautiful eyes."

She leans forward, toward the coffee table, bringing her face closer to the flowers—the bouquet sent by her granddaughter. Sable is leaning back, cellphone raised: "Say cheese!"

When Sable shows her the image, the grandmother nods approval. And with another push of a button, the picture flies off to a cellphone in California.

"That is the reason," the grandmother tells Sable, "they bring me these flowers. These ones here, they are the exact color of his eyes."

*

Brynn tries to describe precisely, for the young dancer, the movements her own body can no longer enact.

While there are various dance notation techniques, the GoFundMe page states, *few choreographers or dance historians know these "languages" (Labanotation, Benesh Movement Notation, Eshkol-Wachman Movement Notation, DanceWriting) sufficiently to record or translate. There is no substitute for **seeing** movements in their full combination, expressed by the body as originally intended. This is why funding these archives is so important.*

They have come to the most difficult section. Down on her knees, then leaping to the sky. Spinning and spinning and spinning, into the indifferent, expanding universe.

"Lead with the hip first, yes, but, no . . ." Frustrating, these failed attempts to describe movements her body no longer obliges. Shapes she can no longer make, compromised gestures carving the air. What she wants to explain is beyond language.

So she stops, just briefly, to think. She is deciding what to do. Then she begins, again, to move.

*

In Palo Alto, the first of the day's subjects has been set free. If she hurries she might make the next tae kwon do class. Or maybe she should skip it and work on her dissertation chapter.

As soon as she leaves the lab, she checks her cellphone, where she finds a text from her sister-in-law. With a photograph.

i love this! she taps back. Just seeing it makes her smile. With a quick push of a button, she displays it on her Instagram account. **My bunica**, she types, **91 years old today!**

By evening, two hundred and ninety people will have seen the photograph of her grandmother with the periwinkle bouquet. One hundred and ninety-seven of them will have "liked" the exact color of Mihail's eyes.

*

Knee popped, Brynn writes to the fans on her blog. She is typing on her iPad in her casual, pokey way, sitting in a firm-cushioned chair in her doctor's waiting room, her bad leg fully, painfully, outstretched. The flight home was tricky, with her leg sticking out into the aisle, annoying everyone. Not to mention the long awkward car ride home, and the depressing drive here today, propped like an invalid in the back seat of her friend's sedan, and then having to use the cane again, like some old lady.

She thinks for a moment, then resumes her typing. *And yes my dears, it was worth it.*

A Guide to Lesser Divinities

Being self-employed, I take very good care of my teeth. Why let U.S. healthcare get me down? The minute I lost my job at the university, I bought a water pick, those rubber-tipped scrapers to get the plaque off, and cinnamon-flavored mouth rinse. Used together, they're quite effective.

This all began three years ago. I was in my mid-thirties (or as some call it, late thirties) and suddenly friends I'd thought no different from me—procrastinators with credit card debt and unpublished doctoral dissertations and boyfriends they'd eventually have to dump—were in charge of things that mattered. School principals! Directors of trade organizations, newspaper columnists opining weekly! Somehow they had parlayed their quaint obsessions and middling skills into actual professions. One lost friend showed up on all the morning news programs, an authority on online dating. I'd done the online rounds myself before meeting Luis and couldn't understand how what, for me, amounted to no more than lost time had become, in the case of my old friend, *credentials*.

How had she done it?

Or rather, what would it take for me to make that leap? To no longer rent a drafty room in a cruddy apartment and teach four classes per semester at a state school in perpetual fiscal crisis. To stop dating a man far too young for me, who texted me photos of himself sunbathing.

Luis. We'd met at the gas station where I was buying lottery tickets; he was filling his Honda, looking cute in his puffy down vest. When he winked at me, I laughed. Being Luis, he just said, "You've got a great smile."

One more reason I take good care of my teeth. I always appreciate an honest compliment, so I handed him a scratch card for his kindness.

"Better give me your number," he said, "in case we need to split the winnings."

Within an hour I'd received a text:

This is Luis from the gas station. Sorry to say we didn't win the 50K.

I wrote back: **Sorry, kid.**

Can I take you to Dinner?

Before I could type **I don't know, can you?** I checked myself. Despite a past event of tragic consequence, I try to be open to what life hands me. **Yes,** I wrote, **you MAY.**

You see, I still believed language, properly employed, might save our careening planet. It's why I made my bewildered students— who enrolled in my Great Books classes not by choice but to grudgingly fulfill their Humanities requirement—learn the difference between *can* and *may, uninterested* and *disinterested, lay* and *lie.* To deny the accuracy of one versus the other, I explained, was a first step toward moral corrosion. I told them how the degradation of language set the stage for ethical misjudgment, that our careful parsing of word choice and allusion were skills to combat despots and charlatans. That the semicolons they so blithely misused might be the last feeble shims propping up our teetering republic.

They seemed to find this amusing. How could such trivialities matter when they were each working two jobs and the babysitter hadn't turned up? They ranged from eighteen to seventy-something, from a new single mother to a Gulf War vet; their daily struggles could not be remedied by grammar. Some would disappear mid-semester, then reemerge a year later without explanation. One woman's family was hiding from the Albanian mafia. The seventy-something was connected, via clear tubes inserted into her nostrils, to an oxygen canister seated intently on the floor beside her. I knew I couldn't solve their problems, but I could try to provide tools for a better life.

The future is in your hands, I'd say, conjugating on the white-board with my one precious dry-erase pen, while the younger students tittered at *laid* vs. *lain*, words fading into nothing as the ink ran low. Please, I'd say, think how happy you'll make me if you remember just one thing I taught you.

*

I was reading my students' homework in the office I shared with two young serfs (or as the university called them, adjuncts) when the program director, Alison, came bustling in. I dislike the word *bustle*—that its implied petty clamor is reserved solely for women—but it is exactly the word for Alison's click-clacking speed-walk along the corridor. She has the most amazing shoes. Strappy pointy things, and leather boots with sinister heels. All her clothes look expensive. Embroidered silk bell-sleeved tops, long slinky velvet skirts, choker necklaces. "Eliana?" She set her hard green eyes on me and asked if I would please see her in her office.

I pretended to be deciding, while the younger of the serfs looked terrified. He didn't know about my longstanding adversarial relationship with Alison—that to simply do as Alison asked would have toppled our sense of world order.

Alison was a tyrant of the micromanaging type. Each semester she insisted on personally "approving" each professor's syllabus and every few months would come up with some new "pedagogical imperative," usually mass-emailed at 3 a.m. and requiring a new "mandatory" teaching sequence that messed up everyone's class plans. I'd learned never to open these emails, but the young serfs would read them and fall into a tizzy. When I once suggested we discuss these matters as a department, Alison reminded me that until I published my doctoral dissertation, I was lucky to have a full-time, salaried, and renewable contract.

The subject I wanted to teach was the topic of my dissertation: the role of the minor gods in seminal Greek creation myths. But each time I broached this with Alison, she said she needed me to stick with Great Books. A professor of American Culture, she was known for her alarmist op-eds critiquing American literacy, which was perhaps why, some years earlier, she had been named director of General Studies. Then a 3 a.m. missive had arrived addressed not to GEN-STUD but ALL-FAC, announcing that while she had for years been fearful of sharing her full truth, she now believed that, despite the risk, it was time she revealed herself as a devoted goddess-worshipper and witchcraft practitioner, as she was now shifting her academic focus to this key aspect of her spiritual and social self, and that despite the history of persecution, she hoped for our full support. Included were two weblinks, one to an explanation of her religion, another to an article concerning the activities of her local coven.

"As if we didn't already know she was a witch," said our chauvinist colleague Rick (who, when I first joined the faculty, kept mistaking me for our office assistant and asking me to make his photocopies). Rick's comment about Alison went ignored, partly because everyone was fearful of saying anything but mostly to avoid Rick, who was known for forwarding emails containing student letter-of-recommendation requests with a note saying, *Hey, I'm pretty busy and you've taught this student* . . .

I wished desperately my best friend, Necee, were there. She would be as enraged as I was that Alison could "shift" her academic focus to *her* goddess while preventing *me* from teaching mine; and I knew Necee, too, would see Alison's message as a play for sympathy by a rich, white, straight, able-bodied, thin, blond woman. "*History of persecution*" *my foot!* cried the Jew in me, whose mother's family had been wiped out in Europe not so long ago. To Rick the chauvinist I simply pointed out that Alison had always been officious and insufferable.

It was to Luis, later, that I voiced my true feelings. But when I described Alison's attempt to define herself as marginalized and become newly relevant, Luis—who taught music at a middle school one town over—said, "Maybe she really did feel she had to hide it, and it was weighing on her."

This was on our second date, at a mediocre bistro where no one would be in a hurry for our table. Luis had used the word *iterative* twice. Even aiming to impress me, he seemed unnervingly laid back, relaxing into his chair and joking with the waitress. I couldn't help wondering if he made a habit of asking out women he met in public places.

"I mean," Luis said, "she might come from a background where being a witch is as bad as devil worship. Maybe she grew up in a conservative family, and what she's doing is a huge sacrilege. So, for her, even just admitting it is daring and risky and . . . frightening."

"She made it sound like she was equating her feelings of otherness with what truly marginalized groups go through—"

"Well, I mean, you never know another person's feelings."

"Luis! Come on, you should be incensed by this."

He gave me a steely look. "I should?"

I stared into my wine. "Not to mention," I mumbled, "the abuse of all-faculty email."

64

He waited a moment before saying in a flat voice, "You're funny."

When I'd stopped feeling like a jerk, I said, "Really, doesn't everyone have personal stuff they'd feel better about if everyone else had to deal with it, too? Yes! Yes, they do! But we don't go around sending email blasts. Well, unless you're Ben Belletti." Talk about misuse of ALL-FAC. Ben let everyone know when he came home early from a conference to find Janine Belletti—the registrar as well as Ben's wife—in bed with the assistant provost.

"What about you, then?" Luis asked. "What hidden truth would your email blast confess?"

Before I knew what was happening, my eyes had welled, my heart shredding. I gulped from my water glass, pretending I'd bitten into a chili pepper. When I'd regained my composure, I said, "I guess I'd have to tell them I'm a heathen."

Before he could press for more, I asked Luis what his message would say.

Looking disappointed, he said, "Maybe I'll tell you later."

"Fair enough."

Then he perked up. "Also, aren't you overlooking the most important part of your boss's message?"

"What's that?"

"The woman's a witch. She can do spells and shit!"

"Well then why did she even need to use ALL-FAC email?"

That made him laugh. I told him how, immediately after Alison's announcement, the university had indeed begun celebrating Alison, as the university's first openly Wiccan faculty member and later as the first openly Wiccan professor to achieve tenure. Articles in the alumni magazine, faculty newsletter, and campus paper about General Studies' new in-demand course: "Pagans, Witchcraft, and America's 'New' Feminism." Not to mention the photograph in constant rotation on the homepage: a radiant, newly tenured Alison in a crushed silk dress, velvet choker, and burgundy lipstick.

65

"I'm just saying," Luis said, "you might try to see things from her end of the broomstick."

It was true we ought to have had enough in common. Not just a shared focus on pagan deities (though I was steadfastly devoted to the Hellenic world). No, what came to mind was that surely, with her long blond hair, Alison, too, had spent her twenties dodging professors' advances, trying to shift her thigh away without offending the person needed to pen a precious letter of reference. Had to cut short her panel presentations after her male co-panelist rambled on for twice the allotted time so that the audience sighed at her impatiently before she even opened her mouth to speak. Had an eminent scholar, after hearing her present her paper, praise her only to follow up with a request, right there in the crowd at the conference: "May I kiss you?"

Yet her brazen use of ALL-FAC email marked the divide between us. I had no job security, had never traipsed through the world draped in silk. My father's Sephardic roots had me dark-haired, olive-complexioned; at the taqueria place, I was invariably addressed in Spanish. Every so often a stranger would speak English to me in an oddly loud, overjoyed, or strangely annoyed manner and only after I answered revert to a relaxed tone and normal decibel.

So, when Alison asked to see me in her office that day, I took my time moseying over.

In a slow, measured voice she said, "What's this I hear about your mother grading your papers?"

I did not say, "How else am I supposed to mark eighty papers at once?" Instead I told her, "I try to find creative ways to motivate the students."

"Enlighten me."

"It's sort of a running joke. Though, to be fair, she's actually quite—"

"Eliana."

I hastily explained. My mother, a Brit raised on the Queen's English, had once—on a visit from the retirement community where she has lived since my father's death—perused some of my students' essays and been appalled. It was true they were pretty abominable. Nothing I said seemed to convince anyone to proofread. It didn't matter that I'd told them about the truckers' union winning overtime pay based on a missing comma in a contract, or the lawsuit over Tiffany "style" diamonds. I thought if I explained linguistic justice in financial terms, my students might care more. I did whatever I could to keep them in the class, anything to hold their attention. Told them about the lesser gods—how Eos, goddess of dawn, turned Tithonus into the very first grasshopper. About Alphito, whose sole power was to inflict leprosy. About Kronos castrating his father, the Furies born of drops of blood from Uranus's severed genitals. The more gruesome, the more it caught their attention. And to motivate them on their homework—I explained to Alison—I told them quite honestly what my mother had thought of their essays. It had become a joking refrain: *What would my mother say*, I'd remark on their more egregious punctuation errors. *My mother would be proud of you!* I crooned when they showed improvement. And when nothing else worked, I threatened to have her grade their homework.

"And might I assume," Alison said coolly, "that this threat is not general classroom policy?"

"She lives in North Carolina. It's logistically impossible."

"Well, I just had one of your students here nearly in tears."

I was shocked. "Someone complained?"

Alison looked pleased to have alarmed me. "Apparently her grandfather passed away and she's behind on her work. She was very concerned. She told me her essay needed to be especially good because your *mother* would be grading it."

Right, I'd received this student's email. *I just got some bad news concerning the death of my grandfather.*

I told Alison an extension could be arranged. She was already standing from her chair, to let me know our time was up. "Glad we had this chat."

I said nothing. One of us had to stick to principles.

*

It was back when Necee was still here that I came up with the idea about the lesser divinities. We were still in our twenties, still had plans to change the world—or at least dismantle the patriarchy—and when we weren't discussing school (she was in the Classics program, too), the subject of love was usually our focus. A marathon session devoted to Necee's off-again girlfriend led to my dissertation topic; I was thinking about the minor gods, that they play as many tricks as the big guns, with just as brutal consequences.

Necee already knew her dissertation topic: comparing all published English translations of *The Odyssey* to the original Homeric Greek, in order to root out inaccuracies caused by decades of sexist interpretations. She had even won a grant to do it. And then one day those laughing gods snatched her up. More precisely, one day, as she and a friend rode their bicycles along Massachusetts Avenue, their bikes somehow managed to collide, so that Necee hit her head on the curb, fell into a coma, and never regained consciousness.

The other bicyclist was me.

*

At some point in the days after Necee joined the gods on Mount Olympus, I managed to get out of bed. I'd gotten somewhat banged up in our collision—of which I had no memory—and was wearing a cast on one arm and stitches in my thigh. I could not make sense of what had happened: that while I had barely a limp, Necee had died. At the funeral, I cowered in the back, though people made a point to be kind to me. There had been witnesses at the accident, and the official report was that Necee's bike had drifted in front of mine without warning and I hadn't had time to stop.

It was too awful. What were the chances that just one of us should live?

I tried to return to my former life. The accident had occurred mere weeks after my dissertation defense, meaning that my PhD was officially complete. I'd been excited about the contract from a university press to turn my dissertation into a published book—but what did such a thing matter now? My computer files remained unopened. Nor could I bring myself to face the friends Necee and I had in common. After a while they stopped calling. Anyone I couldn't bear to see—everyone who knew what had happened—after a time fell away.

I still had to make a living. It was on the basis of my book contract that I got myself hired to teach Great Books. My mother convinced me to see a psychologist, free through my health plan, though I didn't have the energy to make most of the appointments. I tried moving forward, even did some online dating, but somehow the guys never got any older. The gods did that sneaky thing they do: snatch away a dozen years in a single day, so that one morning you're suddenly nearing forty, and nothing much in your life has changed.

*

There was a spark between Luis and me; he must have sensed it even at the gas station. And we were both educators. "Music's a language, too," he'd said on our first date, when I told him about my job, how I hoped to arm my students with the power of linguistic expression. He told me about coded musical language: the sly references and secret meanings a composition might hold—the motifs and acrostics and mathematical progressions, how J. S. Bach liked to spell out his name with corresponding notes on the staff, and that Shostakovich covertly opposed political oppression with his DSCH cryptogram.

His own instrument of choice was the trumpet, which he played in a very loud band every Sunday at a nearby pub, where I soon became a regular. I loved seeing him in action, all confidence and swagger. We also went to free concerts at the fancy university nearby. Luis had his ear out for new pieces he might modify for his middle school students—not the orchestra, which apparently was a lost cause, but the jazz band, which had some talented kids. Like me, even off-duty Luis seemed to carry his students in some active compartment of his heart.

The first time he took me home, some weeks after we'd met, when we entered his building he said, "Now is probably a good time to mention that I live with my mother."

Somehow it didn't surprise me. "Don't worry," I said, "I always get along with my boyfriends' mothers." This was probably because I was often nearly the same age as their mothers, but I didn't tell Luis that.

He had just turned twenty-seven. His mother, Lorena, wasn't even fifty. Apparently she was a math genius who at sixteen had left San Juan to enroll at MIT, where she was promptly impregnated by an engineering major. The engineer had a breakdown and moved back to California, but Lorena had somehow managed to complete her degree, raise Luis, and become a statistician for Gillette. Along the way, she had briefly married but had long ago divorced.

Lorena was a tall, curvy brunette with handsome features and a light Puerto Rican accent. She looked familiar—or maybe it was just that she looked like Luis. Same prominent nose and bow of the lips. She ushered us into the kitchen and put a kettle on for tea.

70

"Luis tells me you're a classicist. I love the *Metamorphoses*. All those transformations. When I was a girl, I wanted to be able to do that."

"It's my favorite book," I told her, "though so much of it is tragic, really." Rape, betrayal, bloody revenge. Damsels fleeing predators, calling desperately for help.

"Yes, but I like the premise," Lorena said. "Well, not to be changed into something, but to turn into whatever I wanted to be."

I, too, had been transported by those tales of metamorphosis, though it wasn't until my freshman year of college that I'd first read Ovid—and my belief in miraculous change was pretty much limited to the scratch tickets I hoped might one day come through for me. "Now I'm more interested in his take on love," I told Lorena. "Because whereas in the pantheon Eros is comparatively minor, in Ovid, love becomes the driving force. It's such a radical twist to have love, this very human emotion, tricking even the most powerful gods."

Lorena nodded wistfully. "Even gods are not immune."

I wondered if she, too, had a lover. The more I looked at her, with her broad, heavy face and strong features, the more I was convinced I knew her. Probably it was because she in some ways resembled a Greek goddess. She had that bold, fleshy, statuesque look of so many classical sculptures.

We talked easily—I would even say we "hit it off"—but Luis was getting impatient. "Mom, it's late. We'll see you in the morning, okay?"

"Next time, baby. I have my Zumba in the morning."

That was it: how I knew her. Zumba class at the gym. She was the big-hipped woman who always arrived late and squeezed herself into the front row. But I said nothing; I really liked that class. I would hate to have to stop going when Luis and I broke up.

*

71

In my classes, I told my students about Aergia, goddess of laziness. Sharing these tidbits always reminded me of back when I felt passionate about my studies, before those antsy gods had their fun with me. And I felt a kinship with second-class goddesses like Aergia, since I, too, was permanently stuck in the minor leagues.

I should point out that none of my students were lazy. They all worked long hours at on-your-feet jobs—bartender, grocery store manager, cashier, waiter—and then dragged themselves to sit in a dingy classroom with a perpetually broken clock. I admit I was easier on them than I could have been. I gave fewer reading assignments and tempered my language when assessing homework. *Your essay*, I would write, *would benefit from more punctuation, particularly commas.* At the same time, I felt a responsibility: to make sure students left my class with skills to pull themselves up in the world. Clarity and grammatical correctness, if not eloquence.

LAZINESS, I wrote on the whiteboard. IDLENESS. SLOTH.

Drita, the woman hiding from the Albanian mafia, had used these words interchangeably in a paper we were critiquing as a class. Though most of the students understood the qualitative differences, few seemed to find it problematic to treat them as equivalents. So I divided the class into groups, asking them to define each word.

The veteran of our war in the Gulf said he didn't see why these small differences mattered. "Isn't it enough if we get the general gist?"

"To be imprecise," I said, "is moral laziness." I pointed at LAZINESS. "Not idleness. Not sloth. Moral laziness. It's a matter of morality because to knowingly misuse a word is a way of lying. And deception is, of course, immoral."

They had no trouble acknowledging this fact when it came to the escapades of the Greek divinities, who always seemed to be pretending to be someone else: mere mortals, or creatures of the animal kingdom, often toward evil ends. When it came to language, however, my students seemed less troubled by such sleights of hand.

72

Perhaps language deployed maliciously seemed a given, one more way that those in charge screwed everyone else over—too obvious to merit comment. Probably my linguistic concerns sounded excessive, or simply irrelevant, when our nation's government was in daily upheaval, and refugees from a dozen ongoing wars were drowning in the cold, cold ocean, and polar bears were tiptoeing on melting icebergs, and killer bees had crossed onto the continent, and every day some cop was killing a black man and walking free.

I shared an example from Necee's proposal, about the twelve slave girls in *The Odyssey*. How would you like it if a bunch of translators called you sluts and whores, when Homer had never said you were any of those things?

A few weeks later, I tried another approach. I wrote on the whiteboard the following terms:

SEPARATE BUT EQUAL

FAMILY VALUES

ETHNIC CLEANSING

PRO-LIFE

ALL LIVES MATTER

Euphemisms as tools of oppression!

We had a lively discussion about connotation and the power of misnomers. I thought I'd made a convincing point. But the woman hooked up to the oxygen tank shook her head, slow and hopeless, as if she had given up on me. Only in that moment did the truth of the oxygen canister fully register: it was what was keeping her alive.

*

By then it was April, and the middle school where Luis worked was on spring break. Luis flew to Bermuda with two musician buddies and texted me pictures of himself reclining on an inflated plastic chaise in the hotel pool. He'd been there just twenty-four hours but already looked tan and healthy. I could see girls in bikinis in the background, their golden, smooth skin, girls who probably still got their periods right on time and hadn't yet experienced the small alarming ways the body begins drafting its resignation. I knew Luis would be enjoying their attention, and while I did feel pangs of jealousy, mostly I felt cold and sallow. The truth was, I'd grown inordinately fond of Luis. I felt his absence acutely.

This wasn't like me. Part of the reason I had no qualms dating younger men was that it couldn't last. I hadn't had a serious relationship since Necee died—back when I was the age of these younger men, more than a decade ago. I wasn't proud of this fact; I'd have liked to change. But it was simpler that way, just doing my own thing, not getting too close to anyone. Normally, I didn't check my phone every hour to see if there was a message.

There was.

I can't say I don't miss you

I read it over a few times. No matter how I looked at it, there was that other sentence inside. **I don't miss you.**

"So he used a double negative," his mother said. "I think you're reading into it."

We were at a club in Somerville. She'd won tickets to see an eighties cover band, and no one else was free that night. Or so she said; while it was true we had grown close, part of me wondered if she might be keeping her eye on me while her son was away. Though, in retrospect, it strikes me she might have been looking out for me.

Now it was intermission, and Luis's text stared up from my phone. "It's linguistic evasion," I said. "He can't bring himself to say straight out that he misses me."

"Have you said it to him?" Lorena adjusted the strap of her slinky top, which made her look my age and was probably why men kept buying us drinks.

74

"If I did say it," I told her, "I wouldn't be all Bill Clinton-y about it."

"What Bill Clinton?"

"You know, *It depends what the meaning of the word 'is' is.*"

"Eliana." She gave me a hard look. "Do you miss him?"

I did. But to admit it would be a sure step toward heartbreak.

"I hear what you tell him," she said, "how he's too young. Like you need some George Clooney—"

"George Clooney!"

"Some older, suaver, richer man. As if Luis isn't enough. You know as well as I do that's not your real concern. It's that you're afraid."

She had said it. So simple. So true.

I was afraid of so many things. The precariousness of love—the capriciousness of Venus and Cupid—and of course our unfortunate age difference. There was also the fact that I hadn't yet told Luis what I, or my bike, had done to Necee.

What I said was, "Wouldn't you be afraid, too? I mean, it's hard enough to make a relationship work—how stupid am I to think Luis won't eventually want someone younger? It feels like a joke, or a trick, for the universe to hand me this laid-back guy who goes through life like he has all the time in the world, and who will probably decide he wants kids years after I've entered menopause." I'd already found more than one gray hair. One day, I knew, I'd wake up withered and alone, with no money saved for an eye lift.

"I do long for grandchildren," Lorena conceded.

I wasn't even sure I wanted kids—one more frightening unknown. I'd been tamping down my own wants for so many years, I no longer knew what it felt like to hope for something. To commit to life, to the future. Gone were the days when Necee and I dreamt of populating the halls of the Classics Department with women, with faculty representing a true cross-section of backgrounds. Yet it was easier to hang things on the age question than to tell Lorena about Necee. "I mean, what are the odds a younger man doesn't eventually abandon an older woman?" Think of Jason and Medea, that great bloody catastrophe.

"Since when do you care about odds?" Lorena was a statistician, after all. "You with those scratch tickets."

I didn't know Luis had told her about that. "It's just for fun," I said, though that wasn't exactly true. Embarrassed, I added, "It's not like I expect to win."

Lorena straightened her shoulders. She glared at me. "You're telling me you didn't win that day? Honestly, Eliana. Think about what you just said. I need to go pee."

I watched her head to the ladies' room. She was right, of course. I felt ashamed. I had insulted her son and laughed at my luck. But in my area of study, love always led to some horrible mistake.

*

When Luis first noticed the scar on my thigh, early on, we were in bed at my place and he was running his hand down my leg. I'd felt his fingers slow down as they traced the long stretch where my stitches had been. "Something happened here," he said.

A great heaviness had come over me. I said, "Perhaps someday I can tell you about it."

But I still hadn't. And seeing Luis's young beautiful bare chest in the sunny photographs he texted throughout the weekend, I knew my jealousy was of more than his vacation flirtations and poolside margaritas. It was of still being unscarred.

Though who knew what he'd had to contend with. Especially in a provincial city like ours. Especially now. I thought of when I'd asked what he would write in an email blast, wondered what it was he had decided not to tell me.

That Sunday I skipped Zumba; I knew Lorena was still annoyed with me. Into the cold drizzle I tramped to the grocery store. As

I waited in what my mother still calls the "queue," I saw, two carts ahead of me, Alison.

I expected her to be dictating something into her phone or checking emails, not wasting a moment of her time. But she was lost in thought, her face relaxed into an expression I'd never witnessed at work. She looked somehow softer. Her hair had blond highlights that must have cost who knew how much.

I never had bothered to follow the weblinks in that email of hers. It was no business of mine which goddess she worshipped or rituals she followed. If her "craft" allowed her to better fulfill her selfhood, congratulations; I felt no solidarity with her. I turned my back and busied myself with my phone, my hair shielding my face. Only after I was sure she had left the store did I dare look up again.

When Monday arrived, I diverted myself from my life by focusing on my students. Pelias, I told them, was warned to beware of a man with one sandal. You see, he was insecure, so he did what many of us do when anxious: consulted an oracle.

I'd done the same once myself, when I was young and in love, at a psychic's on Newbury Street.

The students wanted to know what happened to Pelias. I told them about Jason losing one of his shoes in the mud, and about the Golden Fleece, and Pelias's spectacularly ghastly end after he refused to give up the throne—how Medea duped his daughters into believing she could restore his youth if they chopped him up and boiled him.

If there was one constant in these tales, it was that no knowledge of preordained threat ever helped. When it came to fate, you were simply doomed. Really, I didn't want my students to think that way; I wanted to focus on miraculous acts of self-creation, to believe we could alter our circumstances if we chose to. Or at the very least, appeal for help in such matters.

And yet, in my mind, I heard whispered words from Bacchylides. *It is hard for men on earth to sway the minds of the gods.*

*

On the office computer I shared with the young serfs, I found a note from Alison. *Eliana, please see me asap.*

There had been a complaint—a real one this time. A student whose name was not revealed to me had apparently found it "inappropriate" that I had expressed my political leanings in the supposedly neutral territory of the classroom.

"I wouldn't have thought," Alison said, "I'd have to spell out for you that highly charged political topics must be discussed from a point of impartiality."

What about her witchy "America's new feminism" course? "I was making a linguistic point," I said instead, and explained that our discussion of weaponized language was meant to support the school's mission of informing an educated citizenry.

"Let me remind you, Eliana, that we are a government-funded school paid for in part by tax dollars."

"Look," I said, "we've all had those moments in class where an impromptu lesson is the best way to—"

"You know my thoughts on impromptu class plans."

I decided this was not the moment to point out her oxymoron. Alison was trilling her fingers on her desk, her nails glazed in a burgundy color so dark, only the black enamel of her coffee mug revealed the difference. Tap-tap-tap-tap. Tap-tap-tap-tap. She often affected gestures of flagrant, fearsome pondering. This time, though, it seemed genuine, as if she truly didn't know what to do with me.

At last she stopped tap-tap-tap-tapping. "Eliana. Do you want to be here?"

Trying not to squirm, I asked what she meant.

Slow and cool. "Do you want to be here."

"I guess it depends what you mean by *here*." Here where half the toilets didn't work and, due to fiscal considerations, there was a moratorium on printing from the copy machine? Or here in the classroom, where sometimes, just momentarily, I thought I might have taught someone something that made a difference?

Alison was giving me a look: *You know what I mean by here.*

"Well, I mean, it's my job." It was also my health insurance and dental plan.

"I'm renewing contracts for next year," Alison said. "Something tells me you might be happier when you aren't finding creative ways to circumvent departmental policies."

She had made such statements before, though I'd never thought she would follow through. My course evaluations were always good, and no one else wanted to teach Great Books. At the same time, I'd always imagined that if she did fire me, she would do it gleefully. Instead she looked unexpectedly grave.

"Eliana. My question is not hypothetical. People can sense when someone would rather be elsewhere, just as they sense when someone really is passionate."

Like those pedagogy emails that Alison continued to discharge at 3 a.m.—it was true she was no slouch. Somberly, she said, "I think you could benefit from some serious introspection."

I considered asking what she was insinuating, but she continued. "Eliana, I ask you in all seriousness: What is it you want to do?"

I thought of the moments I liked best. When a student's eyes widened with real interest, or when some tidbit I shared in class left us all walking with more bounce to our step. "I want to inspire people." I said it before I even knew I'd thought it. Immediately I felt like a fool. It was like saying I wanted to be Beyoncé.

Alison was nodding. "A worthy endeavor. I suggest you give some thought as to how you might best achieve that."

"I'm organizing a class trip to the MFA—"

"Not in terms of this job, Eliana. I want you to think *bigger*."

Not in terms of my job? Easy for Alison to say, with job security and a private office with a computer all to herself. Then again—it struck me after I'd left and was about to text Luis—it was true some people grew out of their jobs. Just as they grew out of relationships and even, I suppose, themselves. Even Alison had done something I'd never dared. Given shape to an inner essence. Embraced— announced—her full self.

But to do that would mean relinquishing my rote life. Stepping away from everything I knew. Like Ovid's mortals who cry out to the gods, *Change me!*

It turned out I had no choice. An email arrived the next day explaining that my student had lodged an official complaint with the dean of the faculty and that, given the circumstances, as well as my repeated failure to fulfill my publishing agreement (which had in fact expired years earlier), Alison would not be renewing my contract.

*

With Luis away, and Lorena piqued at me, and my income to evaporate at the end of the academic year, it was a hard week. I told my students how Pandora's box was really an urn, and that an obol was a coin placed over the eyelids of someone who has died. All the while, Alison's question rang in my ears.

What is it you want to do?

I'd entered the university believing it a laboratory of contemplation, a sharp mind the only currency needed for entry. Yet I'd come to see it more as a sanitarium for people who couldn't keep nineto-five jobs—who fell into petty tiffs and seemed to hold as a main aim avoiding interaction with their students (or, as the university had begun calling them, *student-consumers*). In fact, there was much

I disliked about academia: the expensive conferences I'd long ago stopped attending, the knowing chuckles at every bland in-joke, the round-robin sniping in journals. Alison must have sensed this.

Or maybe she had simply grown tired of dealing with me.

. . . some serious introspection.

What about *her*, with her attention-seeking? The thought enraged me enough to search my old emails so that I could read her message again and remind myself how distasteful it was.

This time, though, I found myself reading the information she had included, about her goddess-based religion, with its focus on nature, the seasons, and the earth, giving women an appreciation of their bodies and natural beauty—and that there had been a recent resurgence in the U.S., as a form of feminist resistance to the new president.

I felt something, reading this.

Yet Alison had fired me, a fellow female! So much for supportive sisterhood.

By the time Luis returned, I was really low. Terrified, frankly. Realizing my true market value. I could teach but possessed no other viable skills. Each second was one closer to the moment my auto-deposits would evaporate. I googled old friends, discovered their newfound positions of power, which served only to make me feel inferior. I told Luis I needed time apart, to focus on my job search. Instead of acting crushed, he left encouraging messages, seemingly ready to pick things up as soon as I found employment. But I saw no possible future.

What is it you want to do?

I had one thing: the book based on my dissertation. With some difficulty, I located the ancient computer files. With more difficulty, I managed to convert them into something legible. But the more I read, the more my heart ached, and I knew I couldn't go back there.

In bed that night, I lay sleepless for a long time. Memories returned. My Hellenic studies professor crediting my own comments to a male classmate, how I'd never corrected him. The philosophy preceptor who always breezed into class fifteen minutes late with his coffee and Converse sneakers and ironic tee shirt and tried to chat me up afterward—and that I'd never complained. What would it have taken for me to say something, do something?

To be brave. *Change me!*

I sat up in bed.

For a long while, I thought. Then I called Luis. Told him I knew I had trouble trusting men but that I wanted to work on it, wanted to try to change.

Then I told him my idea. "Imagine if each of us had a personal god or goddess to help us out?" I told him how I wanted to give women the tools they needed to take action, no matter the situation, and that I could use my expertise from my studies.

I was thinking I might put flyers in yoga studios in the wealthier suburbs, give some to my acupuncturist roommate and her healer associates (including a massage therapist who runs a high-end spa) and eventually my client list would grow. I would call the business Inner Divinity. *Channel your inner goddess to realize your dreams.*

My clients would tell me their challenges and desires, and I would locate which goddess from the pantheon best models the qualities for them to work on; then I would help them to cultivate those qualities.

"It's like your name," Luis said, after I had explained my concept.

I didn't understand what he meant.

"Didn't you say that in Hebrew it means . . ."

"*My god has answered me.*"

I don't recall what he said then, because though I had never put much credence in my name before, it did seem, however improbably, as I considered what had been taken from me as well as what had been given, that maybe there was something to it after all.

"What about you?" Luis asked the next day. It was a warm afternoon and we were out for a riverside walk. I had just confessed to him where I'd plucked up the seeds of my idea: that I'd read that link in Alison's email. He didn't seem to think it crass that I was looking to monetize my own obsession. "One of us has got to bring in the big bucks." Then he asked, "Who's your signature goddess?"

I'd pondered that question and had come to a surprising conclusion. "Turns out the character I most admire is a mortal."

With his arm slung around my shoulder, I told Luis the story of Atalanta, the girl from Tegea: abandoned as an infant and raised by hunters. She could match—even beat—any man at any sport. But her greatest strength, they say, was her survival instinct.

"I want to embrace my own survival instinct. Instead of survivor guilt."

And as we walked along the winking river, I told him about Necee, and the accident, and the psychotherapy I'd given up on, how since the day my bicycle collided with Necee's, everything in my life had come to a screeching halt.

It was a relief to tell him. To feel him hold me, to hear him tell me he was sorry about it.

I reminded him that there was something he hadn't told me, too. "Back when I asked what your email blast would say."

He shoved his hands into his pockets. "Ever since I can remember, I've basically had to be my mom's husband. Not romantically, but, you know, it's a lot. Even when you love her as much as I do."

It wasn't what I'd expected. I felt bad for him, and for Lorena. I supposed I was right for choosing Atalanta, though I didn't mention the other reason I liked her: how she didn't want to marry and tried to devise a way to keep suitors from winning her hand.

My therapist and I are working on that.

My therapist says it will take some time. That I will have to learn to allow myself to move forward. That it's not uncommon for people who lose a loved one in such circumstances to cease emotional development at whatever point they were at when the loss occurred.

He also says it's normal that I still talk to Necee. That I'm repeatedly crushed that she never answers me back.

He did not chide me when, exactly one year later, Luis suggested we'd save money by living together, and I explained that economizing wasn't the right reason to make such an important decision.

A year after that, when Lorena was in a relationship we could tell was going to stick and Luis, feeling a lightening of his duty, found his own place and pointed out that as soon as we became official partners, he could put me on his medical plan, I said I didn't want our union to be a mere reaction to the health insurance industry.

Also, they say romance has an expiration date of two years.

But we've been together three years now and I'm still pretty crazy about him. And in these days of abominable news and daily death counts, of constant linguistic shenanigans and semantic treachery, of self-quarantine and social isolation, of terrifying not-knowing, who doesn't need the comfort of love?

Also, Luis said I had better get on his health plan quick, with how contagious this virus is.

Even before the lockdown, I was spending most of my time over at his place. I already had two drawers of clothes there, and my slippers, and a tray of earrings. And the water pick.

So moving in wasn't such a big change. And it was a relief to no longer have to pay rent for my room, though Inner Divinity had gone pretty well, thanks to a feature story in the paper when one of my six clients that first year ran for City Councilor and won; then two more ran for office, and another became a full-time climate change activist. But with the economy tanking, business has taken a hit. Already one woman has asked to defer payment while she's furloughed. I'm charging another half my usual rate, since it's important for us to stay connected, for my clients to stay focused on their goals—whether they're saving the planet or getting a divorce. Some clients tiptoe around what they really want, too shy to even name it. This is where language matters. Clarity and honesty. With the state of the world, we can't stay quiet any longer. I think of my former students, the ones born with losing lottery tickets, without family money, who tended bar and waited tables, and I wonder, with everything closed down, how they're getting by.

In the evenings Luis and I watch the news on television. We listen to the president's people give briefings, each of them standing at the lectern to pronounce their expertise. We hear their circumlocutions, the verbal hijinks and explanations. Some of them seem to be trying to tell the truth. Other times we end up shouting at the television and have to turn it off.

To prevent the possibility of infecting Lorena, we speak with her only via our computer screens. She's really annoyed with us for not having gotten married yet. With the virus, she says, she could be dead any day now. Why hasn't Luis proposed? What about her grandchildren?

"Change rarely happens overnight," I tell her, same as I tell my clients.

The planet might have managed it, this seemingly meteoric shift, everyone having to adapt so swiftly—but usually we humans take a little more time.

Just ask me. I am an expert.

Providence

In the mornings she liked to go jogging. That was the word for it, a leisurely loping across the tracks and up the hill to Highland. She couldn't quite call it "running," not with all the gainfully employed citizens darting past her for the 87 bus to the Green Line. Talia's employment, at a charitable organization where she churned out grant applications and donation requests and received an earnest, disheartening salary, was just thirty hours a week. So she had time for these long jogs.

Past sagging triple-deckers where she had roomed as a student and older, prouder houses high on the hill, up to the stone-and-granite tower marking Revolutionary War battles and Civil War training grounds. Then back down by the pubs and pizza joints and "oriental places" (as her downstairs neighbor, Marsha, wouldn't stop calling them) to her own increasingly unfamiliar neighborhood, with the bakery that sold eight-dollar loaves of bread, and a "luxury" apartment structure where the methadone clinic used to be, and a new, separate, protected lane for "damn bikes" (Marsha again).

Talia's route rarely varied. Except that on this cold spring day, after heading out for her morning jog, she instead found herself in the hospital, with little understanding as to how she had come to be there.

By the time all the tests were done, over a day had passed and Talia had been transferred to a tiny room on an upper floor. The clothes from her jog were bunched into a lump on the window-sill. It seemed ages ago that she had worn them—stepped into the nippy May air with no great worry of dying. But she was forty-five years old; lots of people died in middle age. She wondered where her sneakers were.

The neurologist, a disconcertingly young woman with a posh Indian accent, explained what the MRI had revealed. No tumors—that, at least, was good news. What appeared to have caused the seizure, as far as Talia could comprehend, was a small hole in her brain. It probably had always been there, the young doctor said, her elegant inflection making this appalling fact somehow acceptable. Medication would keep it under control.

"Well. Shit." Talia tried to stay calm. But beneath her shock lay a familiar, simmering panic. Even if this small hole did not kill her, she was quite certain she couldn't afford it.

The doctor was saying something about a prescription and to continue on the blood thinner, and that she would like to see Talia in one week. "And it's best if for the time being you refrain from running."

"Jogging. Really, I barely even sweat. I don't see how it could set off a seizure."

The doctor allowed that the seizure might have been coincidence. "But let's wait a week or so. Now, what questions do you have for me?"

Talia asked if there might be a cheaper room available.

"I'm pleased to report that you're being discharged." Little gold earrings bobbed from the doctor's earlobes. "Have you got someone to accompany you home?"

An acute aloneness seized her. Well, she could probably ask Gordie. Two days had passed since their awkward misunderstanding—which, now that Talia had rubbed shoulders with death, seemed trivial. Still, this was what her life had come to. She had always assumed she would eventually find a companion for the long haul. Instead, here she was, on her own.

And yet. A flickering at the edge of memory. "I think someone was there. When I had the seizure." A presence at her side as she lay on the cold ground. A blanket being draped over her. "Do you know who called the ambulance?"

The doctor shook her pretty head. But the EMTs, she assured Talia, would have a report.

All the way home, Gordie kept asking for details of what had happened. Though he rarely showed emotion, he was clearly upset—even more upset than he had been the other night.

"I'm telling you," Talia said, conscious of the Lyft driver overhearing every word, "all I know is I was jogging and next thing I was in the ambulance. Then I blacked out again." She was aware that she was skipping the part about the blanket being carefully placed over her, but that part seemed suspiciously like a dream.

Gordie kept frowning, his deep-set eyes troubled beneath the swoop of shiny dark bangs. "Superman hair," Talia used to tease him, though really it was his broad forehead and firm jaw that made it look like that. She had to stop herself from reaching over to comfort him. Of the other friends she might have asked to accompany her, Camilla was now the embattled mother of two awful toddlers, and Dani had caved to ever-rising rent and decamped to Providence. Of Talia's series of negligent boyfriends, her most recent lover, discarded a good six months ago, was no one she wished to see now.

Gordie, though, was always around. He lived next door, in the same row house as Talia; his workplace, some tech company run by twenty-year-olds, was mere blocks away, in one of the old brick warehouses that still housed an acrobatics school and a marzipan factory and a film studio and hadn't yet been bought up. He was seventeen years younger than Talia and didn't have many friends. Marsha called him "an odd duck."

Twice Marsha had called Talia an "Angry Black Woman"—but that was another issue.

She told Gordie what the doctor had said, about the hole, the medication. Just mentioning it made her queasy. "No cancerous tumors or anything like that," she said, trying not to let on how terrified she was.

She could see Gordie clenching his jaw, the dimple emerging in his smooth, gaunt cheek. He was ridiculously handsome, not to mention unnaturally smart. More specifically, he was "on the spectrum," though at first Talia had merely suspected that part. He had confirmed her guess one night up in her living room shortly after they met. As the *Eroica* surged from her enormous, prehistoric stereo, Talia mentioned some theory about Beethoven and mild autism, to which Gordie said, simply, "I have that." Which still didn't explain why he chose to hang out with Talia rather than dewy, age-appropriate friends.

Until what happened the other night, she had never seen him upset. Now, watching him chew the corner of his pink mouth, she was forced to admit that despite her doctor's calm demeanor, something really alarming had occurred. And so she acknowledged what must also have been real. "Someone waited with me."

Someone had run off and returned with a blanket. And someone else—yes, there was a second person, too—had remained with her, holding her hand. Saying it, Talia knew it was true.

"I want to find them. To thank them. And let them know I'm all right." But she didn't know who or where they were.

Gordie asked to see the printout from the hospital. It lay on Talia's lap along with her little paper bag of medication. She handed over the flimsy page and watched Gordie read, his brow crimping. He said, "This thing is fucking useless."

That was when he asked if she had taken any pictures along her run. Sometimes she did that, to text him ones she thought might make him laugh, since Gordie didn't smile much.

She took out her phone, but her eyes were too tired. A great weariness overcame her. "I'm sorry, Bug, I can't do this right now." She didn't know why she called him Bug. It was just something she had said once that became normal.

The car had arrived at their block, a strip of row houses built close to the curb, each with a patch of lawn the size of a bathmat. Like the others, theirs was split down the middle by side-by-side front doors like opposing reflections.

Though it was technically one house, Talia's half was painted a periwinkle color, with unlit Christmas lights strung up the side and fake icicles dripping from the gutter, and a screen door whose spring was broken in perpetuity. Gordie's half, owned by an interior designer on the first floor, was slate gray with charcoal trim, its front door painted deep red, with a motion-sensor light meant to look like an old streetlamp. Around Gordie's scrap of lawn, the owner had piled flat rocks to form a quaint stone border encircling pale tulips that, in this coldest, grayest May, were only now fully bloomed. Propped in the woodchips was a sign:

No Matter Where You Are From
You Are Welcome Here

The driver left them there, at the concrete stoop, in front of which Gordie's landlord had embedded some aspirational cobblestones. Gordie said, "I hereby offer my admittedly unexceptional culinary services."

Talia said, "Honestly, all I want to do is sleep." Normally she would ask him up and they would lounge on her nubby sofa and talk until late.

Gordie's cheeks flushed; probably he thought this was still about the other night. He looked away and mumbled, "Well, knock if you need me." He meant on the wall. Talia's living room abutted his bedroom.

Too weary to say anything more, Talia told him, "Thanks, Bug." She wrapped her arms around herself and gave a squeeze, a tradition of theirs, since Gordie's being on the spectrum meant he didn't usually like to be touched.

She told work she was still sick and slept late. Daylight helped her to feel less panicked about the "small hole." She fried up some eggs and spread wheat toast with honey and drank a mug of hot tea. Then she pulled on her exercise clothes, gathered her hair into a high, poufy ponytail, and went out to look for whoever had helped her.

Marsha was on the front steps, heading in with her wad of junk mail.

The first time Talia overheard Marsha calling her an Angry Black Woman was two years ago, as Marsha yammered into a cellphone following an incident involving the volume of Talia's stereo. And though Talia was, technically, just as much an Angry White Woman—with the Norwegian stature, gray eyes, and broad cheekbones of her mother—Marsha was right; it was the Black part that was angry (furious), and the woman part (outraged), while the rest, due to Talia's having her father's bronze skin, went generally ignored by the public.

The second time Marsha called her that, while Talia listened from the stairwell, was to their ancient landlord, Mr. Figueiredo, who lived on the first floor. Apparently Marsha didn't dare confront

Talia about her stomping overhead for fear of approaching an Angry Black Woman. But Mr. Figueiredo was a staunch advocate of Talia. Not only did he ignore Marsha, he hadn't raised Talia's rent in seven years. Talia prayed daily that he would not die—at which point she would surely have to pick up and move to Providence like Dani.

Now, Marsha was squinting at her. "You feeling all right?" For an awful moment Talia thought the hole in her brain was somehow visible. "Gordie said you were in the hospital."

"I'm well enough now."

"Well, good." Marsha let the screen door slam behind her.

Sometimes Talia wondered why she clung to this setup, a bigot literally underfoot. Other times she felt amazed at her luck: a friend right next door and a short walk to her workplace and her plot in the community garden. She even found a certain comfort in the Holmans and DiRuzzas yelling at each other across their rusted chain-link fences, and the skinny MIT kid riding a strange bicycle assembled from junkyard parts, and Neil DiRuzza tearing around in the boxy white U.S. Postal Service truck. It was true that addicts tossed their nip bottles and sometimes needles into the overgrown bushes at the end of the street and that more than once Talia had witnessed a brawl below her window. But it was what she could afford, and most days, it was enough.

Even so, she had begun to look for work in Providence. People said it was what her town used to be, affordable for upstarts and creative types; Dani had bought a condo by the river. In fact, Talia had gone ahead and had an interview, just last week. The position, grant writer for a music program, was similar to her current work, and the interview had gone well. Dani, who for over a year had been pressuring Talia to make the move, kept asking if she had heard back yet.

The interview seemed distant now, something from another life. Talia took a seat on the concrete stoop and checked the photographs on her phone, in case there were clues about her jog. She found two new ones: a scruffy gray dog in front of No. 1 Yummy Chinese and a close-up of two intensely wrinkled men playing backgammon in front of the Hellenic Club.

Both locations were about halfway along her usual route. Since Talia had no recollection of looping back, her seizure had probably taken place somewhere after the Hellenic Club but before the dubious "Lounge" where she usually turned around. It was a lot of territory to cover, but she had all afternoon.

She began at the used car dealership, its dirty plastic God Bless America banner flapping in the breeze. That's how it was now. Rainbow flags versus red, white, and blue; peace sign versus the big red poster with the leftover campaign slogan. Probably it was what had caused her seizure. Not that she hadn't already been livid. But these days it was like being in a constant low-grade war. Even the red, white, and blue pennants strung above the car lot made an angry rippling sound. Talia zipped her jacket and wished she had Gordie with her. Not just for moral support. When she was little, she used to showily hold her mother's hand to put shopkeepers at ease.

Now her parents were far away, having retired to a scenic, vaguely lawless Mexican town known for its cut-rate medical procedures.

"Hello!" A young man inside the dealership looked genuinely excited to see Talia.

Already she felt she was letting him down. "I'm actually not looking for a car." She had never owned a car. She made $36,000 a year.

"Change for the meter?" another, older, jaded man drawled. Talia explained about the ambulance and the fallen jogger. But the words came out oddly, failing to convey that she was the jogger. The omission made her feel deceitful. When it became clear that the men knew nothing of the incident, Talia quickly thanked them and left.

She didn't know why she had dissembled. Probably it was that she still felt a pit in her stomach even thinking of the ambulance.

Or maybe some part of her suspected those men would care more about someone other than herself.

Yet she found herself using the same veiled phrasing not just at the fluorescent-lit liquor store with the big America First poster but also at the hair salon (rainbow stickers on the door), the yoga studio (Tibetan prayer flags strung across the awning), and the florist whose window displayed a handwritten pledge:

> *We believe in Science*
> *We believe in Women's Rights*
> *We believe in Healthcare for All*
> *We Support our Immigrants*

But no one knew of the incident, so that it began to seem all the stranger that Talia herself had not witnessed this thing that had happened to her, which someone, some mysterious other, had. At each storefront she felt a growing wariness, as if this mission were some insanity she had cooked up—even as she tried to assure herself that beneath one of these awnings, behind one of these doors, were hands that had held and warmed hers, that had fetched a blanket to drape over her. Someone would see her and know who she was.

She had come to the block where, on her morning jogs, she always sped up and kept her gaze straight ahead. It was a short one—a vacant lot fenced off for construction and just two buildings, one on either side of the street. The first was some kind of recording studio, with a faded concert poster taped inside the window. Talia rang the buzzer three times, but no one answered.

She looked across to the other building. Red brick, with American flags sticking out all over the place. Each window wore stars-and-stripes bunting, and above the VFW Post 19 crest was a hand-painted wooden sign. ALL LIVES MATTER.

Talia crossed over. The problem, she considered, was that even if they didn't see her the way Marsha did, she could guess—what with her yoga pants and WBUR fundraiser jacket—who they *would* see: one of those bike-riding, latte-drinking, unpatriotic types who used Lyft instead of taxis and bought "artisanal" donuts.

Talia wanted to explain: I've been here twenty years! I helped rebuild the playground when the hurricane tore it up! I volunteer on Flag Day! I can't stand the fancy new donut place!

She also found the new vintage shop exorbitantly priced and the cat accessories shop vaguely immoral. She hated that the bead store was now a vape shop—hated electronic cigarettes emitting scents of chocolate and vanilla, hated the men-children who smoked them. She hated millennials in general.

Well, except for Gordie. Gordie was different. When you asked him a question, he seemed to really think about it before answering. She could let down her guard with him, could tell him anything, even her bleak, unattractive thoughts—of accumulated disappointment and small, sharp wounds, of her dubiousness about the world in general. Sometimes she even saw herself as Gordie did: her archaic qualities as exotic quirks, her clunky stereo system as "cool," and her lack of a television or streaming service as "subversive." Raised on text messaging, Gordie thought her brave for being able to communicate face-to-face, for making phone calls without hesitation. He found it charming that she so rarely texted; once, when he was out front and she opened her window to call down to him, his eyes widened with amazement, as if she had performed a clever trick.

She wished he were here now. But then she recalled his blushing cheeks, his bruised voice.

What had happened the other night was that after eating half an apple pie together up at her place, when they were about to say goodnight, Talia had told Gordie about the interview in Providence.

And though his expression had remained unchanged, he sounded sore when he asked why she had waited to tell him.

"I guess I thought I'd jinx it."

The truth was that Dani had set her up with someone in Providence. An architect named Douglas, whom Talia had met for coffee after the interview. A divorcé, Douglas was Talia's age, with crinkles at the edges of his eyes and a tendency to laugh at his own jokes. His mother was Moroccan, his father from Kenya, and he had lived all over the world. He also ran his own architecture firm and had put his son through college; he was a grown-up. Tall enough, handsome enough, if a bit flabby in the middle. And though Talia hadn't felt a spark, she liked his laugh and in his easy smile had seen, for the first time in a long while, a chance at something so many other people seemed to have found.

In her kitchen with Gordie, though, the meeting suddenly seemed illicit. She found she could not mention Douglas—and certainly not that he had asked her to dinner for the coming weekend, here in town, or that she had agreed.

"I'm sure you'll get the job," Gordie had said quietly, and then lingered awkwardly, not saying goodbye. Talia, nervous, had been about to give herself their little mutual hug when Gordie did something unfathomable. Taking a step so that their bodies were almost touching, he placed his palm on Talia's waist. With his other hand, he touched her cheek. Since Talia was nearly his same height, it didn't take much more for him to lean in and kiss her.

She had kissed him back, their bodies pressed together, Gordie's hand slipping to her thigh, near her buttocks, until the reality of what they were doing struck her—so preposterous, she extracted herself, blurting something about the pie.

Gordie, red-faced, stepped away, while Talia busied herself with searching for the aluminum foil, beginning to understand what she must have been sensing over the past weeks: that Gordie had, in fact, reached out before but each time had faltered. There had been a moment a few days earlier when he seemed on the verge of some kind of confession. Even so, as she found the foil—on the counter right in front of her—she told herself it was impossible, there must be some mistake. She was *old*! Or did he not know just how old she was? People always thought her younger than her age. And so, as she fumbled with the leftover pie, trying to pretend nothing had happened, she said, "In my forty-five years, I've never made such a good pie," feeling ridiculous. She could not look Gordie in the eye as she handed it to him, repeating, "In all my forty-five years—"

"I know how old you are," Gordie said flatly, and instead of taking the pie, left it there, heading down the stairs and out the door, and then back upstairs to his place.

Talia went into the living room, to the wall that abutted Gordie's. For a long time she stood there. She wanted to say something, even just that she was sorry, and leaned her ear against the wall as if to glean some bit of wisdom. She could hear, faintly, the creak of the floor beneath Gordie's feet. With the tips of her fingers, she made a light rippling sound against the wall. She waited, then tried again. Even after she had given up and gone to bed, she lost sleep trying to think how to make things right.

And then came the next morning, her run, the hospital.

At VFW Post 19, behind a metal desk with a placard saying *Be an American Legion Volunteer*, a young woman with many silver rings on her fingers asked Talia if she was here for the youth mentoring training. Talia tried to sound businesslike as she explained about the jogger and the ambulance. She asked if anyone from the VFW might have witnessed the incident.

"You from the *Chronicle*?" The woman wore her hair sheared very close on one side, the other side cut on a sharp diagonal.

"I just want to thank the people who helped out," Talia told her. "Let them know the jogger's all right." She let her gaze shift away. A bright stone from one of the rings flashed as the woman penned Talia's number on a notepad. A diamond; it was an engagement ring. Talia felt herself making a familiar, involuntary calculation: that this woman, too, had managed, like so many others, to find someone.

There had been a boyfriend Talia thought she might marry, nearly a decade ago. She had been with him just over two years when, on his Facebook page one day, he posted a photo of his pale fingers intertwined with her darker ones, and as the image garnered a flood of enthusiastic typed comments, Talia found that this same boyfriend's other self-congratulatory acts, each concerning his union with Talia, swiftly returned to her, a whole flatulent parade of them, until it seemed her love for him, too, must be tainted, and she knew she had to leave him.

"We're having our pancake breakfast Saturday," the VFW woman said, "if you want to bring your friends." Talia was momentarily flummoxed. Did the woman not know what that big hand-painted sign out front meant? Talia heard herself make a sort of grunt. "Thanks," she told the woman briskly, and left.

Even after she had crossed to the next block, though, she felt odd and in some way tarnished for not admitting that she, Talia, was the person who had been taken away in the ambulance.

The next stretch, too, brought no luck. Probably Talia was in the wrong area altogether. Yet some inner thoroughness kept her from skipping more than the apartment buildings set far back from the street and the great brick cavern that was City Hall.

Even when the man in the money-wiring place addressed her in Portuguese (she was sometimes assumed to be Brazilian) and insisted he understood no English, Talia did not skip ahead. She pantomimed jogging and falling and made the whine of a siren, but no sign of recognition crossed the man's face. And as the sun shifted and long thin clouds streaked the sky, everything began to look strange, the shop windows with their signs pressed to the glass— *Cash for Gold* and *Lavender honey gelato!* and *Não Fazemos Remessa.* In front of the CrossFit, grunting disciples hauled medicine balls up and down the gray sidewalk, back and forth, on some baffling mission. Autos convalescing at the Mecânica Brasileira seemed to have gathered for a dreary reunion. In the dry cleaner's, the carousel of hangers sheathed in plastic moved like a procession of shimmering apparitions.

She was stepping back outside when her cellphone buzzed.

Nicole here from the VFW. Just so you know whose number this is. Will see if the guys know anything.

There were two more messages, she saw now, one right after the other.

Hey T, any job news????

Any word from Douglas?????

Dani, in her bright new condo, waiting for Talia to have good news. Talia hadn't yet told her about the seizure. It would only worry her and make the Providence job and decent health insurance and someone to look out for her seem all the more urgent.

Talia stuffed her phone deep into her pocket. She had heard from Douglas twice since their meeting. First a phone message saying he had enjoyed meeting her, then a text suggesting possible restaurants for their date. Now even that exchange seemed like a relic of a previous existence.

She had come to a Victorian house with scuffed front steps and a carved placard hanging from a signpost.

Pierre D. Pierre
Divination Services

99

There used to be a neon Psychic Readings sign propped in the window, but some months ago it had been replaced with this elegant one. Talia pressed the buzzer, which appeared not to function, then knocked on the door, a quick rap-rap-rap. The sound of her knuckles against the wood conjured, momentarily, Gordie on the other side, tapping their private code.

Instead the door was opened by a man perhaps a decade older than Talia, taller and browner than Talia, with thick graying curls that came past his ears. He was wearing a blue tracksuit and carrying a small pajama-clad child.

Well-practiced now, Talia swiftly explained her errand. The child, perhaps a year old, watched coolly from the comfort of the man's chest. "So," Talia concluded, "I'm wondering if you or maybe your neighbors have any information."

There was a flicker in the man's eyes as he nodded. "Please, come in."

At last. Talia stepped into a dimly lit foyer and was waved into a sitting room, its shades drawn. "I return, one minute," the man said, his voice low, his accent mellow, and disappeared down the hallway.

From a back room came the voice of a woman speaking what must have been Creole; she sounded annoyed. Adjusting to the dim lighting, Talia took in a table draped with satiny cloth, where glass bottles of various sizes held flowers with petals of white fabric, and feathers, and a stubby lit candle. On the wall hung a large glittering sequined cloth and an alarming number of posters of Tom Brady in his New England Patriots uniform.

The man reemerged without the baby. "I am Pierre D. Pierre. Please have a seat." He motioned to a smaller table cluttered with seashells, unfamiliar-looking coins, scattered cards, a bell, and many small oval plastic chips shaped like scarabs. Understanding now, Talia said quickly, "I didn't mean I wanted to do a reading."

"Mine are inspired by vodou tradition. You are of Haitian descent?"

"As I said, I just want to know—"

"Divination is not a simple answer to a question. It is the first step toward an answer."

Talia cleared her throat. "I apologize for the misunderstanding."

Pierre D. Pierre handed her a small laminated menu. "My fee sheet."

"I'm sorry," Talia said, "but I don't believe in any of this."

With no change of expression, Pierre D. Pierre took the fee sheet back. He tugged one of the chairs out from the table, sat down. Even seated he was tall. He leveled his gaze at Talia, the gray curls framing his face. "You have been trying to preempt fate."

She should have known a "psychic" would play hard. There it was again, the creeping sense, ever since the hospital, of being punished for some poor decision she didn't even know she had made. "Look, I'm just trying to find out—"

"Often the real question isn't the one we seek to answer." Pierre D. Pierre gestured toward the other chair with practiced ease, but Talia remained standing. "Like when you visit the doctor. What sends you there are merely symptoms. We must diagnose the ailment before we can find a treatment."

At the mention of doctors and ailments, Talia felt a terrible burning behind her eyes. She wanted to explain that she already had a diagnosis: there was a hole—a *hole!*—in her brain. But the thought sent her pulse racing, the simmering fears rising. And now here it came, panic, at the hole and at the great slithering question mark that was her future. At the medical bills, and ancient Mr. Figueiredo dying, and having to leave here, all she would have to give up.

She let herself drop into the chair.

Pierre D. Pierre seemed to decide something. In one smooth motion, he swept the tarot cards, the plastic scarabs, the shells, the strange coins into a small plastic tub. They made a sad clattering sound. Talia watched forlornly, as though she had lost those things, too.

"These are only tools," Pierre D. Pierre told her. "There are times when no tools are needed to access the wills of the spirits."

Talia wanted to shout that none of this was about the will of the spirits; it was about how awful the world was. How, just like that, things could turn on a dime.

Pierre D. Pierre tucked his gray curls behind his ears. "In dark powers, too, we find guidance. I want to help you access that guidance." He closed his eyes and sat very still, just the slightest movement beneath his lids. After a long minute, he said, "You have been running—"

Jogging!

"—from your future. You try to predict. To plan. What the spirits want me to tell you is that fate is not something to fear."

What kind of bullshit was this? She had to plan ahead—her daily survival depended on it. Each day the fragile balance that was her life became harder to maintain. She couldn't afford to be caught off guard. She was provident by necessity.

"With all due respect," she said, "thinking ahead is how I survive." She pushed herself away from the flimsy table.

Pierre D. Pierre opened his eyes. "I'm trying to tell you, you already have divine guidance. But you instead have let yourself be guided by fear."

Talia could feel the fear, deep within her. The suspicion that whatever luck she had had in life had run out. That in remaining true to herself, in thinking she might be loved and understood and met halfway, she had made a lamentable mistake.

"Look," she said, standing, "how much do I owe you?"

"We have only just started." But he stood, pushed in his chair. "You come back, we do more." He did not look terribly disappointed as he accompanied her to the front door. Instead of asking for payment, he took both her hands in his. "You must go to Beauty International."

Talia snatched her hands back.

"They are there," he said. "The people who found you. When you fall down."

Talia could feel her eyebrows raising. "Did the spirits tell you that?"

Pierre D. Pierre shrugged. "In the post office I heard. They were worrying about you."

"Why didn't you tell me?"

"You needed my guidance."

She shook her head at him, furious. But Pierre D. Pierre laughed as if this were all in good fun. Then he said, quite seriously, "I'm very glad you are well."

"Yeah, yeah." Talia was still wagging her head as she stepped outside.

"Good luck, my friend."

"I'm not your friend," she said under her breath, descending the rickety steps. But Pierre D. Pierre called after her, "Please like me on Facebook!"

The air had grown cooler. In the shaded alley at the corner, figures in grubby coats huddled against the concrete. Talia glanced down the street, where afternoon traffic was beginning to clog the intersection. Beauty International was just a block or so away. On Talia's cellphone, there was a message from Gordie.

How are you feeling?

Talia tried to walk and type at the same time, even though she hated when people did that.

Much better! Out walking.

She thought for a moment and added, **Not far from your HQ.**

Maybe Gordie would leave work early and come join her. He did that sometimes. Talia looked for the little answer bubble to light up. Gordie always answered ridiculously fast.

Every few steps, Talia looked down at the screen. She still held, within her, the sensation of Gordie's body against hers, his palm sliding from her hip to her thigh.

The self-congratulatory boyfriend used to pat her ass proprietarily. But no, she told herself, that wasn't how Gordie saw her. And Gordie never would have posted that clasped-hands photo on Facebook.

Her friend Camilla had insisted the photo was no more than an innocent statement of love. But Camilla had no way of ever understanding.

Gordie wasn't like that. Gordie sent deadpan texts that made her laugh out loud. At night he scratched the wall in a light, ruffling way to wish her sweet dreams.

Talia's phone buzzed. It was Carla at the VFW.

You're the runner right?

Talia stopped walking. She read the sentence again. Something seemed to be cracking inside her. There was a bench in front of Momo's restaurant, and she went to it, waiting for the awful cracking to subside.

Yes she typed back. **But I'm better now.**

She stared with surprise at her words.

Carla buzzed right back. **Glad you're okay.**

Talia began to weep. Because it was so wearying, always having to steel oneself against awfulness. Pierre D. Pierre's bogus divination was right: she feared the future and her fate, even as these small warm gestures, like benevolent spirits, seemed to point toward some other, shimmering world.

She tried to stop her weeping. She wished Gordie would message her back. There was one night when she had done a goofy impersonation of Neil DiRuzza roaring around in the post office van, and Gordie had laughed—real laughter, so hard his cheeks turned pink.

She wiped her eyes and texted him.

Would love to see you. Meet in front of Momo's?

His response came, as usual, instantaneously. That little thumbs-up sign. As the scent of frying oil wafted from Momo's, Talia watched the afternoon glare stretch the clouds into brilliant streaks of pink and waited for Gordie.

They went together to the beauty shop, where a skinny woman in an incredibly tight sweater was stacking squat little jars of pomade on a display. Talia began her story, then stopped. With Gordie beside her, she rephrased: "I was jogging by the other day and had a medical emergency."

The woman placed the jar of pomade back on the cart and regarded her. "Is you?"

"Is me!" She didn't mean to shout.

"Wait, you wait here." The woman hurried to the back of the shop. "Lina! Lina! Es ella, la negrita!"

Talia turned to look at Gordie.

"Lina! Está aquí la negrita, del otro día!"

Gordie said, "I think it's a linguistic thing."

A short, plump woman with platinum hair was hurrying out. Seeing Talia, she stopped. The expression on her face was one of terror.

Talia wished Gordie would hold her hand, anything to comfort her. The woman stepped cautiously forward. She reached out and, as if to determine that there really was someone standing before her, let her fingertips graze Talia's.

A sensation came over Talia. Of strong hands covering her. A blanket laid gently across her body.

"No se murió?"

Talia understood, then, that the woman must have thought she was seeing a ghost.

"I came to thank you." Talia's cheeks felt wet. So, she saw, were the woman's. Talia wanted to apologize for frightening her. But she didn't know how to say this, so she reached for the woman's hand. And even as she explained that she was fine, all was well, and that this was her friend Gordie, even as she thanked both women once more and told them goodbye, still her palm pressed those warm knuckles and she didn't want to let go.

The first time Gordie ever knocked on Talia's wall had been by accident. He had just moved in and was shifting furniture around, making a racket. After a particularly dramatic series of thumps, Talia had loudly (perhaps channeling Marsha) rapped the sequence back. The shuffling noises stopped. Then came a series of light, purposeful, rhythmic taps.

Knuckles to the wall, Talia mirrored the rhythm. Two quick taps came back. Talia responded in kind. When Gordie tapped just once, Talia tapped out a long complicated reply.

Then Gordie stopped tapping. She could hear him running down the stairs, and she hurried down hers, to try to beat him to the front door. But when she arrived, breathless, he was already there, looking somehow awkward despite his firm jaw and Superman hair.

He did not smile, did not offer a handshake or hello. He said, "Well, so, how would you rate your skills at figuring out where the furniture goes?"

Outside the beauty shop, he said, very quietly, "Wow."

The breeze was softer now, the sky iridescent. A cloying odor wafted from where a man sat smoking on a bench. "I understood I could have died," Talia said, "but I hadn't stopped to think . . ." She stopped walking, turned to Gordie. "I might have lost you."

"What are you talking about? We almost lost *you*."

She wanted to explain about the other night, to tell him she loved him. That though she knew the situation was far from perfect—not even close—still she wanted to try. But as she began to speak her feelings, the words came out wrong. Because surely there would be trouble ahead; no seer or prophet was needed to tell her that. She didn't know what she was babbling, now, just that whatever she said seemed to be making things worse. Gordie stood across from her, his face expressionless.

Talia gave up and leaned her forehead against Gordie's, even though she knew he didn't like to be touched. Together their heads made a sort of tent. She wondered if he would pull away. She wished he would say something to fill the silence, and listened as their breaths synchronized. Then Gordie lifted his head. "What about Providence? Have you heard back?"

She tried not to picture Dani waiting for her. "No, not yet."

He stood taller. "Then we should probably go make sure Mr. Figueiredo is still alive."

They turned toward home, just the air between them. Talia kept her stride alongside Gordie's. There was a tingling in the space where their hands almost touched.

Egg in Aspic

The bistro was tucked into an obscure corner of the West Village, on one of the narrow cobbled streets where tourists always stopped to look at their maps. Laurel supposed she ought to have heard of it; from her seat next to the window she could see a growing cluster of reservation-less stalwarts shivering outside. Max explained that it had been written up in a magazine, and poured more red wine into her squat short-stemmed glass.

The place was so small, everything had been downsized to fit. Patrons settled on wooden stools at little round tables where tea lights flickered in miniature votives, and cut into their food with slender, weightless forks and knives. With the low ceiling and dark wood beams, it was like being inside a wine cask. At the table ahead of Laurel's, two girls with the angular look of models sat narrowly on their stools, like Egyptian cats. To her right, a pair of white-haired men in tweed jackets were so close she could smell the bitter vapors rising from their tiny shots of espresso. Even the food was small; that was because it was French.

Though Laurel was herself petite, she felt oversized, clumsy on her wooden stool. This was her second date with Max ("short for

Makoto," according to their online exchange), and she was drastically out of practice.

Between them, their first course waited coldly on a little porcelain saucer. Apparently it was the restaurant's signature dish. "The article said barely any places in the U.S. serve it," Max was saying. He was Laurel's age, late thirties, with dark, adeptly disheveled hair that made him look rakish. Online he had written in all lowercase, giving him a busy, no-time-for-capitalization air. Laurel liked him so far. Enough that she had agreed to a second date, and to the oeuf en gelée.

She tapped at it with her fork, dimpling the gelatin. The dark yolk stared up, little green peas hovering in the aspic along with a strip of ham, some parsley leaves, and a truly diminutive cornichon. The ocher tinge of the aspic made them seem ancient, like insects fixed in amber.

"Wait"—Max slipped his phone out—"Don't think less of me." He snapped a photo.

"One of us had to do it," Laurel said. "Though to be honest I don't understand how the cosmos hasn't imploded from all our food photos."

"Right, for all we know they mate and replicate."

"There should be a collective graveyard or something." She didn't mean to sound morbid.

"It's called Instagram." Max lifted his fork. His fingertips were slender, his nails pale and square. He scooped the fork sideways through the gelatin, into the egg. Laurel watched the velvet yolk begin to seep out. There was also a leaf of something green. Max took a bite with a crust of baguette.

"Is it good?" one of the white-haired men asked.

It was as if they were all on one collective date. "Mm-hmm," Max said, still chewing. He didn't seem to mind these strangers observing their courtship ritual. Probably Laurel was the strange one, from having been out of the ring so long. When she first signed up on the dating app, she tried to explain: *I was caring for a sick friend.* Though it was the truth, the words looked wrong, cloying, and she deleted them. If she were a widow she could say, *My husband died,* and it wouldn't sound odd. But there wasn't a word for who she had become. And although a full year had somehow managed to pass without Viv in it, Laurel still felt like a teacup someone had smashed and then glued back together.

"Your turn," Max said.

Beside her, the white-haired men spoke in murmurs. Laurel lifted her nearly weightless fork, the tines clinking against the edge of the plate, and a wisp of thought blew through her, gone before she could catch it. An uneasy feeling—she shook it away, cut into her half of the egg. Her bite tasted of peppercorn. One of the cat girls said, "It's not that I don't like him. It's that I'm morally opposed to him."

With a disk of baguette, Laurel daubed at the yolk. She said, truthfully, "It's good."

Max's eyes brightened. He must still like her, then, to care what she thought of the food. Even so, it seemed to her somehow incredible that they might ever become closer than they were right now, eating from opposite sides of an oeuf en gelée. That people somehow went from being strangers atop separate stools to couples exchanging quiet easy murmurings.

Max helped himself to another wedge of baguette. Maybe he, too, searched, sometimes, for a missing friend in crowded streets. Maybe he, too, held conversations in his head with a dead person.

"I knew an artist," she told him, "who, when everyone was starving in South Sudan, started doing these paintings of food. She had an office job during the day, and she'd come home in the evening and instead of making dinner, she'd do a watercolor of a fruit bowl, or, you know, a loaf of bread." The first painting was a single Macintosh apple; Viv said she had been about to eat one but instead made herself paint it for an hour while her stomach twinged. After that, every evening, she would take some item of food from the fridge and sketch or paint it for as long as she could bear.

"Aren't they still starving in Sudan?"

"Jesus, you're probably right." Laurel took a gulp of the dark red wine. "It's like time compresses. I don't know what's from last week or five years ago."

"But I mean, go on—your friend's paintings."

"She always donated to causes like that, even though she didn't have much money. But it made her feel guilty to just make a donation and then look away. Doing the paintings was different. Although she of course knew her hunger wasn't anything like actual starvation."

Max said, "It was an act of solidarity."

"Except she realized she wasn't doing it right. It took a few days, but she realized she couldn't have the actual food in front of her while she painted. She needed to have to *imagine* it."

Max was nodding. "Was she right, did being hungry affect how she pictured the food?"

"I guess really you'd have to have ones from when she wasn't hungry. To compare." Most of the paintings had gone to Viv's parents, but Laurel kept three. One of the Macintosh apples, a bowl of red peppers so curvaceous they were nearly pornographic, and a hardboiled egg lying pristinely next to a thick slice of bread. Sometimes, panicked that she was already forgetting, she made herself picture the others, too. Though perhaps longing had warped her memory of them. "But yes, that was the idea. That absence would become tangible."

"A presence," Max said, and grinned.

"You can write the exhibition notes." Laurel took another forkful of egg. Even though she had never believed in ghosts or an afterlife, she for some reason had expected to feel Viv about her in some way. Kept waiting to sense some whiff of her. But Viv had been an atheist and refused to make an appearance. Only when Laurel managed to forget to miss her—sometimes for hours, or even, lately, almost entire days—did she think she could sense, like glowing coals, Viv's hot fury at being ignored.

"How long did she do that for?" Max asked. "Painting-while-hungry."

"I don't remember exactly." Viv had kept drawing and painting until there were no more treatments, not even hideous experimental ones, to try. But Laurel didn't want to talk about that. Either there would be time later or there wouldn't be.

Ahead of her, the morally opposed girl was asking for the check. Her perfect face looked impossibly smooth. Max said, "Here, have some more before I finish the whole thing."

Laurel reached with the stunted fork. Again she felt a hint of something barely there.

A tiny platter of ceramic food. A miniature balsa wood table built from a kit. Her dollhouse—she hadn't thought of it for ages, not since she had given it away to a girl she had babysat. There had been a cat that was really a little black pompom with glued-on plastic eyeballs and whiskers of white thread, and a bedside table that was really a wooden spool with a circle of fabric secured over it, and little rubber-limbed dolls with painted-on shoes.

Something in her relaxed now that she knew what the feeling was. That it was a memory, and not Viv's hot fury. She mopped up more egg with her baguette, while one of the men at the next table reached to wipe some crumbs from the other's mouth. An automatic gesture; neither seemed aware. Max had made more progress on his side of the egg, and Laurel quickly took another bite, to catch up before the main course arrived. The aspic was now more like a thin gelatinous border.

"You finish it," Max said.

"Go ahead, I don't mind."

"You can say if you didn't like it. Oh, god—did you hate it?"

"No, no." To prove it, she took another scoop, and what was left of the gelatin crumbled.

Using a scrap of bread to draw a theatrical swoosh through the air, Max swiped up what remained on the plate. "Gone."

*

On the sidewalk, waiting patrons huddled in clusters, monitoring the diners' progress. Through the warbled glass of the windows, the room was a dim chamber of light and shade. A server twisted her way between tables, ferrying a check along. The jellied windowpanes turned the scene dense, ocher tinted. Stooped over their meals and seated so close, everyone seemed to be confiding something. Candle tips winked like caught fireflies.

Vertigo

His father's funeral reception was still in progress when Emil wove past the faces of long ago, the grave pats on the arm, the overly respectful remarks, out to the hotel's front steps. It was a cool April afternoon. Woodsmoke wafted from the courtyard where the reception carried on. Emil took long drags on his cigarette and watched the stupendous mess of traffic. Autos nudged their way along the boulevard, past the town square, inching along until clear of the school.

It hadn't been like this before he left—but that was fifteen years ago, when he was still in his teens. The elementary school remained as he remembered it, pale yellow with square windows and a dark, scalloped roof. Since it was a Monday, the weekly fanfare was blaring from loudspeakers. Emil had heard it once already that morning, from his room in the hotel. He had grown up with the weekly salute—a remnant, according to his father, of Communist cheerleading from back before he was born. But now the blasting trumpets merged with the shrill whistles of the police officers attempting to direct traffic. Blue-sweatered children sifted onto the sidewalks.

"A new family every day," said Ivan Sabow, joining Emil on the front steps. He had been Emil's father's closest friend and was now deputy to the mayor. Emil instinctively stepped away. Ivan lit a cigar and jutted his chin toward the swarming students. "You can't believe how our town's thriving."

Settled by Greeks, expanded by Romans, conquered by Ottomans. A small city, almost, with a university, a respectable museum of historical artifacts, and a good number of scenic town squares shaded by oak trees and neatly pruned evergreens. Sturdy houses of stucco and stone tumbled up into the mountains. "Ever since Milev took office, we're the safest municipality in the province," Ivan announced, as if on a podium.

Emil said nothing. The region was safe because mafia bosses built their estates here, out in the hills at the other end of town, transforming what had once been party-owned lodges into spiffed-up palaces. Not that Emil had understood this, back in his teens. Back then these "special" properties were still being restored, guarded by tall spiked gates and hard-muscled dogs trained to bite and not let go. In order to keep their property safe, the bosses maintained a tight lock on everything, including the local police force—which meant the crime rate had gone well down. As a result, the population had doubled. And so the elementary school was now too small.

But the gang bosses would not invest in a new school. Their children were educated elsewhere.

"Your father," Ivan was saying, "was a great supporter of our administration."

"I've not yet had a look at the will, if that's what you're asking."

Ivan sputtered something into his cigar. Emil had already resolved that if he did receive an inheritance—and he could not be sure of that, not after fifteen years without even a brief visit back here—he would give it to charity.

Ignoring Ivan, he watched the sea of blue sweaters, the girls with white roses pinned to their hair. So many were crossing the boulevard back and forth that the cars had to slow. What had happened was that rather than expand the school, the mayor had decided on

115

two sessions per day. Half the students in the morning, the rest in the afternoon—as had once been standard in every school, back before the changes in the nineties.

And so, every midday, this spectacular traffic jam. Was it that parents drove their children to school? When Emil was a boy, everyone had gone on foot. Looking closer, he saw that while indeed a few were being driven, the others were all accompanied by chaperones—adding to the clot of bodies clogging the road.

There were other changes, Emil had noted. A raised pedestrian crossing by the bus stop, and a multi-level parking garage where the big chain store had stood. A strange bronze sculpture in the main square. In a former bakery, an extremely fit man now jumped around calling out dance moves, with a sign by the open storefront: *Zumba Sport!*

Yet much was as it had been when he followed Daniel through these streets. The motley dogs skulking in packs. The water man clanging his bell through the winding alleys, echoing up the high, close walls.

Those narrow, zigzagging alleyways remained the sole access to many of the stone houses that spilled up the sides of the mountain. Up they stepped, into the tiered gray cliffs, where as a child he had been forbidden to play. Because, he had been taught, up there were witches who turned children into birds and let them fly away.

*

Back then, the blue-tiled fountain in the hotel courtyard spouted water in all seasons but winter. Glass lanterns hung like jewels from the big chestnut tree, and in summer the grapevine cast lacework shadows. The open-air restaurant would vibrate with the trills of Emil's parakeet swinging in her cage, along with vacationers' chatter and the mysterious phrases of the expat poets who gathered daily at a corner table to read their work to each other in droning voices.

It was not a grand hotel like the ones down closer to the sea, which labeled themselves "spas" and charged twice as much. Guests were usually pensioners watching their pocketbooks, taking the mineral waters and mud baths at a discount. Yes, their country was incredibly poor, but it had escaped the wars of its neighbors, and the weather was reliable. Perfect for those looking for a bargain or to holiday among locals. The dark jackets the restaurant staff were made to wear lent the place a patina of elegance, though the quarters were modest, the cuisine merely fair. Emil hadn't known this growing up, running from room to room as the maids swept through—waddling women with aprons stretched across their abdomens, or skinny, scurrying ones who never seemed to stay long. The workman, a roguish-looking fellow named Martin, was always making repairs in some precarious manner, balancing on the slate roof with his faded cap and leather holster of tools.

Not until he was twelve or so did Emil understand that the fat, waddling maids were pregnant, the skinny ones barely older than himself.

His first memory was of that courtyard, of his father's grasp and of steamed cocoa from a ceramic teacup. They had moved to the hotel following his mother's death, when Emil was two years old and the hotel had just been restituted to the family after nearly fifty years of state ownership. "This way," his father liked to tell guests, "I can work from home!" Emil's grandfather had built the hotel, from which he had been banished during nationalization in the 1940s. Now it was Emil's father who spent afternoons in the courtyard when the weather was fine, winnowing his way through the newspaper in carefully pressed pants and thin pullovers, while the wait staff stood at attention in their stiff, dark jackets. The hot-chocolate memory carried with it the way his father held him on his lap—as if to make sure not to somehow lose Emil, too.

There had in fact been a spate of abductions when Emil was in primary school. Sometimes the gangs did it simply for money, while other cases, he understood later, were pressure tactics, like contract killings—often spurred by petty rivalries as much as by business disputes. It happened to a girl in the high school, her parents paying up their life savings in ransom. The hotel maids, protective, told Emil the stories about mountain witches turning children into birds, to keep him from straying. His father, less imaginative, said only that he was to stay close to home, out of the alleyways and away from the hills.

The stories hadn't truly frightened him. But at night, when his father tucked him into bed, he had pretended to be afraid of monsters, to keep his father with him as long as possible.

"What monsters?" his father had said, the first time Emil mentioned them. "I don't see any monsters."

"They're invisible, Papa."

"Well, then, lucky I happen to have these invisible monster traps. Invisible even to invisible monsters. You tell me where you want them."

And so every night Emil would point—there, and there, and there—until every possible entry point and hiding place was protected. But something odd began to happen: the more he performed this ritual, the more necessary the traps became, until, for a good stretch of those early years, only in the light of morning did he feel fully safe.

Ivan Sabow was often there in the courtyard with his father, the two men playing dominoes and discussing adult matters. They had grown up together, and when Emil was still very small, Ivan would say that as soon as Emil grew big enough, he would buy him his first cigar. Emil wanted to grow up fast, since Ivan also couldn't wait to teach him how to drive a car and to dance at his wedding.

If ever a waiter fumbled, or a napkin or silverware fell to the floor, Emil's father would just laugh: "You know what they say, the dirtier the tastier!"

Later on, when he started wearing finer suits, Ivan would add, "Same goes for women." When he laughed, you could see his gold fillings, from a dentist in the capital city.

*

Back in the courtyard, the shade umbrellas had been folded shut. Tablecloths twitched in the breeze. Even the old rosebush, rife with white blossoms, seemed to shiver. Men were buttoning their suit jackets, women wrapping themselves in scarves. One by one they said their goodbyes, until finally Emil was alone, just the waiters clearing the food away and sparrows dive-bombing for crumbs.

He took a seat in one of the heavy wooden chairs. He did not regret never having seen his father again. He did not regret the cursory letters, the tight-lipped phone calls on holidays. What more would he have said? That he could not stay in this place where appearances mattered more than truth. That he refused to live off his filthy money.

Across the courtyard, a janitor was sweeping up. The place hadn't changed much, though the tiles around the fountain were chipped. Odd that no one had bothered to have them repaired. And that the fountain was no longer running. Surely his father had the money. A room here cost three times what it used to.

Emil let his eyes close. Heard the murmuring of the waiters, the chink of dishes being stacked. If he kept his eyes shut, he might be back there. Leaning from the balcony, searching the courtyard. Hearing, like magic, his own name floating up.

*

Early the next morning he headed out to the alleyways that cut into the mountainside, up to the house where Daniel had lived.

Though each alley path had a name, few could be found on any map. Wedged into the cliff walls were stone houses with slab-stone roofs, hand-rigged antennae, and every so often, a morose dog on patrol. At first the paths were broad, their stones smooth from centuries of foot traffic. It was refreshing to rise away from the street noise and car exhaust, from the church bells clanging like an angry cook rattling copper pots. But soon the steps became high and blocky, the alleys maze-like, intersecting at each plateau. Emil had to pause every minute or so to catch his breath. It was his vertigo, he told himself, not that he was out of shape or smoked too much. He was only thirty-two. Shielding his eyes from the sun, he could glimpse the outer loop that led back down the mountain—an incline so steep that parked cars propped heavy stones behind their rear wheels.

He was up high enough now to have reached a tiny convenience store, the sort found at these heights, just soda and basic necessities. Tacked to the façade, a jumble of flyers advertised cellphone services, used cars, missing persons. Drawn by muscle memory, Emil turned onto the next alleyway, where the houses were taller, narrow, two stories instead of one. He heard voices, the scuffle of feet. Not far from the house where Daniel had lived, children were playing soccer. Three of them, kicking the ball as if the ground were horizontal and the alley a stadium, then running frantically as the ball threatened to plummet into the abyss.

They wore the blue sweaters of the school uniform and glanced only briefly at Emil. He continued to Daniel's house. No longer the proud establishment he remembered, with the nameplate declaring *Teodor Sali, Shoes*. A poor dwelling now, rusted grilles over the windows. The concrete steps were chipped. As Emil drew closer, the door opened.

A little girl stepped out. She wore the school colors, and a big white ribbon-flower in her hair. She said, "He was waiting for you."

Emil felt faint.

"For a long time."

He tried to catch his breath. "I beg your pardon?"

"You're too late. He left."

Emil was still having trouble breathing. Again he asked what she meant. But the girl seemed wary and hurried away.

"Wait!" He meant to follow her but felt dizzy. He had to pause to steady himself. Of all the times for his vertigo to act up . . . He waited for the spinning to slow. When he looked down the alley, the girl had gone.

He squatted, dropped his head between his knees. He could hear the boys at the other end of the alley scrambling after the soccer ball. As the vertigo subsided, he reconsidered the girl's words. Clearly, her parent or relative had simply been stood up by someone, and she had assumed Emil to be that person. He felt ridiculous for having tried to follow her.

The dizziness eased. He dared to cast his gaze across the other houses and rooftops. Searching. As if Daniel might be here.

*

It was springtime then, too, the rosebuds still tight. Easter break, a full week, meant the restaurant needed extra hands. With his waiter's jacket, Daniel looked proper, dashing, not quite the tousled boy Emil saw at school. They were both fifteen years old. Emil glimpsed him on the first day of the school holiday, from the table in the courtyard where he was pretending to do his mathematics homework. "Look at my boy," Emil's father boasted to Ivan Sabow from where they sat with their dominoes. "Studying even on holiday!"

Really it was an excuse for Emil to eavesdrop on the expat poets. He was determined to erase the distance between the mincing English he uttered in his class at school and the version he heard the expats speak. Encamped at their corner table, the poets—there were seven of them—sounded nothing like his teacher, who spoke with a mortifying accent. Even the Danish couple seemed fluent. The others were English and Canadian. Who knew how they had found this hotel.

"Sublime," the Englishman would say when he liked something. "My, my . . ." he proclaimed when he did not. The Canadian woman wrote about her garden in Vancouver, where she returned each summer to grow wisteria, clematis, day lilies, pansies, and other flowers whose misspelled names Emil jotted into his notebook.

That Monday it was one of the Canadians' turn, a poem entitled either "When I First Saw a Robin" or "Birdsong"; he welcomed input on the matter. Emil was listening when he noticed a new face in the courtyard.

At first he didn't recognize him. At school Daniel's hair was perpetually ruffled, and he was always laughing, playing at some sport, making dramatic saves and theatrically falling to the ground, until he was scolded by a teacher—briefly, indifferently, because teachers didn't expect much from alley children.

All Emil knew, in the way that townspeople knew these things, was that Daniel's father was a cobbler and his mother, like Emil's, long gone. Now here he was, balancing tumblers on a tray. When Daniel smiled, Emil looked down at his dictionary.

It was later that day, as Emil returned from the restroom, that Daniel said, "I know you." Flustered, Emil said, "I guess we're both trapped here." It was disingenuous, as if he, too, had to work for his bread. Daniel seemed about to laugh—but the head waiter barked an order and he had to return to work.

Over the next days, Emil spent hours in the courtyard, waiting to glimpse Daniel, trying to think of something clever to say. Since Emil's friends were mainly acquaintances whose parents were friends of his father, he was glad to avoid them.

At the end of that first week, rains came, confining the wait staff to the indoor restaurant. With fewer tables available, Emil was discouraged from lingering. He took the parakeet to his room on the second floor and tried to teach her to say, "I'm hungry." He reviewed his growing vocabulary list from the poets. All the while he kept his door open, in case Daniel stepped out to the courtyard. But it kept raining and no one came.

Even when the rain let up, it was too wet to sit outdoors. Plump droplets plunked from the chestnut tree onto the tiles of the courtyard. Emil brought the bird back down, hooking her cage back onto its branch. She loved the water splattering from the leaves and flapped her wings so that beads of water rolled down the feathers of her back. The rosebush, too, had responded to the rain, buds opening into messy white frills.

"Say 'I'm hungry,'" Emil ordered the parakeet, loudly, hoping Daniel would hear and come out.

"Good day!" It was the first phrase Emil had ever taught her.

"I'm hungry," Emil pronounced, loudly. "I'm hungry."

"Good day!"

Emil heard someone—but it was Martin the workman, who fetched a forgotten hammer and returned inside.

Emil's hair and sweater had become damp from the mist. He lingered, willing Daniel to step out, until he gave up and headed back up the stairs. Even then he took his time, wishing Daniel might somehow materialize. He couldn't have said what had come over him. At the balcony, he paused, leaning to gaze down at the courtyard.

That was when the awful thought came to him: that with the rain slowing business, Daniel had been told he was no longer needed, and been sent home.

Hopelessness gripped him. He turned away.

"Psst—Emil!"

In all the years since, he has never experienced anything like it. His own name rising to meet him. The quick bright shooting leap in the core of his chest. There at the foot of the stairs, Daniel with his winking eyes, grinning.

He said, "I'm off until seven if you want to get out of here."

Stupefied by the granting of his wish, Emil just blinked. Since he knew how his father would react to see his son and the busboy together, he suggested they meet at the fountain. Daniel would know which one, in the town center, the giant shallow goblet where pigeons congregated and streamlets of dirty water trickled over the edges to the corroded basin below.

The afternoon sun was chasing the last clouds away when Emil reached the fountain. Seeing Daniel, he felt awkward and threw a pebble at the pigeons.

"Now why would you do that?" Daniel gave an exaggerated pout. "They get a bad rap because they're city birds. But if you don't think of them that way, they could be beautiful."

Feeling chastised, Emil said, "C'mon, let's go," though he had no plan and suspected Daniel didn't either. From the fountain, they headed up to the scenic overlook. Tourists from nearby towns slid coins into magnifying viewfinders and bought bottled water from pushcarts.

This really was the best view of the town, everything at just the right angle, the white columns of the university appearing, from this distance, clean and bright, rather than covered with pigeon droppings. The sharp tips of church spires seemed to pierce the sky, and the rounded arc of the mosque gleamed gold and silver. Even the call to prayer sounded different from here, secrets breathed over a magic kingdom. Daniel lit a cigarette and went to peek through the unclaimed viewfinders.

"Sometimes there's extra money left on them." At the third one he said, "Ah, here you go," and stepped away so that Emil could look. "Our beautiful homeland."

From his tone, Emil couldn't tell if Daniel meant it sincerely or not. He peered through the binoculars, startled to find his world suddenly magnified—and caught sight, shockingly clearly, of one of the expat poets. Frizzy red hair, baggy pants, and the grubby cloth bag she carried at all times. Though he supposed he should be taking in the panorama, he instead looked to where the north tunnel burrowed out of town, and heard himself say aloud what he had never confessed to anyone. "I want to go to Kansas City, USA."

Daniel looked about to laugh. "Kansas City, USA! What wonders await you in Kansas City, USA?"

Emil had a second cousin in Kansas City, from whom they received an annual Christmas card containing a few bland words. "Or maybe Dresden, Germany." The head waiter had a sister in Dresden and made it sound like paradise. Not that anyone needed a reason for wanting to leave this place. The only jobs that made any money were in the crime gangs; everyone knew that. Even so, Emil said, "I want to see the world."

Really that wasn't it. The truth, if he were to admit it, was that he had feelings, sometimes, that overwhelmed him. A deep longing and strange elation that he didn't want his father, or anyone else, to know. A longing he felt right now, with Daniel beside him.

"You mean," Daniel said, in his winking way, gesturing out at the panorama, "this isn't the whole world right here?"

*

Daniel's father, it turned out, was not a cobbler but a shoe manufacturer. He had bought the equipment, Daniel explained, for almost nothing, from a Greek company upgrading to automated production. The old machines filled the first floor of Daniel's home and allowed Teo to double his output of the sturdy black shoes he was known for: clunky ones of inflexible leather, with reinforced lace holes and nearly indestructible soles. Devoted customers returned every five years or so to replace their old battered pairs with new stiff ones, and everyone in town knew in one glance not just who made their shoes but whom they voted for or against.

This was because—Daniel explained that first afternoon, as Emil followed him up the alleyways—Teo headed a proletariat group known for its anti-corruption campaigning.

Emil had never followed politics, though his father, as the town hotelier, was friendly with the local administration. Daniel, meanwhile, said Teo didn't want him participating in his group's activities until he was out of school.

A heavyset man, Teo worked for long stretches at his shoemaking operations, fortified by toxic inhalations of epoxy glue and polyurethane. Visiting Daniel, Emil would steal glances into the shop, where rows of narrow shelves held pairs of wooden feet in each size. The walls and countertops displayed animal skins spread and waiting to be cut. In exchange for his politely muttered "Good day," Emil would receive a glance from Teo, then head up to Daniel's room. On days when Teo used the hole-punching machine for the lace holes, Daniel's bedroom shook.

That first day, dizzied by the fumes, Emil followed Daniel up the narrow staircase. His heart thumped horribly as he entered Daniel's room. Daniel shut the door and, as if it were the simplest thing, said, "Come here."

*

His walk down from the cliff alleys was less taxing, with no episodes of vertigo; Emil easily made it back to the hotel in time for his meeting with the lawyer. The two of them sat at the corner table where the expat poets used to convene. What happened to them? Perhaps time had aged them so that they could no longer make the trip. Or was the spiffed-up town now beyond their reach, the rent too high, the restaurants too dear?

There was a new set of expats now. Dutch, he would guess, two boyish-looking men in pastel shirts and three well-preserved women wrapped in light scarves. They sat closer to the chimney and instead of reciting poetry were drinking fruit brandy and discussing a novel they apparently all found too long.

The lawyer, from the firm that managed Emil's father's accounts, slid the pages of the will from his briefcase. "You're a lawyer, too, I hear."

Emil was the in-house counsel for a large advertising firm in Edmonton. Lucrative, uninspiring work—file cabinets full of documents with fine print. In law school he used to dream of returning here in aid of justice, to help those who hadn't been given the chance he had. Now he listened to the lawyer explain that, according to his father's will, the hotel and all assets had been left to Emil.

No matter that Emil had left and not come back; he was still an only child. No other relatives whom his father would have thought to endow. Emil's mother's relations in Kansas City quit sending Christmas tidings as soon as his aunt died.

What surprised him was the figure the lawyer quoted. The amount seemed to Emil oddly low. It must have seemed so to the lawyer, too; he mustered a false-sounding joviality, as if to cover for the meager life's savings.

"There is also a small sum left to a Mr. Nelson Schiller." The lawyer seemed to expect Emil to recognize the name. "Of Naples, Florida, and Blainville, Quebec. We have been unable to reach him."

Emil had never heard of him.

The lawyer showed only brief consternation. "Not to worry. An inheritance tends to bring even the most long-lost relatives out of the woodwork."

"I imagine so," Emil said, a sick feeling inside. The breeze carried the scent of the old rosebush from across the courtyard, too sweet.

"If you think of anything that might help us," the lawyer said, "please let us know. And we're available to help with any negotiations in your absence."

Emil stood abruptly, overtaken by shame. The lawyer took his cue and followed him to the front exit. Now that it was midday, the traffic jam had started up. Tough going for anyone to find their way out of that mess.

Emil watched the tide of blue, the bobbing white flowers, listened to the bright voices caught one in another as parents ushered their children back and forth from the school.

When he was a child, he had just a one-block walk from school to the hotel and went on his own. But now, watching the lawyer take his leave, he understood: only alley children made their way to school unchaperoned. Everyone else was chauffeured back and forth, most on foot, some by car. Because parents didn't trust that their children wouldn't be snatched away.

That was why this swarm of bodies slowed traffic all the way to the town square. This great knot of traffic was fear. A parent's fear, multiplied many times over.

*

At school he and Daniel rarely spoke. When the last bell rang each afternoon, they would separate and begin the climb up the blocky stone steps of the alleyways.

They had a meeting place. A small overlook along the first tier, not far from the ring road. From there they would continue on, buying snacks from one of the high-up corner stores and heading to one of their hideaways, which were not secret but felt that way, perhaps because Emil had been forbidden to venture there.

He knew by then that the concern was not witches who turned children into birds but the dirt and rust and darkly etched poverty of those alleys. The desperation and casual violence of people who had never known good luck. "Witches" he understood as shorthand for all unspeakable things.

The birds fly away and can never go home.

Some afternoons the two of them went off with Daniel's friends to play soccer, but other days were for Emil, wrestling out on the cliffs, or in Daniel's room. The pleasure of it didn't diminish even when these meetings had been going on for one year, for two.

His father no longer asked about girlfriends, had stopped mentioning the names of his acquaintances' daughters. And then one evening, when it was just the two of them dining at a table under a heat lamp in the chilly courtyard, as the flame of a small candle wavered between them, his father said, "When I met your mother, it was like a flower was blooming in my chest. If you had held a gun to my head, I couldn't have stopped those petals from opening." He cleared his throat, lowered his voice. "Son, I know that in matters of the heart we can find ourselves at the mercy of powers beyond our control. I just ask that you be careful."

Emil could feel his face reddening. He could not look at his father—could not even trust that those words meant what he thought they did. He was grateful when a breeze blew the candle out and his father, back to his usual joking, said, "Our cue to go back inside!"

As for Daniel's father, Emil spoke to him only in greeting, always trying to look serious, since surely Teo knew who Emil's father was. Everyone did. In the past, Emil had liked that his father was on a first-name basis with the mayor, included in town planning meetings, often present at ribbon cuttings and ground breakings. Despite the country's reputation for corruption, their town had never been scandalized. But now there was a plan for a casino, which Emil's father supported and Teo's group opposed. Emil's father was angling for the casino to be built as an extension of the hotel, though there was little space for expansion, not to mention the elementary school so close by.

One afternoon Emil and Daniel found an envelope propped against Daniel's front door. Teo's name on it. When Daniel handed the envelope to his father, Teo's face paled.

"There was another one like that last week," Daniel whispered as they climbed the stairs. "Anonymous."

Emil asked what the messages said.

"He won't tell me." They spoke of it no further. But Emil thought of the letter a month later, when he and Daniel found, in the same spot, a mangled pigeon. It lay there like a gruesome offering from an overzealous pet. Then the bird twitched. Daniel whistled through his teeth. He reached down, took the bird in his beautiful, perfect hands, and in one swift movement broke its neck.

*

Nelson Schiller. For hours that day, and again the next morning, Emil searched his father's rooms, his desk, the thick address book. Must be someone from after Emil left town. He went through all recent accounts and ledgers. Flipped through notebooks, smoothed out crumpled slips of paper, anything that looked like it might hold some key to the truth.

Nothing.

Just as strange was the fact that, according to the books, the hotel had indeed continued to make an enormous profit in recent years.

The increased income had begun back when the defunct government properties were being renovated. Emil's father, too, had decided to upgrade. Every day, it seemed, Martin was tiling, painting, refinishing scuffed wood, lugging in some new piece of furniture.

It was Daniel, with an offhand comment about "your wrestler guests," who caused Emil to understand.

He meant the men with thick wallets who breezed in and out of the hotel. Because the hotel was where they stopped in town to monitor progress on their properties in the hills. "Wrestlers" was slang, due to so many former athletes joining crime syndicates after the changes left them with few options. Some had done quite well. The province was a main entry for drug transport in and out of Europe, the country often referred to as a "gateway" for smugglers—though Emil had never consciously considered himself connected to that world. But with Daniel's comment he reconsidered the men at the hotel for whom his father transformed into an obsequious host, understanding in some primal way that his father must have little choice. He thought of every gift his father had bought for him over the past year, and of the hotel's newly renovated kitchen.

"Open your eyes, friend," Daniel said. He was wearing the green Adidas jacket he had saved up for and rarely parted from. Then he touched Emil's temple, lightly, to show he didn't judge him.

These days, Emil considered, the smuggling would be of immigrants without papers as much as of illicit drugs. Traffickers were often state security agents or border police. Sometimes, when people learned where Emil was from, they made comments or asked questions—about dysfunctional law enforcement, murdered journalists, rackets of every kind; some even knew just where his country ranked on lists of corrupt governments. Other times they knew nothing about his country at all. Emil still wasn't sure which was worse.

Going through his father's account books, it seemed even now the hotel continued to turn a profit. Yet there was little money left. An even smaller sum of which was to go to this Nelson Schiller.

If anyone would know who he was, it would be Ivan Sabow. Who, it occurred to Emil, had not been mentioned in the will. Only now did he savor that fact. Well, Ivan wasn't family (though he had been the one, after tracking Emil down, to inform him of his father's heart attack). And yet this Mr. Schiller *had* been included.

Emil picked up the office phone and pressed the button with Ivan's name on it. Just touching it felt like a betrayal of himself. When the voicemail picked up, he left his number, asking Ivan to please call him back.

*

He and Daniel were seventeen before the first of the mansions was completed.

Construction teams hammered at roof tiles and balconies. "Those guys have so much money," Daniel said, "their biggest problem is what to do with it all. Have to hide their cash as much as their contraband. My old man says they'll have full hold of this town in no time."

Emil understood by then about government contracts awarded to family members, corruption investigations that led nowhere, newspaper headlines that eventually disappeared. About crimes never solved, erased from official record. People joked that the main work of the local police was not safety but public relations. Pep rallies and concerts, schoolchildren singing on bleachers in orderly rows. Public forums with a microphone passed around—to boost public morale when tensions bubbled up.

"Building trust and confidence," Emil's father called it. He was in a delicate position. He had stopped advocating for a combined hotel-casino and now lent his support to a gaming place to be constructed near the tourist overlook, with a funicular running up the mountainside.

Daniel said the gangs and the administration were basically one and the same. And observing the mansions being constructed, Emil sometimes imagined he and Daniel were spies—though all they saw, usually, were laborers on ladders, sweating. Until one day, as he and Daniel lounged on an overlook, Emil caught sight of someone he knew.

Ivan Sabow. Standing on a terrace with another fellow in smart clothes.

Sunshine bathed the hillside, making Ivan Sabow all the more visible. Emil realized he recognized the other man, too. Had seen him at the hotel. And then Emil saw, stepping into the pool of sunshine, his father.

He wore a suit and stood with his hands in his pockets. If he said anything, he was too far away for Emil to hear.

Daniel remained silent. Emil forced himself to watch. There was a terrible throbbing in his ears. When the three men had finished their discussion, they went round to the other side of the building.

Daniel looked almost shy. He touched Emil's hand. "Let's go."

Ears ringing, Emil followed Daniel up the alleyways.

It was a few months after they saw Emil's father at the mansion that a new memorial was unveiled at the scenic overlook. A sculpture (interlinking circles of shiny silver) and plaque in honor of some long-ago uprising. Emil's class was made to attend a tedious ceremony of names read aloud while students who didn't care if they got in trouble snuck off—which meant Daniel was nowhere to be found.

They were nearly eighteen by then, Daniel lanky, his muscles tight. Any time he skipped class, petty thoughts besieged Emil—of Daniel off with the guy who worked in the cheese shop, or one of the determined, misinformed girls who flitted about him at school. These were not mere imaginings. He knew Daniel did such things, had even caught him, once, with the cheese-shop guy.

Awful thoughts overtook him as he waited through the ceremony with the mayor and his entourage under the throbbing sun. Ivan Sabow was there. He held some titular post representing the tourist district. In fact, Teo's group had named him in a complaint alleging some kind of collusion between the town and a city magistrate. Emil's father said the charges were baseless. The newspaper had stopped reporting on the subject.

When at last the ceremony was over and the officials dispersed, and the students were allotted a break, Emil bought a soda and watched a couple trying to appease their children by giving them a look through a viewfinder. The children squirmed at the binoculars, and the parents gave up.

There would be money left on the timer. Emil went to look through the binoculars. The colorful houses, the white pillars of the university, the radiant dome of the mosque, the sharp spires of steeples and the minaret. He peered left and right, and realized he was searching for Daniel.

He couldn't help it. Even as he peered through the lenses, he recalled that first day here. And in that moment of recollection saw, in the distance, Daniel, in his green Adidas jacket.

The timer clicked off, and the view disappeared.

He must have imagined it. As if he could will the vision into existence.

At school the next morning, milling around out front, his classmates seemed oddly quiet. Emil asked why everyone was whispering.

"They found Daniel Sali. Out by the mansions."

The world spun. The classmate was still talking, said laborers had noticed vultures fighting over something. A body. Already picked apart.

Somehow Emil managed to speak. "Then how do they know it's him?"

"It's him."

Emil ran then, out past the square and up into the alleys. He ran until he was panting, his feet no longer so quick. The higher he climbed, the stranger he felt, until the air around him seemed to waver. When things began to spin, he had to stop and close his eyes.

He had never suffered such symptoms before. Only when the spinning ceased and the air no longer quavered did he continue, gingerly, to Daniel's house.

The nameplate beside the door declared *Teodor Sali, Shoes* as if nothing had changed. Perhaps if Emil wished hard enough, nothing would have. His heart hit hard at his ribs.

There came a sound then, as he stood there. A whispering. So soft, he strained to hear it.

It came from above. From the pale gray rocks of the alley wall.

He looked up, at the gray stones jutting from around the house. The stones were whispering.

One of them moved.

A mourning dove. Pale, purplish gray. Must have been there all the while, roosting between the rocks.

Emil stepped back, and there came more rustling. Three, four more birds nestled among the jutting rocks, camouflaged by their dark gray mottling. Emil's movement had disturbed them.

The sweep of their feathers against the stones made a *shhh, shhh* sound. *Shhh.* Clucking softly, they tucked themselves back into hiding.

Emil was trembling. He saw that the front door was open, forced himself to step through it. Paused before the stairs he had climbed countless times. Just seeing them made him mildly dizzy. He could see the wooden lasts along the shelves in Teo's shop, the animal skins splayed on the walls. Slowly he made his way up to the main floor, where people were speaking in low voices. Teo was seated on the sofa, looking somehow smaller than his actual size.

Heads turned toward Emil. They would know him as the son of the hotelier—some would have seen him in the restaurant over the years, just as they saw his father and Ivan Sabow leaning over their dominoes.

Martin the handyman was here. For a moment Emil was confused.

Teo pushed himself up from the sofa. Came to stand before Emil, his eyes bloodshot, his face gray. He reached out, and Emil waited to be strangled, punched, dragged out of the house. With a heavy arm, Teo pulled Emil close, and a great sob rose between them.

Emil felt Teo's thick hand rubbing his hair, his heavy arms clinging to him. He let himself be held, let the sobs escape. From across the room, a voice rose up.

"But his father . . . !"

Teo tightened his grasp.

Emil felt their eyes on him, their hatred, until Teo loosened his grip and stepped away. Without looking up, Emil fled.

At the hotel, wrung dry from crying, he told the maids he was ill and went to bed.

He knew no one cared what happened to the son of a shoemaker, that even if Teo found those responsible, there was little anyone would do about it. What future would Daniel have had, anyway— did any of them have, in this land without prospects? He thought of the carcass picked apart, told himself it might not have been Daniel at all. But then he pictured Teo's eyes and knew it was true.

The maids brought him broth with rice. When his father poked his head in, Emil pretended to be sleeping.

He heard his footsteps, felt the mattress shift as his father sat beside him. Lying with his back to him, Emil tried not to move. In his mind he heard the voice from Teo's, saying, *his father . . . !* He felt his father's hand brush his hair. The hand was trembling.

The mattress shifted again, and his father laid his cheek against Emil's temple. Emil shoved him away.

"Son—"

"Go away!"

The mattress shifted again, and his father left the room.

Emil waited until the third afternoon, when his room had taken on a close, dank smell and his father would be out at his weekly luncheon, to go downstairs. It was a gray day, and the poets were in their corner. They nodded gravely.

So they, too, had heard the news. Of course; it wasn't every day that a student was murdered. Though who knew what the newspaper would call it.

Emil ate his soup meekly. Already it was late enough that the poets were finishing up. The Danish couple left first, then the Canadians, along with the Englishman. The woman with the messy red hair came to take a seat at Emil's table.

"We heard about your classmate," she said in her British accent. "I'm so very sorry."

Emil felt a fly on his cheek and swiped at it. His hand came back wet.

From her cloth bag she pulled out her notebook full of poems. Tore out a page. Emil watched her scribble a name and a number. She folded the paper, pressed it into his hand. Looking him softly in the eye, she said, "In case we can be of help."

Emil heard himself thank her. With his napkin he wiped at his eyes, his nose, his ears. It seemed everything was wet.

In his room later, Emil looked at the piece of paper. Stared at the number, trying to imagine how the woman and her husband might be "of help." Though he was the hotelier's son, he had no money of his own. Everything in his daily life was paid for, yet he could afford little more than a train ticket. He thought of his relatives in Kansas City, wondered if he might somehow contact them. No, they would surely tell his father.

All he understood, after calling the number the woman had written, was that there was an opening in a university somewhere in Ontario, Canada, a work-study program with a scholarship for room, board, and tuition. Because of the woman's connections, Emil need only apply.

It seemed too strange, the timing too perfect. Probably it would turn out to be some religious thing, like those groups bussed into town center. Yet if it would get him away from here . . .

He packed little, wrote a terse note, and called his father only after he had arrived in Toronto, the Brits having spirited him to London and paid for his ticket out of Heathrow, arranging for the husband's cousin to meet him on the other side of the Atlantic. After that, a chain of generosity and serendipity helped him to stay afloat. When he was accepted to law school, he somehow qualified for full funding. At the time it was a blur. Only after being hired for his first job as a lawyer did he appreciate the ridiculous luck involved—that the red-haired woman, by giving him that number to call, had set it all in motion.

He hadn't seen any of them since.

*

Ivan Sabow called to tell him to come by his office.

Emil made his way to the main square, where the municipal building stood across from the fountain. The air smelled of roses. Tourists sat on benches, or posed with the strange new statue. A bird, he saw now—sleek, abstract.

Inside the municipal building he was directed to Ivan's office, and wondered vaguely if Ivan still expected to have been named in the will. It gave him a bitter pleasure to ask, instead, if Ivan knew anyone by the name of Nelson Schiller.

Ivan looked at him without expression. Then he said, slowly, "Ah. Yes."

Emil waited. Ivan said nothing.

"Well, who is he?"

"Those writers. Used to come for the winter, always sat at the table in the corner."

He didn't remember anyone called Nelson Schiller. They had all gone by other names—comically short ones, single syllables. *Chip. Dick.*

"Your father worried something would happen to you. He asked them to get you away from here." Ivan's voice turned sharply triumphant. "You didn't know that, did you? How your poor father worried. I'm not surprised his heart finally gave out."

He was speaking louder now. "Who do you think made sure you could attend college? Law school? Your father gave the funds to those poets, had them arrange everything."

Impossible. How could there have been enough money? And with the hotel in disrepair . . . The missing tiles on the fountain, the nicked bricks of the fireplace. The same heavy wooden chairs needing varnish.

Emil hung his head, then, understanding.

Ivan seemed to be standing taller. "You think good things just happen? That they aren't always paid for in some way?" Ivan laughed, then—a mean, sad laugh. "I will miss your father, boy. I already miss him. Now maybe you will, too, hmm?"

Emil's legs somehow carried him out to the corridor. Sounds from other offices echoed down the hall.

His father had known, then, which schools Emil was attending, where to send money. And Emil had known nothing. Just the grudging vows to visit, never fulfilled. His father could have cut off his assistance, even come to find him. Instead he left Emil to his freedom.

Shaking, Emil stepped back outside. A concert was taking place on the green, schoolchildren standing on risers, singing some warbly song. People sat in folding chairs, listening stoically. Emil made his way toward the other end of the square, the children's voices following him.

Emil began to run. Up the narrow paths, terrace by terrace, into the alleyways. It was nothing his mind told him to do; his body carried him forward. A few times he had to pause, feeling the dizziness coming on. At any moment he might plummet off the cliffside. But he fought through it, his feet propelling him onward.

As he neared Daniel's alley he saw her—the little girl. She stood in her blue sweater, a big white rose in her hair, and slipped round the corner before he took his next step.

He was panting now, trying to keep up. He thought he heard her voice just ahead of him. *You're too late, he left.* Yet when he rounded the corner, the girl wasn't there.

Only as he neared Daniel's house did he see it, on the ground a few feet away. The white flower from her hair.

He reached down to pick it up—but it wasn't a flower at all. Just a crumpled piece of white paper.

He unwadded it. From behind the creases emerged a face, a name. One of those missing-person flyers.

Shhh, shhh.

Emil closed his eyes.

Shhh.

Daniel, he meant to say. He meant to whisper, but his voice broke loudly.

"Papa!"

Birds shook themselves out from the rocks. Emil felt the paper escape his grasp, and watched it follow them up into the air.

Three Times Two

It was a bed, not the mountain, that would cast its hex on the hikers that August, but they did not know that yet. There were six of them—three couples—and so far, the one thing they all agreed on was that it was an ugly mountain.

Massive and brown, with trails lined by scrappy, wilting foliage. No berries or butterflies. Only occasional birdsong. Markus, a mathematics post-doc, had been the one to plan this year's holiday and perhaps felt accountable. He kept joking to Lynn, his girlfriend who was visiting from America, that they must be on the wrong mountain entirely, since this wasn't how the guidebook described it.

Already his twin sister, Bettina, had mentioned last year's mountain, which had been so much nicer. And despite the occasional cool patch of forest or brilliant view of another mountain's crimped peaks, the trail also led to things like dried-out dung of unknown origin, or the rotting carcass of some field mouse or badger.

The mountain even had an ugly-sounding name, which Lynn kept forgetting, because she didn't speak German. But she knew it was ugly because Markus and his friends said it was. They were Austrian, and to them the mountain's brutishness seemed a consequence of its being across the border, in Germany.

This was a long time ago; they were still in their twenties. Lynn was living in Boston, completing a PhD in philosophy at a university that wasn't Harvard. Though she had yet to defend her dissertation, she had just accepted a lectureship at a college in the suburbs.

She and the two other girlfriends walked together behind their men, chatting, wondering if the mountain might improve. Maybe it was some biological instinct that had them grouping off by gender. But it was also a matter of courtesy. Bettina and the third girl always made a point of speaking in English so that Lynn could join in.

A few meters ahead, their boyfriends were a handsome sight, three young healthy men with square shoulders and light brown hair, lugging their packs on their backs. Markus was the tallest, with the broadest shoulders and messiest hair. His school friend Wolfgang was thinner and wore wire-rimmed spectacles. Bruno, the clarinetist whom Bettina had been dating for three years, was whistling, which he often did, and which made people think of him as a jolly sort of fellow, which in fact he was. His whistling seemed to lead them forward, up the mountain.

*

Later, when he was in his mid-thirties, Wolfy would try to write a poem about it. The cool mountain air and the dark black night. He was taking a poetry class for fun, taught by the friend of a former lover, and found himself intrigued by terza rima. Clever, the way the interlocking rhymes turned three-line stanzas into a linked chain. He had been in America for a decade then, working in Silicon Valley, and the class on poetic form appealed to his mathematical side.

But the poem sounded strange, and he did not show it to anyone.

*

142

Not knowing the language or the city, Lynn had felt at a loss the moment she stepped foot in Vienna. En route with Markus to the apartment on Something-strasse, she quickly saw that she looked like a tourist in her loose American clothing, and wondered if Markus noticed. The physical qualities she knew he loved—her large round breasts, the very Americanness of her braces-straightened teeth and her long hair full of blond highlights—seemed crass and excessive in this city of prim, cobbled streets. The women were thin boned and neatly dressed, like Bettina, who had the same greenish-brown eyes and sandy complexion as her brother and whose wispy hair and slightly crooked teeth managed to look, on her, chic. Lynn, with her cleavage visible at the V of her tee shirt, felt freakish. Also, she had been apart from Markus for over a month by then, and at first they were awkward together. When she told comical anecdotes of her job tutoring high school students, Markus looked increasingly perturbed and would not laugh.

The reason he didn't laugh was that he could not stand to picture Lynn having fun without him. But she didn't know that, and neither, actually, did he. She had gone and cried in the shower, while Markus busied himself with preparations for the hike.

His sister witnessed these painful stirrings with only slight surprise. She knew well her brother's delicate ego and casual cruelty. They shared the small apartment their parents had bought for them, and she had on numerous occasions—even in the few weeks since her brother's return—observed how he was with women. Sometimes she even felt she knew what he was thinking.

Not that she could read his mind. Fraternal twins, they shared no secret language or telepathy, but they had been paired together all their lives. Twinhood simply meant that Bettina's fight for attention, for privacy, for recognition, for affection, for sustenance of every kind, had begun much earlier than for most siblings. In the womb.

A third or so of the way up the trail, they rested in a patch of shade, eating the lunches they had packed—another world ago, those gray dawn hours before the train ride and bus trip and trudging up from the mountain base.

There were sandwiches (liverwurst pressed between crusty white bread) and hard-boiled eggs and little runty-looking apples. The pines gave off a faint, bitter scent. Bettina, peeling one of the eggs, recalled her dream.

"I was at a house"—she said it in English, for Lynn—"where there was a doll that could talk. I had just to play a record player, and the doll's mouth moved, and she spoke."

Markus, seated beside her on a wedge of rock, told her it wasn't a dream. "We went there. The doll museum. Aunt Carolina took us." He took a bite from one of the sandwiches, and crumbs fell around him. When Bettina asked why he remembered it if she didn't, Markus gave a shrug that suggested this was only natural.

Bettina couldn't help frowning. "Aunt Caro must have taken you and not me." The dream seemed less charming now that Markus had inserted himself into it.

"There were *two* talking dolls," Markus continued, "and a gramophone for their voices."

Bettina looked down at the boiled egg, to prevent her face from revealing that in her dream, too, there had been not one, but two, dolls. A blonde and a brunette. But only the blonde had spoken.

Bruno, passing around a big plastic bottle of lime soda, asked why she would suddenly dream of the doll so many years later. Everyone mused aloud while Bettina's cheeks grew hot; it seemed to her suddenly obvious that the doll must symbolize a child.

But the others were already debating dream interpretation. Wolfgang's girlfriend—the latest in a never-ending series—owned a book on the subject. She was a wispy thing, a few years younger than the others. Apparently the only bit she recalled from the book was that broken teeth signified death.

Wolfy wanted her to feel comfortable with his friends and was making sure to give her lots of pecks on the cheek and drape his arm around her. They had been together less than two months and had slept together a handful of times. He suspected she viewed the invitation to the hike as a step forward in their romance. Really, these days on the trail were a way for Wolfy to uphold his role as boyfriend while having a convenient excuse not to have sex.

Next to her, Lynn sat cross-legged, so that she wouldn't have to look at her hiking shoes. Like her big American body, and not knowing German, the shoes embarrassed her. More like padded high-top sneakers, they were a bright magenta color, with thick waffle soles and fat neon yellow laces. Markus and the others had old-fashioned stiff brown leather boots.

Wolfgang's girlfriend asked how it was that Lynn and Markus happened to have met.

"We were both lost," Lynn told her, and Markus, looking somewhat imperial on his slab of rock, said, "I had a meeting but was in the incorrect building. Lynn was trying to find where her professor was giving a lecture."

The girl brightened. "At Harvard?"

"No," Lynn said, "at Markus's school. MIT."

Though Lynn's school was perfectly respectable, on this trip its not being Harvard seemed to have become a shortcoming. On the connecting flight from Frankfurt, the woman next to her became excited the moment she heard "Boston" and "PhD"—and then looked disappointed when Lynn corrected her.

"I asked Markus for directions," Lynn said now, "and then we stood talking for an hour." Soon they were spending all their time together. Markus's postdoctoral fellowship was supposed to continue for a second year, but when the funding wasn't renewed, his visa couldn't be extended. Frantically he had searched for some other post, but nothing had panned out. When the university in Vienna made an offer, he accepted.

Lynn had considered dropping out of her program to follow him. She had pictured a quaint Viennese apartment in the center of the city, and a job teaching English as a foreign language, or whatever menial employment an ABD in philosophy might secure.

But Markus hadn't asked her to come with him. Which hurt her feelings but was also something of a relief.

*

It was five or so in the afternoon when they at last spotted the guesthouse. The faint clanging of cowbells grew louder as they wound their way out of the forest. On the grassy plateau the hollow jangling sounded like the call of some enchanted species. Cows moved slowly about the broad green pasture, occasionally releasing a disaffected groan. The bells hung like medals from their necks.

It was cooler here, out in the open. Bettina found the wool pullover she always brought on their hikes and tied her bandana around her neck like a scarf. She was a month pregnant and felt things more extremely now.

She hadn't told anyone her news. The pregnancy was unplanned, and she was still deciding how she felt about it.

The guesthouse was a chalet complete with a peaked roof, ginger breading, and window boxes crowded with yellow flowers. The proprietors, a nervous-looking couple of middle age, pointed them toward a path that led to a vista they absolutely must see—now, quick, before the sun set.

Lynn, aware of new blisters blooming inside the magenta sneaker-boots, wanted to rest. But dutifully she and the others followed a tree-lined path to a breezy ledge where there was, indeed, a view. Distant cliff walls blushed in the slant sun and took on the subdued colors of a bruise. The wind made everything feel colder. Lynn pulled on the V-necked sweater she had borrowed from Markus, which was somehow both too large and too tight across her chest. Markus took out an identical one in a darker gray, while Bruno pulled on a windbreaker. Wolfgang wrapped his arms around his girlfriend, pulling her close.

The view, it was agreed, was not as good as last year's mountain. Lynn, in her best deadpan voice, said she would try not to feel cheated—but it came out sounding less like a joke than a grim truth.

Bruno said it was one more strike against Germany. Many German cities, he reminded them, teemed with unexploded ordnance from World War II. "Buried underground," he said as the group turned away from the view to head back to the inn. "All these bombs, and they built right over them."

Allied bombs and grenades, five, ten thousand of them. Bruno was still explaining as they arrived back at the guesthouse, where the nervous-looking wife was dusting the outside windowsills. The other guests—loud jolly red-faced Germans seated at a long picnic table on the patio—had already settled in and begun their drinking.

Thousands of tons of buried bombs, Bruno said. Who knew what might set one off.

*

The poor wife seemed to be dusting or sweeping some floor or surface the entire duration of our stay, Lynn would write in a letter to her mother from the airport five days later. Funny how easily facts and emotions could be flattened, neutered. The letter would reduce the weekend to yet another comic anecdote. Only after she had mailed it did Lynn understand what she had done—belittled her own experience—and wish she could take the letter back.

*

Their reservation had been made for six people, but when the nervous-looking wife showed them to their room, there was—to Lynn's surprise—just one big square bunk bed.

Made of wood and broad like the floating dock Wolfy and his cousins used to dive from in summer. On each bunk a flat futon-like mattress was rolled like a scroll against the wall.

Lynn said, "German way to ensure there's no hanky-panky?"

"Ah, but if we were in France"—Markus slung his backpack down to the floor—"it would be a *ménage à . . . six.*"

Wolfy, grateful for this communal bed where only the merest cuddle could take place, kicked off his hiking shoes, pulled off his dusty socks, and took his sandals from his pack. The first two times with his new girlfriend had been in the missionary position, but the third time she had been on top, which Wolfy never liked, the way the breasts hung in his line of vision. It had taken him a long time, and he had resorted to fantasies that, afterward, deeply shamed him. Only on the fourth occasion, when his body had failed to comply, had he dared to ask her to use her hand instead, so that he could close his eyes and take refuge in his imagination.

*

There was an outdoor shower—a big wooden box around a high tap—that they took turns at. Lynn wanted Markus to join her there, to have a brief moment alone together. Maybe that would make things feel less "off." It would also give her a moment to tell him, in private, about the lectureship.

She had meant to tell him ever since arriving. But each time they were alone she found she didn't want to ruin the moment by introducing thoughts of the future. "How about a shower?" she said now, smiling in a way she hoped he would understand.

"You go ahead." Markus unrolled the mattress on the bottom bunk so that he could flop on top of it, and let out a dramatic sigh.

Lynn blamed the awful magenta sneaker-boots, and having forgotten to bring a sweater. Otherwise she would not seem so ridiculous, and Markus would still want to be with her.

Really she knew it wasn't that simple. From the moment he accepted the Vienna post, Markus had been quietly dialing down his love. That was why she had taken the lectureship. It had seemed a way to save the both of them: Markus would not have to admit that he no longer loved her, and she would not have to feel she had been left behind.

But first she would have to tell him.

*

They ate dinner out on the patio, under the stars, and wrapped themselves in heavy blankets when the air grew cold. Then they moved inside, where the room smelled of woodsmoke, and the nervous husband brought them a tray of little shots of schnapps, each a different flavor.

At the other side of the room, the Germans had joined two big tables together and were singing loudly. Bettina and the others looked at them with envy. They could never be like that. They were Viennese, correct and culturally proud, if old-fashioned. Their idea of a wild time was, for instance, the New Year's Eve when at midnight they had danced a minuet instead of a waltz.

But they had fun sipping the schnapps, guessing which fruit was which. They even ordered more of the plum one, because Wolfgang's girlfriend said it was lucky. She instructed everyone to make a silent wish.

Bettina wished for clarity about the baby situation—that she would know what she wanted to do.

Lynn wished Markus would love her the way he used to.

Wolfy wished for what he knew he could not have.

They raised their glasses and drank. Lynn was still wearing Markus's sweater and pushed the sleeves up, feeling warm and rosy

149

from the schnapps. When Bruno asked what classes she would be taking come fall, she told him that at this point she was just finishing her dissertation.

"Might you come here, then?"

Lynn felt herself shift in her seat. "Well, no, because I've accepted a lectureship."

"At Harvard?" Bruno perked up.

"No, a college outside Boston." She said it casually, but already saw from Markus's face that she had made a terrible mistake. She felt her own face reddening as she told them about the job offer, that these positions were hard to come by and that the lectureship would greatly help her future prospects.

Markus appeared to be gritting his teeth. Lynn wondered if it were possible that he had, unbeknownst to her, intended to ask her to join him here. Or perhaps his tense jaw was due to her having announced her news in front of his friends, instead of in private.

When the others moved over to the big stone fireplace, Lynn lingered behind with Markus, her face burning.

"When did you take this job?" His voice was loud enough that surely the innkeeper-wife, sweeping the floor a few tables away, could hear. When had the offer come, and when had she planned to tell him? Etcetera. No pause between the sentences, as though Lynn weren't meant to answer.

And in fact, when she opened her mouth to speak, Markus cut in. "Why are you even *here*?" He stomped off to the other room, as if unable to be near her.

*

On the big smushy sofa in front of the fireplace, Wolfy was polishing his spectacles with the bottom of his shirt. He scooted himself over to make space for Markus, who slouched into the cushions in a bodily pout. When Markus crossed his arms, one elbow lightly

150

brushed against Wolfy's. At the warm surge that swept through him, Wolfy pulled his arm away.

He had always found Markus handsome, but then, who didn't? Many a time Wolfy had tried to reassure himself this way. Other times he was certain everyone must know what he felt. Now, as Bruno continued to explain to them something about the opera house in Barcelona, Wolfy felt another awful surge, and stared into the fire.

The first time he ever felt such a surge was as a child on a sailboat where another boy, a teenager with curling blond hair, had smiled at him—no more than that—and his body did something it hadn't done before. Then there was a boy at camp he couldn't stop looking at. After that came the fantasies. But in moments like this, when the shivers came, he pushed them away.

Even so, he could not help wondering if Markus's arm might again accidentally brush against his.

*

Dregs of the schnapps stained the bottoms of the little glasses. Lynn sat alone at the thick wooden table, shifting from guilt and despair to anger and petty regret: at spending the precious funds to come here, and at having bothered to wax her bikini line. It was one thing to have a bad time on a vacation, quite another to know that it ought to have been wonderful, and that it was only you—the two of you together—who had rubbed out that possibility.

And now here she was, nowhere to escape to, because she was stuck on a mountain.

A fucking *mountain*!

Had she been truly alone, she would have allowed herself the indulgence of tears. But the Germans were right there, joking and singing, and the innkeeper-wife was dusting the bookshelf across from her. The rest of her group was over by the fireplace, where

Bruno, perhaps in an effort to keep up with the Germans, had ordered another pitcher of beer. The pain of her aloneness was all the worse for being surrounded by so many other people.

She left the table and went to the rented room. Under the yellow light of the too-bright bulb, she opened her backpack and found the journal in which she had intended to record her daily adventures but had yet to write a word.

On the big square wooden bunk bed, the rolled-out mattress was flattened from so many past bodies. Lynn covered it with one of the sheets, tucking the edges underneath. Then she lay on her stomach, opened the journal, and in messy script wrote encouraging words to herself. Soon she had filled an entire page. She was well into the second page when Markus came in.

She looked up at him, not caring if he saw her tears. But it was the journal he had noticed.

"What are you *writing?*" As though the act of writing, in a moment of heartache, were an affront.

Lynn leaned over the notebook to shield it, then realized how it must look: as if there were something meaningful written there, something secret, something about *him*—when really there was just the one bland sentence, again and again. *This will soon be over.*

She would keep that notebook long after other diaries and letters and postcards had been tossed away. She wanted proof that her heart had been broken, and that she had survived.

*

And how did they decide where, on that bed, each of them would lie?

It wasn't a decision so much as the fact that Lynn had already fallen asleep on the bottom bunk, and that Wolfgang's girlfriend, concerned that she would need to pee during the night, didn't want to climb the ladder in the dark. She lay down next to Lynn, leaving space for Wolfgang on her other side.

152

Bettina pulled herself up to the top bunk, exhausted in a deep, pressing way that was utterly new to her. With the last of her energy, she scooched over to make room for Bruno.

But he had drunk nearly the entire pitcher of beer all by himself and was too sloshed to manage the ladder. He plunged heavily onto the bottom bunk, next to Wolfy's girlfriend, and immediately began snoring.

Bettina, too tired to care, heard her brother sigh, and felt the bedposts creak as he hoisted himself up. He lay next to her, heavy and still, and even as she drifted toward sleep she felt sorry for him; she had witnessed his anticipation in the weeks leading up to Lynn's arrival, had seen his face glow whenever he spoke of her. No wonder he was hurt.

As everyone slumbered, Wolfy pulled on a clean tee shirt and pajama bottoms and stood staring at the bed. He took a deep breath, removed his glasses, and climbed up.

Everything was blurry, and he had to squint to find the light switch, leaning precariously to flick it off. Since Markus was lying on his back, Wolfy turned his body away from him, facing out. But he could still smell the eucalyptus scent of Markus's soap.

His skin tingled. He tried not to inhale the scent, not to feel the heat from Markus's body. He tried to think instead of unpleasant things, like his poor girlfriend trapped next to snoring Bruno. He felt sorry for her, for the inevitable letdown that lay ahead. Because it would be only so long, he knew—a month or two more, probably—until she began to suspect. There were only so many times, he knew from experience, that he could do certain things, or fail to respond, until a woman began to take things personally. Until her disappointment became palpable, and Wolfy would experience another type of guilt—not at who he was, but at the hurt he had caused some poor woman to feel.

Wolfgang's girlfriend was one of those people who in their sleep spread out like a starfish. Lynn, facing the wall, felt a leg, and then a full-fledged kick that shoved her own leg over. Then an arm flopped itself across her face. Lynn didn't care. She wasn't sleeping anyway. Each time the girl flung her limbs around, gradually rotating, diagonally, across the mattress, Lynn told herself it would be over soon.

Up top, Wolfy was still wide awake. Even when he at last managed to doze, it was a half-sleep, aware all the while of Markus. And when the opaque glow of dawn began to show itself, Wolfy drifted into a terrible, wonderful dream.

He was with Markus in an enormous bed, their bodies moving together.

He awoke with his cotton pants stretched tight. Behind him, breaths faint from sleep. He realized that Markus had spooned against him, one heavy arm around his torso. The shallow breaths were warm against his neck. And against his buttocks Wolfy felt the firm pressure of another man's morning erection.

It happened so swiftly. Even as he tried to shift his hips away, there came the pulsing rush—the swell and surge and the horror of it.

*

The morning sky was cloudy, the air oddly cool. The Germans were already outside at the big picnic table, drinking tall mugs of beer. The nervous wife was sweeping the entranceway, apologizing for dirt that Bettina, rushing to breakfast to stave her nausea, couldn't see.

Lynn, who had woken to find herself lightly pinned down by Wolfgang's girlfriend, was last out. Stepping onto the terrace, she noted the eerie stillness of the air and heard the proprietress saying something to her.

She shook her head. "I don't speak German." One more of her failures.

"Ah, right, you are American." The proprietress asked where Lynn had come from.

"Harvard!" If nothing else, she would live up to this woman's expectations. She hurried to the table where her group was already eating their fruit and muesli.

"Your eyes look strange," Wolfgang said. "You are allergic?"

Lynn reached up and touched her puffy eyelids. "It's because Markus made me cry."

Markus, pleased to be bestowed such power, leaned over to kiss her cheek.

Lynn accepted the kiss but envied the others—Bettina and Bruno so firmly in the hold of their relationship that they did not even need to speak to each other, and Wolfgang and his girlfriend in the bloom of new love. Thinking of the long climb ahead, she said, "Maybe I'll stay here today. I have a book to read. I can join you on the way back down."

Immediately she saw that Markus had taken the suggestion as another rejection. He pulled away as Bruno asked, "You do not want to reach the top?"

"My shoes are no good." She gestured at the magenta sneakers.

"Maybe I'll stay here, too," Bettina said, to show solidarity with Lynn, and because her morning queasiness was surprisingly worse today. "It's so cloudy—will there even be a view?"

Wolfgang said, "But we weren't going to come back this way, remember?" The innkeepers had told them about a return route that went straight to the base camp, where they could rent a cabin for the night.

And so the six of them dragged themselves up the dusty trail. Markus and Bruno were at the head, Markus storming forward as if the entire enterprise were pointless now that Lynn had taken a job in America. A few strides behind them, Wolfgang and his girl-friend walked side by side, and then came Bettina and Lynn.

Bettina watched her brother march angrily ahead. Next to him, as if he weren't a bit hung over, Bruno was whistling an aria from *L'Italiana in Algeri*. As the melody spun through the air, a strange and terrible thought came to Bettina. It was that she did not love Bruno.

This thought came to her so swiftly, so clearly, she stopped, and heard Lynn ask if she was all right. Yes, she said, even as she wondered how she had spent three years with him already. It seemed obvious now that her affection had only to do with their shared love of music and friends in common, as well as the perk of having Bruno's apartment to go to when she needed a break from her brother. In fact, the more she thought of it, as they continued along the path, the more it seemed to her that she did not even really like him. The qualities she had once admired—his constant cheerful-ness, and the way he seemed to know, or have an opinion about, basically everything—suddenly seemed irksome.

By late morning the path had narrowed, each switchback sharper than the last. Every so often they passed hikers already making their descent. One was limping. Some had scrapes where brambles or sharp stones had scratched them. Some shook their heads and laughed: "Sure you want to keep going?"

Wolfgang's girlfriend called out, "I think Lynn had the right idea, to stay at the inn!"

Next to her, Wolfy watched Markus stomp ahead. In bed, he had known the very second Markus awoke—because Markus pulled away as if having touched a hot coal.

More hikers were coming down now. One had a bloody knee. Trailing at the back with Lynn, Bettina called out, "We can still turn back!" She wished she were at the inn, napping on the big square bed.

Yet they continued on, even as another batch of battered hikers descended. "What an awful mountain!" they all joked, to make it seem less true.

Higher and higher they climbed, until the morning's guesthouse seemed like something from a long time ago, their jumbled night in the big square bunk bed no more than a strange dream.

*

The final stretch of the trail was very steep. "Orthogonal," Markus and Wolfgang joked. Bars like handles had been attached at some of the tricky places, to help hikers haul themselves up.

Wolfy stayed close to his girlfriend in case she stumbled. It seemed to him the expedition had become something more than a mere hike—a dangerous quest, or perhaps a punishment. They continued to climb, not really talking any more, too out of breath. Bruno had quit his whistling. They had to pay attention to where they stepped; some stretches were little more than ledges of stone like shallow stairs. There was even a sort of rope ladder near the top.

When at last they reached the summit, the sky had filled with clouds.

Markus dropped his pack, raised his hands above his head and bellowed into the air, a theatrical howl—but in the expanse of gray it sounded more like a lone wail. Then he plunked himself down and leaned his elbows on his knees. Lynn sat down beside him, and the others flopped down where they were, except for Bettina, who gingerly took a seat next to Lynn and immediately began rummaging through her pack for something to eat.

"You're looking in your sack," Bruno said, "when you should be looking at the view!"

Bettina raised her eyebrows. "What view?"

Everyone laughed, because what else could they do? No view, just a world stuffed with cotton batting. Bettina was relieved to find a package of biscuits in her bag.

We are in the clouds. If you said it that way, Lynn thought, it sounded mysterious, ethereal, rather than just cold and gray.

With pocketknives they sliced dry sausage and peeled more of the runty apples. Triangles of cheese wrapped in foil were passed around. Like in those children's tales Lynn used to read, where the hunchback would be tested by a sorcerer disguised as an old woman asking to share his lunch. *I have just some stale bread and a thermos of beer, but you're welcome to it.* Lynn, too, felt humble, unworthy, there on the cold gray peak. An American girl who had waxed her bikini line yet hadn't thought to pack a sweater. Perhaps she, too, was being tested—how long could she stand the rebuff of this boyfriend who no longer loved her.

Bruno was telling them about trepanation. He had seen a documentary in which a man trepanned his own skull.

"And filmed it himself at the same time!" Markus said, in German. He had spoken only German all morning.

"He used a dentist's drill," Bruno explained, "straight into the frontal lobe."

Bettina, finishing off the last of the biscuits, looked into the thick wall of clouds and knew she would leave him. The thought frightened her. Because she also knew that she would keep the baby.

The man drilled the hole, Bruno said, to achieve a "higher consciousness."

She would end things as soon as they were back in Vienna. No point in waiting. All that mattered was that she could raise this new being with pure love. She hadn't known, before, that she could feel this way.

"A sort of lobotomy," Bruno said. "But in ancient times it was to rid the patient of evil spirits."

158

Markus said something in German then—something that made everyone laugh.

"Markus," Lynn said, her patience gone, "please stop being a prick."

Markus stared at her.

"How about acting civil until we get off of this mountain," she said, "and then I can take my leave?"

To her surprise, Markus did not frown, or turn away, or stomp off. He knelt down and took her hands in his. Head bowed, he took an audible breath, then looked up.

"Lynn, please don't take that job. You could stay here with me. We could live together."

Lynn was aware of the others watching. She was aware that Markus was asking her to stay with him—and also that he had not, in his phrasing, *asked* her. He had made no clear statement of desire. Which seemed to her a symptom of some larger problem. Something unsolvable.

She considered saying something prudent: *Let's discuss this in private.* Instead she gave a small but clear shake of her head.

For a moment Markus just knelt there. Then he stood and stepped away. Standing apart from the others, he brought his hands to his face.

Slowly, quietly, everyone began to speak. Murmurs. They finished eating, and stood and stretched. Wolfy looked over at Markus, and it seemed that Markus was crying.

Wolfy went to him then, and touched his shoulder.

Markus flung Wolfy's arm from his. "Leave me alone, you faggot!"

The words echoed in the sky. For a moment Wolfy could not move. But his feet took him back to where his girlfriend waited. He touched her elbow. "Let's go."

But she was squinting at him. And even after they had pulled their rucksacks up over their shoulders, and were heading down the mountain, she seemed to look at him differently.

First there were more of those handlebars, and then an incline of dusty pebbles that rolled underfoot. Lynn, in her magenta sneaker-boots, slid and slid, and sometimes fell, feeling all the more a stupid tourist. Markus, at the head of the file, never stopped to ask if she was all right.

Soon they were all quite dusty, their shins a chalky white. Wolfy, hanging back in self-imposed exile, thought of the invisible dust the German innkeeper-wife had been constantly sweeping. It had seemed like obsessive compulsion, but now he wondered if there had been something there, something none of them could see. Perhaps she only sensed it, the tracked-in dirt of so many guests. Perhaps that was what made her so anxious. So many filthy thoughts.

Bettina, slip-sliding behind Lynn, didn't mind the dust. Each pebbly, rolling, tripping step brought them closer to the base camp, and bus ride, and train, and then home, where she could begin her new life.

Bruno, ahead of her, pebble-surfing behind Markus, kept up his whistling, as if to insist to the world that they all were absolutely fine. Bettina winced to hear it. She envied Lynn with her puffy-from-crying eyes, and Markus so upset he could not speak—that they could feel so strongly for one another, become upset over each other that way. It seemed a crime that Bettina had never felt that strongly about Bruno. No great anger or sadness or desperate longing.

She did not know, yet, that she and Bruno would fight passionately for many years ahead. Long litigations, loud vituperations, a fervent sparring over their son. In fact, their fighting would be more impassioned than their romance ever had been.

As for her brother, when, one day long after the hike, Bettina mentioned the mountain to him, Markus (by then married, to a woman a decade younger) claimed to recall only two things: that the view from the peak was a disappointment, and that he had not been kind.

*

Lynn had been married for over a decade when she told her husband about the hike.

Not that she had purposely withheld it from him. She rarely had reason to recall it. When she did, it was with the understanding that she had been as bad as Markus—too prideful to state her wishes or speak the truth.

She and her husband were looking at a map of Germany with friends who had been cycling through Bavaria. "I just remembered this awful hiking trip." She pointed to a section of the map—"Somewhere here"—and looked for the mountain with the ugly-sounding name.

Her husband pointed at a mountain that wasn't the right one.

"No, that's not it." Her eyes searched the map. Perhaps they hadn't been so close to the border after all. Perhaps it was further west.

She bent closer, searching for a name she recognized. She even borrowed her friend's reading glasses. But it seemed the mountain had disappeared.

*

"There was this giant bunk bed," Wolfy told the man with whom he would spend the final thirty-four years of his life. "The kind you see in those lodges."

They were sipping wine on Wolfy's patio. He was in his mid-forties by then but had never told anyone about the hike. Now he described the sound of cowbells greeting them when they emerged from the woods, and the shimmery dew on the grass the next morning, and his feelings for his friend. "I wrote a poem about it," he confessed, and told of the poetry class taught by the friend of his former lover.

Though the hour was late, he went to his desk and found what he had written. It was still there where he had hidden it years ago, in a folder at the back of the bottom drawer.

The braided tercets seemed to him to have been waiting. With the typed-up poem on his lap, he settled next to his new friend, and together they read it aloud to each other.

Seeing

It had been this way for over a month now, ever since the mid-July evening when Kristin, her feet comfortable in thick socks and cushy sneakers, her cotton shorts and fresh tee shirt light and soft, had gone on her usual evening walk. She liked to stroll for a half hour or so before dinner, to stretch her legs after long hours at the town clerk's office, where she spent each day in a chair of orange vinyl, dialing telephone numbers, attempting to collect on delinquent water and sewer bills. Evenings were her own, watching the smooth folds of the Sangre de Cristo Mountains bend sunshine into a series of dark shadows and glinting slopes of light. Many of the dirt roads along her walk seemed to head straight into them. Though she would have liked to follow those paths of winding gravel past farms and cattle right into the land itself, she never did. She was a young woman alone on an evening stroll, and those country roads were possibly dangerous, ruled by mangy, unleashed dogs defending no one's territory, and handmade crosses where loved ones had died in car wrecks.

That Friday evening in July had been a pleasant one, the sun hitting her neck like a kiss. Kristin was going on three years here in New Mexico. Before that she had lived in Arizona, with a husband who cheated on her and a mother-in-law who defended him. The move had allowed her to look at her past as though it belonged to someone else. She chose her friends more carefully now, taking her time, living quietly, enjoying her solitude and the modest adobe casita that was her home.

On her walks, she always kept to the street that ran parallel to the main road. Though fairly well-trafficked, it was narrow and sparsely inhabited, passing nothing but private residences, a shady ravine, and an expanse of scruffy fields. Even the bright clear sky could not penetrate the ravine full of shadows, brush, and snakes. No one ever went there except escaped convicts from the local penitentiary. Such escapes happened fairly often, since the jail was badly run, with poor ventilation that caused the guards to leave the doors and windows open. It was not an uncommon sight to see men in bright orange jumpsuits scurrying along not far from the highway, hoping to miraculously blend into the silver-green sagebrush. Because the ravine was their favorite hideout, it was where they were most often apprehended. The reliability of this fact meant that, instead of causing fear, the ravine held for Kristin a certain pleasant familiarity. Its darkness was a refreshing contrast to the flat, parched fields that followed.

Shade shifted to brightness as she continued past the ravine and emerged into full light. Prairie dogs stood at attention, then scurried off to disappear into dusty brown holes. A few men in pickups passed, calling briefly to Kristin, their dogs yapping halfheartedly at her from trailer beds. Kristin had grown used to this. No matter where women went in this town, men drove by in menacing, oversized trucks and leaned out of tinted windows to whistle at them.

"Hey, baby!" It was Kristin's policy to ignore such comments, but this was a voice she recognized. "How goes it?"

In the other lane, coming toward her, was Leroy Sanchez, from the town clerk's office. He was in charge of property taxes and was nice enough. Kristin waved at him as he slowed his car, a silver two-door in poor shape.

"Taking some exercise?"

"Gotta keep fit!" Kristin said this even though she had serenely resigned herself, ever since the move here, to always being somewhat plump.

"All right, you do that!" called Leroy. "But don't forget you're bringing the donuts Monday!" A car was coming up behind him, so Leroy waved and drove on.

Kristin didn't want to think about work now; she was settling into her weekend mood. She concentrated on the warm breeze and the angle of the light. To her left were those preternatural mountains—so immense, they rivaled the sky.

From behind her, she heard a clattering sound, and the helpless noise of a broken muffler. The noise approached slowly, with difficulty. When it sidled up to her, Kristin saw a shiny red truck, badly dented, its windshield an enormous web of cracked glass. The driver, a man in a blue bandana, leaned over to ask, "Want a ride?"

"No thanks." Kristin had been taught to be polite. When her mother died of stomach cancer, five years ago, Kristin had found herself thinking the tumor a consequence of her mother's impeccable manners. All those years of false smiles and white lies, all the things she had never allowed herself to say—her true, impolite, feelings—had grown into a malignancy, eating her up from the inside.

And yet Kristin found herself just as polite.

"You sure?" asked the man.

"Yup."

The truck continued on. Its wheels were those mini ones. They stuck out slightly to the side of the truck's body, lowering the entire vehicle so that as it crept away and turned down a side street, the truck looked to Kristin like a pregnant cat attempting to stalk a bird, its belly grazing the ground, tailpipe dragging behind.

Kristin had to give the guy credit for daring to even think someone might want a ride in that thing. His truck looked not only uncomfortable but illegal.

Ahead, an older man on an equally rickety bike was approaching. Passing her, he gave Kristin a somber nod. She nodded back. Along the barbed wire fence that marked the fields beside her, magpies muttered at each other. The chirping of a million crickets made it seem the fields themselves were singing. And then Kristin heard, again from behind her, the same clatter of muffler and tailpipe. The glossy red truck slowed beside her. "Get in," said the man with the blue bandana.

"Excuse me?"

"Get in." He did not sound particularly insistent. Kristin ignored him.

"Get in so I can fuck you," he added conversationally.

For a moment she did not feel threatened so much as affronted. Perhaps she had misheard. She couldn't help but look at him.

The man's face was relaxed, and he wasn't old, maybe her age, twenty-five or so, with brown eyes, shiny skin, and thin eyebrows. He coasted alongside her as if the pickup were a pet that needed walking, so that Kristin knew she had not misheard. Adrenaline shot through her. But then a car came from behind, and the man was forced to continue ahead.

He was sure to come back, Kristin decided. That was clear from his eyes, which had been filled not with determination but with boredom. They indicated that he was driving simply to pass the time, and that in discovering her the man had found the temporary motivation he usually lacked. She could guess what he would probably do next: drive to the end of the long paved road, turn right once, onto a side street, right again, onto the main road, right onto another side street, and then back toward Kristin.

To continue on her usual walk would prolong the situation, especially since her route ended in an office park sure to be abandoned at this hour on a Friday. To turn back meant an equally long stretch of unpopulated landscape, but at least she could count on a steady, if thin, stream of traffic.

Annoyed, Kristin turned back, and soon, as expected, the clanking, low-bellied truck was next to her, this time coming from the opposite direction.

"You've got nice legs," the man said. "I'm going to open them wide."

Kristin kept walking, wondering whether to answer him. Perhaps he was one of those only slightly criminal men who were easily scared away. The kind who wouldn't be riled to anger if you told them to go fuck themselves.

The man leaned farther out the window. "You've got nice tits. Don't you want these hands on your tits?"

The pretense of ignoring what both she and the man knew was happening seemed ridiculous. Kristin stopped and looked at him.

His face was smooth, his jaw and forehead unworried. Kristin tried to read his eyes, lusterless but not particularly cold. Maybe he wasn't much to be frightened of. "C'mon with me, baby," he said innocently, expectantly, as if this tactic usually worked for him.

Another car came, forcing him to move on. Kristin exhaled, thankful, as the red truck clanged away. But it was no real relief. The man would certainly come back. And Kristin had yet to pass the ravine, with its messy brush and dark hiding places, no one there to help her. What had once seemed cool and beautiful she now understood to be the ideal spot for a man in a blue bandana to pull over, park, and attempt an assault.

The cops tended to take too long to respond to complaints (and she could already hear how her call would sound: silly, generic, petty, as if she were some kind of prude who couldn't stand up for herself). But she could call her friend Melanie to come pick her up—although she would have to wait an awfully long time for Melanie to get here. Better to call a ride, if there was a driver nearby.

Kristin took her phone from her pocket, hailed a car, and prayed for luck—though already she saw on the map that there were (no surprise) no drivers out here.

Cesar will arrive in 15 minutes in a black Honda Accord.

She took deep breaths. She couldn't stand here waiting. Think, she told herself. And be prepared to scream bloody murder.

Just past the ravine were private homes. On a Friday evening with weather as fine as today's, people were sure to be outside, drinking beers, tossing balls to their poorly behaved dogs. Someone will hear me, Kristin told herself. And I have my phone . . . Approaching the ravine, she became convinced that she could scream, that she would be heard, that there were people all around to save her.

And then she saw one, a savior. He was a young man on a bicycle, wearing a helmet and little biking gloves, looking very serious. It was an all-terrain bike with thick tires and various pieces of equipment strapped on. Kristin knew what to do: wave to the cyclist and explain her situation, ask him to please accompany her for a few minutes in the other direction, back into civilization. The man peddled toward her expertly, and Kristin prepared her brief plea.

When the moment came, something happened: Kristin doubted herself. Who could say she was truly threatened? She didn't want to be a fool. Her ex-husband often told her she was too jumpy. One time when he was drunk and fell down the stairs, she ran to him faster than she knew she could, screaming as loudly as she ever had, certain he had broken his neck. When he saw how worried she was, he laughed and stood up, showed her he was only bruised. Maybe now, too, she had gotten carried away. Maybe she was being stupid. If something happened, she could call 911. Otherwise, why create drama, as her ex-husband would have called it.

The cyclist looked so intent on his Friday evening ride. Seeing him made Kristin feel safe again, reminded her that this was a street like any other, where people walked and rode and drove. Who was she to make this person turn around and ride back with her, out of his way, just because she was afraid of some silly man in a blue bandana?

Nothing bad was going to happen to her. She simply wasn't that sort of person. She had lived for twenty-five years keeping out of trouble. And so she watched the man peddle past her, hunched intently over the handlebars. He did not appear to see her.

Crickets chirped with alarm. In mere seconds, the hopeful feeling floated away. Kristin tried to slow her heartbeats, told herself she was in control. She made her way forward. A minute passed. As if it had been waiting for the bicyclist to leave, the red pickup slunk around the corner, coming from the narrow side road that circled the ravine. Seeing Kristin heading in his direction, the man in the blue bandana pulled over ten or twenty yards ahead of her, on the opposite side of the street, his back to the ravine.

Kristin considered her options. Just a few feet in front of her, to her left, was a wide side street that led to the main road. She could keep straight ahead, toward the man, or she could turn down this street. If she ran very, very fast, she might make it to the main road before the man could catch her.

But her legs were shaky enough already, and she knew better than to consider herself a runner. And then she understood: running down that street was precisely what the man wanted her to do. Because on the side road there were no other cars, no cyclists to yell to, no houses nearby to hear her scream. That was why he had put himself ahead of her. To scare her into a less protected area.

That meant—Kristin considered, still walking slowly toward the man—two things. One: he was not entirely stupid. Two: he was not entirely convinced. As long as she stayed on the street they were on right now, he was uncertain of his own capabilities. He knew as well as she did that not far ahead were houses where people might hear them, and that any minute now a car might drive by and witness him there on the other side of the road taking off his shirt, as he was right now, saying, "Don't you want this body on top of yours?"

He's not sure, Kristin told herself. He's not entirely sure.

Taking a deep breath, she continued past the side street, in the man's direction.

He was walking out into the middle of the road now. "What's wrong with this body, huh?"

If I don't look scared, Kristin told herself, he'll wonder why not. I could even record him on my phone—no, that might just egg him on. Maybe if I keep my hand in my pocket, he'll wonder if I have a weapon.

"Oh yeah, baby."

Look like you have a weapon.

Look prepared to use it.

Kristin continued toward the man. She looked straight at him and placed her right hand inside the other pocket of her shorts. In this pocket was a small flat key tied to a shoelace. She had never liked carrying all her keys with her on her walks, took just the house key along. Now she balled her fist around it, the tip pointing out for self-defense, and, looking right into the man's eyes, walked straight ahead. Never had she allowed herself to feel so preposterously confident.

The ridiculous thing was that it worked. The man began to back away, toward the other side of the street, where his truck loomed like a sore bully.

The moments after blurred into Kristin's rushed heartbeats. All she knew was that, as she made her way past the ravine, the man retreated into his truck, his window rolled down, saying things to her that she would never let herself repeat. It was then that Kristin ran, faster than she had ever run, toward the houses and families and driveways waiting a short distance ahead. Her legs propelled her as if of their own accord, and she realized that she was doing something she had never done before. She was running for her life.

*

"Have a good weekend, Kris?" Leroy Sanchez didn't wait to put the box of donuts down before helping himself to a vanilla cream. This was his week to buy snacks, and he had selected, as he always did, all sorts of flavors no one else liked.

"Good enough," Kristin told him. "I went to Santa Fe with Melanie." The two had spent an afternoon shopping the back-to-school sales. They had also gone on a mildly depressing double date with two Navy Seals Melanie had met at a bar the previous weekend, but Kristin decided that wasn't worth mentioning.

"Carol and I took the boys for a run in the ski valley," Leroy told her. By "boys" he meant the eight dogs he and his wife left unattended in their yard all day. Sometimes they acted as vicious guard dogs, growling and baring their teeth, and sometimes they just lay around on the shady parts of the driveway. "You ever go hiking there?"

Kristin, leaning back in her chair of orange vinyl, did not reply. On the ceiling, she had spotted a speck of blood. The blood was red and fresh, right near the edge of the wall above the window. It appeared to be expanding.

She stared at it, wondering if it would become a puddle. That was the one image she remembered from reading *Tess of the d'Urbervilles* for her English class back in high school. Now it was happening right above her, here in the town clerk's office. She wanted to say something but did not want to cause alarm.

She decided to phrase it as a question. "Doesn't that look like blood up there?"

Leroy looked up. "Yeah, remember, all of the window frames were that color."

Kristin shook her head.

"Must be left over from when they first painted the windows. I guess it was before you started here. Thank god they repainted them. This place felt like a barn."

Kristin thought she might cry. All the time now she witnessed horrible things, only to be told they did not exist. The blood was only paint, and the moaning sounds that last week she thought were the gasps of a dying man were only her next-door neighbor having sex with his landlady. She did not dare mention to anyone the terrible things she saw all around her: the dead baby lying on the side of the road; the deformed boy weeping at the movie theater; the blond teenager strangling his girlfriend outside of the burger place. These turned out to be, respectively: a crumpled paper bag, a perfectly normal boy teasing his mother, and lovers kissing. But for a few terrifying moments they had been those other things.

If only the police hadn't told her. Kristin had called them, back in July, as soon as she caught her breath, calmed down, and felt safe, to report the man in the blue bandana. She did not call Melanie, or her godmother (who lived in Utah and worried about everything), or the guy she had dated briefly last year and now sometimes met for beers or a movie. Instead she had called the police, watched the first two episodes of a new series on HBO, and gone to bed early. The next day the police informed her that the man was in their custody and they needed her to come to the station—where, after identifying him from behind one-way glass, she was told she might have to testify in court. The previous night, the man had raped a woman and left her for dead.

The victim was in an induced coma, recovering from surgery. Kristin could not stop imagining what the other woman had gone through, what it would take to come back from that. What it would take to move forward again. The more she pictured it, the more afraid she felt—more afraid than when she had been running for her life. Not only might she have possibly prevented this disaster, if only she had called the police earlier, while on her walk, but that woman could have been *her*.

She was now one of those people, the ones she read about in the paper, recounting brushes with tragedy or horrible accidents they had witnessed or suffered. She always thought of them as "those people"—the people bad things happen to. Catastrophes too awful to dwell on. Things no one should be forced to contemplate.

So, she decided to never again mention the man in the blue bandana. She did not tell anyone at work, just as she had not, in the weeks since, mentioned the other horrible things that she—and only she—witnessed. Often she thought of the cyclist peddling so swiftly by on that July evening, how he seemed not even to see her.

He did not see because he could not. He wasn't one of those people.

Sitting at the town clerk's office in her chair of orange vinyl, Kristin knew that only a few people were able to see. Now she, too, because of the man in the blue bandana, saw.

Leroy munched contentedly. Kristin waited for the tears to recede behind her eyes, so that she might, every few minutes, monitor the red fleck above her.

Communicable

The first time it happened—though she didn't exactly take note—was when the plumber reemerged from the basement to report that the water was back on. He wore the kind of mask that protruded like a snout and kept to the border of the kitchen, directing his comments only to Leland, though Marlo had been the one to make the appointment and usher him inside. As though Leland really were the man of the (rented) house and not a lover arrived just days ago. Marlo watched from the heavy oak dining table that had become her office, wearing knit fingerless gloves to compensate for the feeble heating. Something fluttered just beyond her knee. But when she looked, there were only the scratched wooden floorboards, with dark knots like misshapen eyes.

"I'll see if we've got the part in stock," the plumber said. "With shipping delays, orders are taking some time."

From behind his own mask—of wrinkled fabric—Leland asked about using that bathroom. He had a habit of hunching his shoulders to accommodate those shorter than himself, and against the persistent chill wore the padded jacket a friend had given him—apparently retrieved from a dumpster, washed, and, failing to fit his friend, handed off to Leland. It was deep blue like his eyes, with sleeves a half inch too short. His wrists poked from the cuffs, making him look as much a child as his true age of thirty-six.

While the plumber delivered what to Marlo seemed a preposterously lengthy response to a simple question, Leland nodded along, pausing to tug the cotton mask back up to the bridge of his nose. In their weeks apart, Marlo had often pictured him—the tousled hair, the violet flecks in his eyes—and the word that came to her was *dreamy*. But with the mask, his eyes looked severe rather than a frankly penetrating blue.

It was as he again reached up to adjust the mask, hiking the somehow ludicrous jacket above his waist, that she saw another shadow. More like a flicker. The moment Marlo sought it, it disappeared. She glanced at the overhead light. The house possessed many quirks. Marlo had found it online, through a real estate agent, after everywhere she could afford had been snatched up. She had waited too long to leave the city, hesitated even as provisions dwindled and hospitals filled—had put off her decision because of Leland.

They had been dating only a few weeks before the lockdown and when Marlo finally left had slept together only twice. The first time was the night before the email from Marlo's company directing employees to bring home all they needed to work remotely. And as Marlo filled a cart with cans of soup, sacks of rice, and dried beans precious as ancient beads, her next thought, beyond panic, had been, *Will I ever see Leland again?* He lived with roommates in a fifth-floor walk-up on a grim street down by the Manhattan Bridge. With fears of even a shared subway car, the distance between their apartments became a vast and perilous gulf.

Now, she watched him show the plumber out and checked the time. Marlo was director of marketing for a company that designed office furniture, and endured daily meetings with her boss (a mildly infuriating man who had already contracted the virus and survived). Leland ran his own nonprofit, the Community Project. In normal times he spent his weekends documenting whatever activity he had organized (pop-up tuba concert; barbering classes; painting murals on a stretch of city street), to post clips on his social media accounts. Marlo usually found such look-at-me behavior cloying—but this was to bring in donations. Leland's posts garnered hundreds of hearts. He also belonged to an online network of people who recycled their belongings not simply to reduce waste but also to avoid spending money. If someone needed a new cellphone, say, they asked if anyone had an old one to give away. Same for sofa beds, wrapping paper, wart remover. No request was too large, small, or strange. Marlo knew this because Leland had invited her to join the network, where she saw people posting photographs of trash on a street corner: *Found this free armchair, just missing one foot!* with the geographical coordinates, no seeming worries of bedbugs or otherwise. Leland and his roommates had furnished their entire apartment via the network—perfectly nicely, though Leland had no mirror or desk. Marlo couldn't help wondering, if he were ever to give her a gift, if it would come from this list. But four years had passed since her divorce and she was tired of the dating apps, the disappointments. She liked Leland's energy, his keen mouth and hands that even the first time knew just how to touch her, and wanted to do things differently.

"Here, fuel to get you going." Leland had removed his mask and slid a bacon-cheddar scone before her.

She was supposed to curb her salt intake due to high blood pressure, but she didn't want to sound defective; she took a bite. "Mmm, delicious."

Yawning, Leland took a seat across from her. Marlo reached over to wipe the residue of sleep from his lashes. "Trouble sleeping again?"

"Yes, but it doesn't bother me." An edge to his voice. Apparently, he had experienced insomnia for years.

"I was hoping the country air would be a soporific." She said this even though she herself found the bedroom somehow unnerving. She wondered if Leland had noticed the strange feeling in the room but hated to mention it if he hadn't.

He said, "The key is not to stay in bed if you can't sleep. That way you don't associate the bed with lying awake."

Marlo had been aware of Leland leaving in the night. "What do you do when you get up?" She had been wondering this since his arrival two days earlier.

"Read, or stretch, wait until I feel sleepy again. Last night I did some tai chi." He took a sip from his coffee mug. Like Marlo's, it was glazed a morose shade of green and chipped at the brim. "In the past, some women I was with weren't able to deal with it."

The mention of previous women had her sitting up straighter. "You mean—your insomnia bothered them?" (It bothered her, too, but she was determined to acclimate.)

"I don't know exactly. They decided they weren't comfortable with it. You know how some people are."

Some people. Informing Leland about the rental, Marlo had been ashamed—at her desperation to escape her sleek building (especially the elevator), and at how easily she had shelled out no small amount of cash for a scrappy cottage three hours from the city. She once heard a friend say of her that she *threw money* at problems. Marlo was single, childless, and made a good salary—not to mention the divorce payout, after Reggie's affair with a paralegal from his firm. The staggering shock, after six years of what she thought to be a happy marriage, was worth something after all. Marlo did not live grandly, but if something broke, she paid someone else to fix it. If disaster struck, she bought a ticket out of it.

Yet money could not mitigate the fundamental awkwardness of being thirty-nine years old and dating during a plague. It was hard enough getting to know someone new. Frightening, even. Marlo's friend C.J. had already told her she was moving too fast with Leland. She said the virus was a perfect excuse to slow things down.

"But I'm afraid of losing him."

"Lose him—where's he going to go? The entire planet is on lockdown."

"We're just getting to know each other. If we don't stay close, he could lose interest."

"Shouldn't you be focusing on figuring out how *you* feel about *him?*"

C.J. was such a killjoy. No wonder she was still single.

It was Marlo's main partner at work, Pamela, who convinced her to invite him—not that Marlo would have admitted it to anyone. People thought Pamela was batty because she did things like claim to be *mildly psychic* and, if a coworker ever did something obnoxious, sent the person a *forgiveness memo* stating why the behavior had been hurtful and that *this memo is meant to be open and forgiving* because she believed that failing to be truthful about one's feelings caused them to manifest in other, harmful ways, drawing out residual emotions lingering in the atmosphere—to say nothing of the fact that, upon receiving the company email about the building closing due to the virus, she had used Reply-All to urge everyone to rinse their sinuses with a mixture of salt and lukewarm water. She had also, once, refused outright to work with an employee she claimed had conducted himself deceitfully. Actually, Marlo privately admired her for that. Another time, Pamela declared herself *unable* to work on a textiles partnership because she had a *bad feeling*—and, sure enough, the textile company's owner was accused of embezzlement. In her late forties or early fifties, Pamela was VP of communications and had an enviable aura of calm about her, plus she was brilliant when it came to marketing campaigns; probably her uncanny ability to read people was what she meant by *psychic*. She was the person who, during team brainstorms, would serenely watch everyone work themselves into a corner, and then suggest, *Or we could just . . .* Always something simple yet right—which, Marlo supposed, was how she got away with all the nutty stuff.

Marlo and Pamela worked in tandem and often chatted together before and after meetings. Soon after Marlo had bought the used Honda to relocate to the farmhouse, she found herself telling Pamela, at the end of one of their calls, about Leland. Was it too soon to invite him along? Friends told stories of boyfriends who turned out to be nightmares, or simply annoying. Either way, it scared her.

Pamela said, "Listen to your intuition, not your fear. Intuition allows us to take action. Fear paralyzes us. Let it be *you* deciding— not your fear."

Taking another bite of scone, Marlo decided she would simply tell Leland she liked less salt. Easy enough. Problem solved.

*

The shadow-flickers returned a day later while she was on a call for work. On-screen her coworkers appeared less polished, some with unmade beds in the background, some with pets, small children, sulky teens sidling up, to be briefly indulged then swatted away. Her sales strategist (huddled in a laundry nook to escape household noise and her children) was constantly having to tell her youngest, *Not now, sweetie, I'm on a call.* And each time Marlo glimpsed his little head entering the frame, a pang went through her, at not having her own child to sweetly bat away.

She hadn't dared tell Leland she hoped to have children, for fear of scaring him off. She hadn't told him about the painful, expensive process she had undergone to have her eggs extracted and frozen. *You know Marlo: throwing money at a problem . . .*

What would frugal Leland make of an extravagant medical procedure for a purely hypothetical possibility?

Her friends found it incredible that Marlo had yet to hold the do-you-want-kids conversation with Leland. Was it the fact that Leland had yet to ask *her*? She hated to sound like one of those women simply looking for someone—anyone—to father a child. There was also the matter of her true age, which Leland did not yet know. On the dating app she had entered her age as five years younger, since everyone told her men wanted younger women. And it turned out to be true, the men who chose to meet her uniformly believed themselves older than Marlo. She had intended to tell Leland her real age the night she met him—but by the time she remembered, that fact, too, felt like something she needed to introduce at the right moment.

"For the semi-opaque ones, I'm thinking something like 'Refuge'?" her marketing manager said. He wore his signature bolero hat with a blousy silk shirt unbuttoned to mid-sternum, so that some wispy chest hairs were visible. Though still in his twenties and possessing no great talent, he had been prematurely promoted, apparently because he reminded their boss of the younger version of himself.

From the laundry nook, her sales strategist said they needed something less literal. "What about 'Aura'? Like a cloud, rather than a divider."

Because of the virus, they were having to reconceive their entire product line. Community spread meant no more shared office spaces, no more hot desks. When people returned to work, it would be in cubicles, as if it were the nineties again. Today they were naming a line of plexiglass partitions easily erected between desks.

Marlo watched as the marketing manager pontificated in front of what looked to be a professionally stocked bar. The sales strategist had turned her screen off, which meant she had at least one child seated on her lap. Pamela sat in calm solitude before a bed on which posed a subtly shifting black cat.

"Mar?" Leland poked his head in, hair mussed in his youthful way. "Have you seen my jacket?"

Marlo smiled, gave a little shake of her head; he would understand she was in a meeting. Leland whispered, "Sorry!" and disappeared from her view.

Something flickered at Marlo's elbow. She kept her eyes on her monitor. "Okay, how about these ones with storage?"

As possible names were tossed back and forth, Marlo involuntarily checked her hair in her little box on screen. (There was only so much longer that she could keep touching up her roots; soon she would have to re-dye, risking Leland noticing.) She swept a stray lock behind her ear. Though she no longer wore her sleek jackets or sharp-heeled boots, she still used a hair iron and eye makeup before her meetings. She could not imagine attempting her role without them.

Meanwhile, these men with their five-o'clock shadows and unmade beds . . . and the marketing manager with his stupid hat and bare chest . . . When he turned off his video, his black box was replaced with a photograph of him in semi-profile, wearing sunglasses (though the photo was clearly taken indoors) and the flat-topped hat but with a different—tapered—shirt, also unbuttoned to the level of his nipples, his chin angled dramatically toward his shoulder, his one visible eye peeking over the rim of his shades. If Marlo used a picture like that—if she wore a bolero to work with her blouse unbuttoned down to her bra—she would be laughed out of town!

The sight of the photo, like the hat and unbuttoned shirt, brought on the same low-grade resentment she could not help feeling at Leland's ill-fitting jacket—that he could wear a coat found in the trash and be taken seriously, while she had to iron her hair and swipe on eyeshadow. On his video calls Leland rotated the same two faded button-down shirts, plus the scrappy padded jacket, without being mistaken as destitute or insane.

What about the young men his program helped? she wanted to point out. Would he send them to an interview in threadbare shirts and too-small jackets and expect anyone to give them the time of day?

"File-r-upper ..." the marketing manager was saying.

"Smorgasboard," said her sales strategist, hunkered in the laundry nook.

From the hallway, Leland pantomimed: Could he borrow the car? Adding, in a half-whisper, "Must've left my jacket at the post office."

Marlo pointed to where her purse (which held the car key) hung from the doorknob, as something flitted past her hip and a notification popped up on her screen. The network, someone in her neighborhood in the city asking if anyone had a spare desk. Even with the nation wiping down groceries with antiseptic cloths, leaving mail to sit for forty-eight hours, people were still exchanging items.

Marlo clicked the notification away, trying to focus, as Leland thanked her and left.

When at last her meeting ended, she and Pamela purposely lingered. Pamela looked tired. She asked Marlo about life in the country and, when just the two of them remained on-screen, "How's it going with Leland?"

"Great—really well!" Marlo told her how it felt to have his help shopping at the grocery store, Leland keeping a place in the long, slow queue while Marlo foraged for flour, bouillon cubes, boxes of pasta in strange shapes that were all that was left on the shelves. Back at the house, lathering their hands under the rushing spout as hurriedly as if they had touched a corpse, Marlo felt, she half-joked to Pamela, like a real couple!

But something on Pamela's face looked—what? Disappointed? As if she didn't quite believe it? Perhaps Pamela was envious. After all, she was a good decade older, not to mention still single. Marlo asked, "How are you holding up?"

"It's been hard. Home alone, day in and day out."

This was something else Marlo liked about Pamela. Never the reflexive *Fine, and you?* Marlo wished she could be like that.

Pamela said, "You know, I'm used to a balance of solitude and socializing. I had the perfect life. I sang in a choir, I swam on Mondays, took a blacksmithing class on Wednesdays—"

"Blacksmithing!"

"—and Friday was Lindy Hop night. Now all that has evaporated. Sometimes I'm just . . . sad."

Her voice through the computer audio was hollow. As if her voice, too, were caught in a square black box. Marlo wanted to reach out and hug her. She felt herself about to invite her to join her and Leland in the country house. But no, that would be crazy. She said, "That sounds tough."

Pamela said, "You were smart to invite Leland to come out. Everyone who has someone with them right now is lucky."

"Well, except for people stuck with people they can't stand."

"True," Pamela said. "The grass is always greener."

For a horrible moment Marlo imagined herself alone in her own apartment, without Leland to accompany her through the torrent of emails, the online meetings that managed to bleed into every hour of the day. With everyone working from home, she now found herself scheduled for meetings at all hours, five in the morning with a London distributor, seven thirty in the evening with the Seattle sales team . . . To go through this alone, no one else in her box of an apartment to turn to, would be hell.

"I do feel lucky," she told Pamela. And though not usually superstitious, Marlo rapped on the wooden chair, just in case.

*

She asked Leland about children on a suddenly warm afternoon on the south patio. While the north side hadn't yet shaken the bleakness of winter, here one could feel the sun and watch bumblebees dawdle in the bushes.

She was glad to be outdoors. To escape the eeriness that lately seemed to have spread throughout the house. Something not quite right . . . Though she tried to tell herself it was nothing, the sensation affected her concentration—just when she needed to prove herself, with the consolidations at work. Yet she hesitated to mention it to Leland, wanting to preserve the even rhythm they had created. Also, it was the kind of thing some eccentric spinster like Pamela would say.

In the sunshine, her unease floated away. Marlo felt less burdened. Reclining in the wicker chaise, laptop balanced on her thighs, she was mid-email when a shadow-flicker swept through her periphery.

This time she took full note. "Did you see that?" she asked Leland, who was working at the wrought-iron table, munching on a cider donut from an orchard he had stopped at on one of his drives.

"No, what?" He wore the pale blue sweatshirt she loved, that made his eyes twinkle. In just over two weeks, his hair had reached his ears, thicker and lightly mussed, like a teenager's.

Marlo indicated the area by her leg. "I thought I saw something."

"Chipmunk? I think they're planning a coup."

It was true the chipmunks were hard at it. Each seemed to have its own fiefdom; interlopers were chased away in what looked like adorable skirmishes but were probably incisive territorial battles.

Leland held the bag of donuts out to her. She waived the grease-stained thing away. She couldn't eat baked goods as he could, without repercussions. Leland was always bringing home bread products, having taken over most of the errands now that Marlo headed her company's digital division, too. While Leland's patronage of small-town grocers near and far was sweet, he had somehow managed, so far, to always let Marlo be the one to fill the gas tank.

Another shadow-flicker—quicker this time. Marlo knew it wasn't a chipmunk. She was about to say, "There, see"—but stopped herself. She didn't want to sound insane. She told herself it had to do with the way the sun was passing through the clouds. She looked up. There were no clouds.

Please don't let it be eye trouble. Not now, when all the doctors' offices were closed. Probably it was from too much screen time. The consolidations meant Marlo spent even longer hours on her computer. Not to mention that her boss had made *her* do the layoffs.

She tried to remember what the eye doctor had told her about torn retinas, or was it macular degeneration? Something about "floaters" or dark spots. Was that what these flickering shadows were? She couldn't ask Leland. That sort of thing was an old-person problem.

She was suddenly terrified that there was something really wrong.

Leland yawned. "Time for my post-prandial nap."

Marlo tried not to show annoyance. She had begun to suspect that his naps contributed to his insomnia. But the one time she suggested he try to push through, Leland had looked at her with affront, as if her insensitivity to his malady were a sign of hard-heartedness.

He also checked his cellphone in bed, though the light from such devices was known to interfere with sleep. He was always posting on his various social media feeds, to keep people engaged in the foundation while its activities were stalled, since he had lost some large donors. He called it the KEEP CONNECTED CAMPAIGN. Marlo had seen some posts: the gothic-looking turkeys, the solitary deer that liked to nibble placidly on one unfortunate tree, a garter snake peeking out from a rock . . . Leland did not feel the need to hide his abandonment of the city. He came up with comical tag lines for his photographs (for the turkeys: *Sure, it's beautiful, but I miss the city—here no one ever seems excited to see us*) always with a link to the Donate button. Apparently, each brought in a slew of small donations.

Was that what he worked on in the wee hours?

A chipmunk, cheeks bulging, ran right across Marlo's foot. They really were cute. Marlo watched it scurry to the stone wall to fit itself into a dark little hole, its perky tail upright like a flag. And in that moment, Marlo managed to blurt out, "Have you ever thought about having kids?"

"Yeah!" Leland said it brightly, as though recalling a fun leisure activity. "I've always thought it'll happen however it's meant to happen."

Men could do that, wait and see. Her ex—six years older than Marlo—had done that. He and the paralegal (whom he had gone ahead and married) now had twin daughters they dressed in absurd matching outfits. Never mind that the paralegal had been a subordinate; Reggie's indiscretion had not prevented him from making partner at the firm. He got the whole enchilada, as C.J. had put it.

C.J. always knew how to make Marlo feel a blow.

Pamela had told Marlo she needed to rid herself of her resentment. That if internalized, it would warp how Marlo viewed the world. Of course, *Marlo* would be the one whose attitude had to change. Not cheating, paralegal-poking Reggie. (While *Pamela* could outright refuse to work with that guy *she* no longer trusted, and completely remove *herself* from a project based on a negative feeling!)

Marlo was prepared for Leland to ask if she wanted children of her own, but his phone pinged. Though his projects were stalled, he still fielded plenty of calls.

He reached over to give Marlo's hand a squeeze. "Sorry, Mar, I have to take this."

His phone was a small, refurbished one acquired through the network. As he spoke, Marlo secretly congratulated herself: she had asked the dreaded question. The answer wasn't anything other than what she ought to have expected. She needn't worry anymore.

*

When she and Leland went walking together, they rarely saw a car, let alone another human, just the occasional fleeing deer, or a hawk lifting with the wind, or cows whose tails spun like dials. If they did cross paths with someone, it was usually the old man at the farm down the hill, standing at the opposite side of the road to chat while his three dogs barked ferociously from behind an invisible electric fence.

Leland asked the man about the house they were renting, where the owners had gone.

"Been empty a good year now. Guy had a landscaping business, but must've had trouble. One day he up and left. Wife and kids, too."

When she and Leland continued on their way, Marlo wondered aloud if the couple still owned the house, whom exactly her rent went to.

"I wonder if they're still a couple," Leland said. "Maybe they were splitting up." He slung his arm around her. "A few of my friends are going through that now. Relationships I thought were rock solid. But I guess after a certain amount of time . . . who knows. Must be rough." He let go to pick up a bright rose-colored stone from the road, examined it, tossed it aside. "What about you? Know anyone who's been through a divorce?"

Marlo kept her eyes on the pebbly road before her. The problem was that when your husband left you for another woman, it sounded as if you were insufficient—a reject. She said, "No—well, maybe I should say *not yet*." She tried to laugh.

"Yeah, well, you're a few years younger than me. Give it some time." Leland took her hand in his. She held tight, as noisy birds clamored in the trees, and said nothing more.

Later, at home, Marlo thought about what the man down the road had told them. It made sense that the family's finances hadn't been good, when she considered the state of the house—the weak plumbing (the part for the toilet had arrived only last week), constant draft, whole place needing a fresh coat of paint. She always emphasized these facts in her phone catch-ups with C.J., who had gone to take care of aging parents in a house in Vermont and sounded cold and lonely. Bitter, too; her brother wasn't helping one bit. Marlo had told C.J. about searching for a plunger in the basement and discovering a stash of empty vodka bottles—twenty, thirty of them—behind a panel near the washing machine. Dusty, some covered in cobwebs. Was this why the landscaping business had gone under? "Someone was hiding their drinking problem."

"Drinking while laundering," C.J. joked. "Depressing."

"Leland brought them to the dump. He says the important thing is to take action, not get emotional. When I'm heartbroken over the news, he talks me down. It's such a breath of fresh air compared to what I'm dealing with at work. They just furloughed another fifteen percent of the company. Leland makes everything seem manageable."

"He's your knight in shining armor."

Marlo couldn't tell if C.J. was being sarcastic. She decided to keep the tender moments for herself. The (loving?) way Leland held a buttermilk biscuit to her lips on one of her now nonstop days. Eyes lighting up when she emerged from her shower, as if she were an odalisque and not a nearly forty-year-old in a fuzzy blue bathrobe. Dancing around together to old rockabilly songs when they cooked dinner, how he paused to brush her hair from her face and kiss her.

She wondered what small, unconscious actions she might have taken that pleased him without her knowing it.

"How's his insomnia?"

Of course C.J. would go there. Marlo explained that though he still had some trouble, after nearly five weeks of this, it no longer disturbed her. "I mean, half the time the coyotes wake me up." There was a wolf in the pack now, she had noticed. A lower, deeper howling than the others.

Sometimes, seeing the empty spot in the bed, the void seemed to chide her—for all she still did not know, did not understand, about this person she wanted to be close to. As if it were some error on her part. That if it weren't for the lurking unpleasantness of this room, of this house, Leland would be here in bed beside her.

One day, Marlo noted something to perhaps support this notion. It happened during a work meeting, the morning after Leland's question about divorce. A shadow flickered near her elbow. And on-screen she saw—was certain she saw—Pamela's eyes dart to where the shadow-flicker had been.

She saw it, Marlo thought with a jolt. Saw, and then couldn't see—just like me.

There was no time to chat after the meeting, and Pamela didn't mention it. But Marlo had seen her eyes. This gave her confidence to say something to Leland.

She waited until dinnertime—Leland's spaghetti, steam rising into the chill air. "Don't you think this house has a weird energy?"

He was twirling his noodles around his fork, a miniature hay bale. "What do you mean?"

Marlo felt a small deflation, that he had not picked up on the strangeness. "I think something happened here."

Leland seemed to really be thinking. "You mean—because of what the plumber said?"

The plumber. When he at last returned with the missing part, Marlo had noticed the way he paused in the entryway to glance around the combined living-dining room, as if looking for something. She had ventured: "Did you know them?"

"Family that lived here? Nah. Must've been doing their own plumbing. Or *trying* to."

"Did something happen to them?"

"Other than the business failing? Not that I know of. Small enough town, I'd hear about it. Cops had to come here a couple times. Wife was a screamer."

Marlo stared at him. "What do you mean?" She asked even though she wasn't sure she cared to hear his answer.

"Guess they liked to bring the local brass into their marital spats. Some folks like an audience."

She didn't like the plumber at all, then.

To Leland she said, "Maybe that's what I'm thinking of."

Because anything else would just make her sound like a madwoman, and she didn't want him to think of her that way.

*

By mid-May, peonies were blooming on the east side of the house, heavy wadded pink clumps. Marlo cut stalks to bring inside. Despite the signs of spring, the air still nipped at them; Leland wrapped himself in a wool blanket (he never had found his padded jacket), and Marlo still wore her fingerless gloves. The peonies leaned in a tall vase near her desk so that their sweetness infiltrated her meetings. The petals crawled with shiny black ants.

Today's meeting was just Marlo, the marketing manager, and Pamela; to Marlo's dismay, her sales strategist had been furloughed. Worse, it seemed she did not intend to return. With her children home, and summer camp likely to be canceled, and who knew about school come fall, she said she could no longer do two jobs at once.

190

She was probably right about school. Today's meeting was for the company's "At School At Home" campaign—office furniture repackaged for domestic use. Secretly Marlo wished the marketing manager had been furloughed instead. If you told him (twenties, single, childless) you needed him at a sales conference in Grand Rapids, he would make a wincing sound and say, "You know, I just don't think I can fit it in." Whereas her sales strategist (thirty-seven, three children) would take a long deep breath, pause, and say, "Okay, I'll see what I can do."

Marlo's favorite graphic designer, too, had been let go. She was a single mother with two young sons, one of whom had some severe condition that required him to live in a residential facility, which had closed due to the virus. Marlo had no idea how she was managing.

On small calls like this, Marlo liked to arrange her screen so that she could view everyone at once. Through the open dining room window came a robin's expert whistling, and the cute interrogative whine of goldfinches.

Not now, sweetie.

Even in the warmer weather, the marketing manager wore his bolero hat, with a shiny blue shirt unbuttoned to mid-chest. Marlo adjusted her earbuds as Pamela said, "We want to sound upbeat but not false. None of these kids *want* to be home." Behind her the cat, regal, eyed the camera distrustfully.

Marlo heard the door open. Leland must have woken from his nap. He asked if she had the car key.

She turned to give him a quick wave and indicate her earbuds. Her purse, in which her keys were buried, hung from her chair, but something stopped her.

"Sorry to interrupt," Leland whispered. He pointed to her purse as he approached her, made a key-like gesture.

Pamela said, "Is that Leland? Handsome!"

"Yes!" How proud it made her, to be able to say, Yes, he's mine!

As he hovered behind her, Marlo reached into her bag for the keys, tossed them to him. A pillow-crease marked his cheek. He thanked her and ambled out.

"So *that's* what lured you out to the country," the marketing manager teased.

But something was happening to Pamela. She was no longer smiling. Her eyes were blinking. Her mouth was open. She seemed to be staring at something.

"Pamela?" the marketing manager asked.

Marlo looked behind her. There was nothing there. "Pamela," Marlo asked, "what do you see?"

Pamela rolled her chair backward, as far from her desk as possible. The chair bumped the bed, startling the cat. It leaped away, off-camera.

The marketing manager said, "Is there something happening on the news? Is that what you're watching? Marlo, are you on Facebook? I'll check Twitter."

"No, I'm not," Marlo snapped. "Pamela, what's wrong?"

But Pamela's little on-screen box disappeared.

"I'm messaging her," Marlo said, as her marketing manager, scrolling through his phone, said, "I'm checking my feed, there's nothing happening."

"Let me call her."

There was no answer. No one was able to reach Pamela for the rest of the day.

*

It was like she was hallucinating, they explained on their group call the next day, when Pamela still hadn't returned any messages. Though one of the designers who lived in her neighborhood had tried to check on her (at Marlo's urging), Pamela hadn't answered

192

the intercom. When Marlo suggested contacting the police, their boss said it was Friday, "let's give her the weekend—you know how Pamela can be. She logged off on her own, so she hasn't had a stroke or anything. Maybe she just needs some time."

The fact was, everyone seemed to have expected this. Hadn't Pamela always been crazy? Clearly pandemic isolation had driven her over the edge.

Meanwhile, ever since that day, Marlo had been seeing, all around her, the flickering shadows. They gathered round in swarms.

She never had spoken to Pamela about the shadow-flickers. Since Pamela hadn't mentioned them, Marlo hadn't dared ask what she had seen that one time. Now she tried to recall if those circumstances had been similar. This time Pamela had seen Leland walk in, and then: what?

She tried texting Pamela again.

I'm worried about you. Do you need help?

Silence.

There was no sign of Pamela on Monday. But when Marlo asked about contacting the police, her boss said he had managed to reach Pamela and not to worry—then refused to say more. Marlo forced herself not to dwell on it. But by Friday, when Pamela still hadn't returned, Marlo, desperate, called her boss to ask, "What's going on?"

"Oh, I meant to tell you. Pamela got in touch a few days ago. She decided to take the severance package."

The early retirement package being offered to more senior employees, to help reduce overhead.

"You mean, she's not coming back?"

"No, she said she's done here."

It was a slap—a punch. "But—"

"She said she's been wanting to start her own consultancy. That this way she could take a break first. Have a rest."

It was true Pamela had mentioned wanting to go out on her own—but now surely was not the time!

Marlo immediately texted her.

Are you okay? Know that you can share with me what happened.

And hours later, when Pamela had not responded:

Pamela, you can tell me what you saw.

All week, the flickering shadows had grown so frequent, so teeming, it seemed impossible Leland didn't see them. But he sat peacefully at the other end of the dining table, typing into his laptop, the fuzzy wool blanket wrapped around him.

When she could no longer stand the shadow-flickers darting round, Marlo typed:

Pamela, if what you saw has to do with me or Leland, I beg you to tell me.

The reply came within minutes.

You haven't been forthright with him

Marlo stared at the message. She was considering how to respond when Pamela wrote again.

Rage attracts past rage

Lies breed & proliferate

Marlo turned off her phone. This was no time for that kind of crazy talk.

"You okay?" Leland placed his palm on her forehead as if taking her temperature, then leaned down to kiss her before taking a seat next to her.

"Pamela quit." She could hear her voice shaking.

Leland gave a tsk. "She have kids at home, too?"

"No, she's not—"

"Oh, right, the kooky one."

They were Marlo's words, yet they sounded wrong. "She wasn't just kooky."

"I meant . . . isn't she the one who, like that time someone was dishonest—" Leland stopped himself. He leaned back, away from her.

Marlo felt herself stiffen. "Yes," she said, "all of that nutty stuff."

Leland slid his chair back. The violet flecks in his eyes looked like sparks. For the briefest moment, Marlo was afraid of him.

"She took the early retirement package," Marlo said quickly.

Leland said nothing. Marlo could not look at him. She looked down at her phone with its darkened screen.

At last Leland said, "Well, I guess that would explain it."

"Yes. I suppose I'd take it, too."

She dared to look up. Leland's gaze pinned her to the chair. Marlo said, "More work for me. Yippee."

Leland gave a quizzical look. When Marlo looked away, he said, "Just don't burn yourself out."

*

That night in bed, the coyotes woke her. It always happened this way, a single coyote's cry, then another's excited yapping, and another, as if the yowling were contagious. In her half-sleep, she envisioned the house's former owners out there, somewhere among them, howling.

Wife was a screamer.

She could hear the wolf now, too, its deeper howl. Rolling to her side, she saw that Leland had left the bed.

The skirling outside was wild, pagan. What had they killed out there?

"Do you hear that?" she called to Leland.

She threw back the covers. The floorboards were cool and rough, and she hastily pulled on her socks before stepping out to the dark hallway. A dim light issued from around the corner. She followed it, to the door that led to the basement.

"Lee?"

The bulb above the basement stairs had gone out. The only light came from below, a dull amber glow. Marlo waited for her vision to adjust before finding her way down the steps—wooden slabs that gave small groans under her feet.

A single yellowish lightbulb left most of the basement in shadow. Across the room, past the washing machine, a figure hunched over something.

In the dusky shadow the figure became Leland. He was kneeling, crouched in a posture that at first confused her. His shoulders sloped, his head bowed over what seemed in the haze to be a torso.

Leland looked up. In a pained voice he asked, "Why did you hide my jacket?"

For a moment, Marlo could not speak. She found she could barely breathe. How could he not see *why*—though she struggled, now, to find words to respond to his question. Even in the dark she could not look at the jacket. She asked, "How did you know where to find it?"

He gestured at the crawl space where she had found the vodka bottles those weeks ago. "Isn't this the hiding place?"

The shameful place. Everything she hadn't dared say aloud. Her resentment, her lies. He had sniffed them out.

"I'm sorry, Lee. I don't know what I was thinking." She realized she was whispering.

He was still crouched on the floor, shoulders drooping. Calmly, he said, "I'd like to try to understand. But right now I just need to figure out what I want to do."

She felt her heart racing, chasing after him. "Please don't leave me here."

"I just need to borrow the car and take a drive or something. Clear my head." He placed the plywood cutout back over the crawl space. Stood and brushed the dust from his pajama pants. Tenderly, he draped the jacket over his arm. Then he walked past Marlo, toward the stairs, without looking at her.

In the amber darkness, she watched him make his way across the room. With his long limbs, his pajama pants exposed his knobby ankles, visible only as he passed close enough to the light, before darkness hid them again.

She watched him retreat back up the steps. The squeak of each wooden board was like a tiny cry. Around her, the shadow-flickers gathered, flitting frantically back and forth. She stroked them, and caressed the tops of their heads, before swatting them away.

Oblivion

It was thanks to her aunt Lucille, who had gone to typing school and worked for the phone company, that Joan had her first chance to move up in life.

Bell Canada was looking to hire students over the summer, to help with a system upgrade. Aunt Lucille explained: it would mean exaggerating Joan's age a bit, but that was a small thing. Joan was often mistaken as older than twelve; she had the height and poise of her father (whom she had never known). Her mother, who worked for a manufacturer of roasted nuts, agreed she ought to interview right away, to be sure to be at the top of the list come summer—though it was only February, the streets of Toronto thickly shellacked with frozen slush.

The day of the interview, it snowed. Thick wet flakes came down fast. She did not own a winter coat, only her softball team jacket, an ugly rust-red satin thing with the team's sponsor—Avon Sportswear—spelled out in yellow felt across the back. The letters were stained, grimy, and Aunt Lucille said the jacket would not do. Instead Joan was lent Lucille's enormous green wool coat, which, by the time she arrived downtown, dragged wetly at her ankles.

At the central office, she went straight to the ladies' room and locked herself in a stall. Shook the snow from her drenched toque and mittens and scarf and, with numb, fumbling fingers, peeled off her soaking ballet flats. They were her only good shoes, the leather now sodden, her stocking-toes stained black from the dye. From under her tiered skirt she removed her garters and rolled the freezing wet stockings down from her legs. Briskly she rubbed her shins and calves and toes, trying to warm her numb skin. She shoved the stockings and garters into a coat pocket and tugged her ballet flats back onto her bare feet. At the mirror, she tried to fix her hair. Pearls of water dropped from the tips. She could not stop shivering. But she carried the limp toque and mittens and scarf to the personnel office, where she signed in with the receptionist and took a seat far in the corner.

There were two other people in the waiting room: an older man reading a newspaper and a young woman sitting primly near the door. They saw her and quickly looked away.

When a woman stepped in to ask who was next, the secretary said, very quietly, "Her." And Joan, staring down at her reddened feet, heard, quite clearly: "*That* in the green coat?"

The woman's words obliterated everything that came next—the interview, the paperwork, even the fact that she would be hired. Back home that evening, in the apartment where neighbors' voices leaked through the walls, Joan draped the damp, sprawling coat over the clanking radiator and waited for her toes to thaw. Already she could feel a fever coming on. When her mother, scrambling eggs at the kitchenette, asked how the interview had gone, she just sulked over to the sofa to tug the mattress up—it took three heavy lunges to get the thing out and flat—and crawled into bed. She would have done anything for a door to slam.

At Aunt Lucille and Uncle Wesley's house, her cousin Russell had a door—an entire room of his own. Really, it was just the enclosed back porch, which everyone called the "sunroom" and traipsed through to get to the backyard, but still: he had a door to close, and lived in a *house*. On Clinton Street, in a crowded block of red-brick houses. Two stories if you included the attic. The kitchen had a nook with a bench and wooden table and cream-colored wall-paper on which a shepherd, etched in violet, called to a small herd of sheep again and again. In the living room, the first television Joan ever saw sat on its very own table. Uncle Wesley had fashioned a leaf of translucent rainbow-tinted plastic to fit over the screen, to transform the picture from black and white to color. On Sunday nights, Joan and her mother would cluster together with the neighbors to watch Ed Sullivan, whose face was always green.

Uncle Wesley planned to make a fortune selling his television-tinting device, but that hadn't worked out. Joan's mother—widowed by Wesley's brother, who had gambled away her savings—said this happened to all of Wesley's inventions and was why Aunt Lucille still worked for the phone company.

But they had a *house*. Windows trimmed in white, and a pleated awning that reached over the porch like a starched skirt. A real house of their own.

*

Now, the white trim had flaked off, leaving dark cracks where paint had been. Joan thrust her hands in her coat pockets, the arthritis in her knuckles already reacting to the cold, and noted a torn window screen curling stiffly at its corner. The porch slouched alarmingly.

"So, there you have it," the young neighbor, Rena, declared, with a carefully executed sigh that did nothing to mask her glee at being the one to reveal this cataclysm.

To hide her shock, Joan said only, "It's so small." Fifty-something years ago, when she was a little girl, it had seemed huge, an entire house for one family. She shivered, no longer used to cold

200

weather, and marveled at the scrap of front lawn glazed in refrozen snow.

"I'm so sorry." Though Rena seemed to want to look concerned, her forehead remained oddly still. Joan was reminded of some actress or celebrity . . . invisible wrinkles treated by injections. So, Rena wasn't as young as she thought. Joan glanced at Rena's hands for confirmation, while Rena said, "It's so sad." Her tone carried an accusatory *See what we've been putting up with?* Her own house, of real brick, not the fake wraparound siding that sheathed Russell's, sat directly across the street, with this ruin as its view.

"The caseworker said the place is uninhabitable," Rena was saying. "The nurse flat-out refused to go inside. She said there's no running water."

"He must have stopped paying his bills." But that didn't make sense. Joan had telephoned Russell just last week to wish him a happy New Year, and on Christmas, too. Both times the answering machine had picked up. She hadn't thought it odd that he hadn't responded; Russell hadn't answered her calls or letters for a long time now. No more faux-obscene Christmas cards with jokes about the Virgin Mary, no birthday wishes sung to her voicemail, rhyming "cake candles" with "love handles." Joan lived in San Diego and hadn't been to Toronto in a decade. The last time she visited, Russell had suggested they meet at the museum. Now she wondered if that had been to prevent her from seeing the house. Clearly, even then he hadn't been keeping it up.

"Garbage all over the place," Rena continued. "Cat feces. That's why his hand got infected again. The nurse couldn't change the bandage—she refused to step foot in there."

Rena was the one who had taken Russell to the hospital and somehow managed to track Joan down, a coup considering the splintered nature of their small family. Joan had immediately packed and left word with her husband, who, as usual, was in meetings all afternoon. She had rushed to the hospital first thing this morning. Now she asked Rena, "Do you know how he hurt his hand?"

"Who knows? He asked to borrow some milk, said he'd taken in a stray cat. I saw his hand was swollen. You could see it had been wrapped, but the bandage was unraveled and totally filthy." Rena lowered her voice dramatically. "He said the school nurse bandaged it."

Joan watched Rena attempt to raise her eyebrows. She wanted to explain that it wasn't necessarily a childhood reference, that Russell had been a high school English teacher. Still, even then, his comment didn't make sense. He had retired years ago.

*

The doctor—male, of middle age, shielded from Joan and Russell by a sleek desk—said it wasn't Alzheimer's. The tests showed standard progressive dementia. "What happens is that long-term memory remains comparatively strong while short-term memory weakens."

"I think that's what his mother had." Aunt Lucille had been younger than Russell when her symptoms began, but Joan had moved away by then.

"And your relationship, again?"

"We're cousins!" Russell, proud in his ragged pants and filthy flannel jacket, his hand freshly bandaged by a hospital nurse, had not lost his cheer and at times seemed fully lucid.

"Our fathers were brothers," Joan quickly added, to make clear that any senility genes came from Lucille, not Joan's side of the family. It was what she told herself in those moments when she forgot things, or made an unthinkable error. Composing an email at work the other day (she was associate director of campus recreation for the university's athletics program) she had typed *uv* for *of*—and for a split second this new spelling made more sense than the correct one. And she had wondered: Is this how it happens?

202

Was that how her dashing cousin had turned into a perplexed sixty-eight-year-old with tussocks of gray-black hair sprouting from the sides of his head? His once-firm stomach had become a soft-looking lump. On his right cheek was some sort of contusion. Had he fallen when he hurt his hand? If not a bruise then an age spot, or a lesion presaging something more deadly.

The former Russell would never have shown himself in public like this. He cared about his appearance to the point of vanity, plucked his eyebrows where they threatened to meet, shaved twice a day if he was going out. With his dark Welsh looks, he favored his father, whom everyone had compared to Tyrone Power, hair shiny and black and rising in a peak above a broad forehead.

The doctor said, "I understand that, given the circumstances, live-in help is not an option." He handed Joan a sheet of paper. "Here are some numbers to call."

Joan pretended not to hear Russell say, "I'd really just like to go home."

*

Well, they did have to go back to the house, to find his financial documents. The front door barely opened against the piles of unread mail. As Russell slipped inside, Joan smelled, already, the odor: of wet animal, decayed food, mildew. She stepped delicately past the stacks of yellowed newspapers. A fearful decorum prevented her from glancing at their dates. "Good lord, Russell, no wonder the nurse refused to come in."

He said, "I hope the cats are okay."

"I thought there was just one cat!"

Smartly, he ignored her.

Along the kitchen's perimeter were many stacks of empty cat-food tins. Had he cut his hand on one of the lids? "Why didn't you throw this stuff out?" She was furious at what he had allowed to happen: the grimy walls, the rooms clogged with trash, with egg crates and empty toilet paper rolls—and the big healthy ants parading jauntily across the windowsill.

Yet Russell had no difficulty locating his financial documents, handed them over in their ancient manila folders as if it were only natural he should be so organized. Of course, his papers had been here for decades. He had moved back home during the final stages of Aunt Lucille's dementia, a few years after finishing his Master's in education. Everyone said what a good son he was, so doting, so responsible—conveniently forgetting whatever estrangement had occurred in the meantime.

With the automatic deposits from his school pension, and barely any debits from his account (just telephone and electric and, every so often, an electronic payment to his credit card) Russell had a decent cache of savings. To Joan's surprise, the documents also revealed a mutual fund and a large brokerage account. No matter that everything reeked, that the furniture and artwork were surely unsalvageable. Knowingly or not, her cousin had managed to prepare for disaster.

*

Her summer job at the telephone company began the day after the school year ended.

She had just turned thirteen. At the downtown headquarters, she and the older girls were corralled into the center of a cavernous room, where a circular arrangement of open card files held five-by-eight-inch note cards cataloging every residence, business, and corporate switchboard in central Toronto.

Aunt Lucille and the other typists were distributed along the periphery in front of each of the offices. But in the pit—as Joan came to think of her area of desks and open files in the center—there were women wearing headsets, perched on stools in front of switchboards. Since this was the downtown exchange, entire extensions were dedicated to Eaton's and Simpson's and to the insurance companies on University Avenue. The ladies in headsets were always busy taking calls from the outside world, where all manner of things caused communication failures.

A line was down. A bird's nest was in the way. A basement flooded. Coffee on the switchboard.

COS the women would write—or *No DT* (no dial tone) or *CCI* (can't call in)—and then pass the cards over to the men, who were the technicians. The cards contained all information on any given telephone number, from number of extensions and where the feed line entered the building, to whether there was a cat or dog in the house.

Joan and the older girls sat at the desks by the files, hand-copying all the addresses and telephone numbers from the five-by-eight-inch note cards onto smaller, narrower cards with punch holes down the sides: this was the system upgrade. Monday through Friday Joan sharpened and re-sharpened her pencils, neatly printing the information onto the new, slender cards. Her fingers carried the bosky scent of pencil shavings and by the end of each day were cramped from pressing the lead tips just so. She had always been a good student—had skipped grade three and spent a miserable year having to catch up. (Then came her growth spurt, and the hand-me-downs from Russell that made her feel like a boy, her scuffed shoes pressing against her toes, and free cartons of milk at lunch, so that everyone knew she was on assistance.) She had no choice but to try harder. No matter how many hours her mother put in at work, there was never enough money.

At the table with the older girls, she listened ravenously to talk of boys and crushes and dates, the glorious chatter a great bubbling wave that rose, swelled, crested—and abruptly stopped when the floor supervisor told them to keep it down. At which point the

crescendo would begin anew, gradually building, rising, bursting
. . . and then the pattern would repeat once again. All the while,
Joan observed the older girls, the hue of their lipstick, how they
curled their hair. Tried to see what it would take to become one
of them.

*

When she asked where he might like to go for dinner, Russell told
her, "the Inn," which was no help. Prodded for more information, he
allowed that the Inn was not far from Dundas Street. "I could stay
the night. It's a friendly place."

Joan gave up and instead they went to a cafeteria-style eatery.
Made conversation, somehow, though even as she spoke, she could
feel the past lapping at her. Moments she hadn't thought of in ages.

After the meal, she brought Russell to her suite at the hotel, where
he could have his own big plush bed. While he sloshed around in
the hotel room bath, she called home to tell Ted about the house,
the cat-food tins, the odor. "Honestly, I don't know where he even
sleeps. There's no room left. There's stuff I think he found on the
street. He took a whole wad of napkins from the place where we
had dinner. I didn't realize until we got back here."

Ted asked if Russell's hand was healing. There was a slight pause
before each of his sentences, which meant he was playing solitaire
on the computer.

"I suppose it's healing, but every time I see the bandage I want
to cry." She told Ted goodnight, pulled herself into bed. In dreams
sometimes she screamed at someone—vituperations so hateful she
woke exhausted. But that night she slept dreamlessly. When she
greeted Russell in the morning, he reacted with surprise and joy, as
if she'd just arrived.

*

Their supervisor in the pit was a trim, sandy-haired man in his thir-ties named Bob Buell. The switchboard ladies liked to joke about him in a way that made it clear they in fact admired him a fair bit. Each Friday, as soon as he handed her the envelope enclosing her check, Joan would march straight to the bank, a block away, and with the bills loosely folded, so as not to crease them, continue around the corner to Simpson's.

Her favorite department, on the main floor, near the handbags and not far from the gloves, was called Notions. Change purses of puckered leather with little clasps that clicked together just so, and lipstick cases with a slender mirror fitted into the side, or ready-made collars of different styles and fabrics, to clip onto a dress or a coat.

Last autumn, on their annual excursion to Eaton's for school clothes, as Joan tried not to stare at a pair of saddle shoes she wanted more than anything but knew they could not afford, her mother had been pulled aside.

"May I see your handbag, ma'am?"

There were stockings there, still with their flimsy cardboard tag. The officer led Joan and her mother to a back room reserved, it seemed, for this precise humiliation, and in that windowless room Joan felt something awful bloom inside her.

The truth was that she had seen her mother steal before—in the grocery store, little jars of this or that dropped into a coat pocket, or a wrapped package of meat she slid up her sleeve. Joan hadn't real-ized, when she was little, that it was stealing. Later, she pretended not to know, or that her mother would remember to pay when they came to the register.

Not saying anything made her feel like an accomplice. And ever since the Eaton's incident, she hadn't set foot inside.

In Simpson's, with her telephone company money, she made small purchases, saving up everything that was left. When summer ended, she went back and bought herself a pea coat of dark blue wool.

*

The nursing home said they would have a room for Russell by Thursday. He could move in any time after nine in the morning.

She raised the topic multiple times, to help him acclimate to the idea. "We should get in touch with your friends—anyone who should know you're moving. Do you want to make a list of who might like to come visit?"

Asking, as they drank fragrant tea in the hotel's "breakfast room," she felt the awkwardness of her teenage years, when she first understood that Russell had a life without her. His friends were the clever ones who sang solos in the choir, who were called to the podium to accept awards and recite speeches. Joan had friends, too, but they were teammates, fellow athletes. And though she always attended Russell's performances, and met him backstage after curtain, she sensed that he led a separate existence.

Even as an adult he had never spoken with her about his personal life, had never once mentioned a significant other. A boyfriend, Joan assumed, though Russell never said so. Back in high school, girls went with him to dances, and fell in love beside him in musicals, but nothing came of any of that. Then, toward the end of grade thirteen, there had been some rift between him and Uncle Wesley, and Russell had moved in with a friend.

Now, he said, "You mean, my friends at the Inn?"

"Which inn is that, Russell?"

He just sat there. The tussocks of graying hair made him look distraught. She had a vision of debilitated charges dollied about in wheelchairs—the "droolers and screamers" as Ted (whose father had achieved obsolescence in a nursing home) called them. The ones with bars crosswise at the sides of their beds. She reminded herself that the home Russell would be going to—a neatly maintained network of brick buildings near a park—looked sunny and welcoming, and that she had arranged for a private room.

"We could bring some photos," she said, "make it feel homey. We'll look through everything at the house, see what you want to keep."

Russell nodded gloomily, and she reached out to hold his good hand. The other one wasn't so swollen now that it had been pumped with antibiotics. "How did you hurt yourself, anyway?"

Russell looked at his hand and seemed surprised to discover that it had been injured.

*

The following summer, the year she was fourteen, she was again hired by the telephone company. It seemed a stroke of luck, since the system upgrade to punch cards was fully in place. Most of last year's girls were gone, and the new card system now included pre-coded ones for all possible "telecommunication incidents."

Dropped call. Crackling wire. Scrambled connection. Testing would determine if the incidents were internal (at the home offices) or external (a problem on the wires, or in customers' residences or buildings). If external, the cards would wait in the pending bin while the dispatch office was called.

Joan's new job was to tabulate how many incidents occurred in each category each day, along with their resolutions, completion times, and whether or not the complaint had been made before. At the edge of the new cards, beside each code, was a small hole; when an incident was called in, the repair operators punched the holes matching each reason for the call, leaving a notch.

The coded cards made Joan feel like an archivist in charge of data that only a select group understood. Which, in a way, was true. To sort the malfunctions at the end of each day, she was given an instrument that looked much like one of her mother's knitting needles, but with a handle like that of a screwdriver; she stacked the cards and skewered them at a given hole ("circuit problem in central office"), and cards without a notch punched through the edge would dangle from the needle, the others falling away. She could then count the fallen cards, repeating the process for each code, and send the final tally on for further analysis, so that next morning the previous day's "Repair Index" appeared on a chalkboard over the technicians' workstations.

Her floor manager was still Bob Buell, and her pay had increased. On her excursions to Simpson's, she was joined by another summer girl, Maxine, a slender redhead a few years older than Joan (though Maxine didn't know that). As much as Joan still loved Notions, Maxine favored the sewing department. And though they were not quite the same size, they swapped patterns for blouses and skirts and smart dresses that Joan would piece together on her mother's Singer. There were slender packets of piping that looked like long slim packs of cigarettes, and seam bindings of lace in every color, and little envelopes with needles pinned to shiny colored rectangles of paper like chocolates in a box. Selecting ribbons that shimmered when they caught the light, and satin cording soft as caterpillars, and zippers like the long thin tongues of flamboyant snakes, Joan always took her time. It was the first time in her life that she was able to wear just what she wanted.

*

They were back at the putrid house, sorting through drawers and cabinets for anything worth saving, when Joan heard knocking at the door.

Rena from across the street stood on the porch, in a long sweater and tight jeans and those ugly shearling boots that had been the style for what seemed an unreasonably long time. Joan draped her coat—boiled wool, warm without the bulk—over her shoulders to step outside. Her own boots were cowboyish ones of supple leather, "handcrafted" (meaning that she had disposed of the receipt rather than let Ted see what she had paid).

"So, it occurred to me," Rena said, "to tell you that my brother Michael is a developer. He might want to buy the house."

Joan shivered beneath her coat cape. "But I mean, is it worth buying?"

"Well, the property, yes."

Of course. Joan exhaled and saw the ghost of her breath. Of course they would tear the place down. It was the Annex location that was valuable, not the house. She willed herself not to cry in front of Rena.

Rena said, "It could make things easier for you. To not have to deal with, you know, real estate agents."

Though she did not want to give in so easily, she supposed Rena was right. "Maybe. I'd be happy to speak with him."

"Great! Okay, I'll email you his contact info!" Rena headed briskly back to other side of the street.

Joan remained by the moldy door, dreading returning inside. It wasn't just the smell and Russell's cryptic remarks. It was a creeping fear. That just as Russell had slid from reason to oblivion, she might, somehow, by some trick of time, slide back into childhood, or to some murky place between then and now. All day long, memories had come at her unbidden. Her mother with the stockings in her handbag. Lyrics Russell once sang: *Be ahead of every goodbye, as if it were already the past. Like winter, which even now is passing . . .*

She had spent much of the morning contacting his friends, explaining the situation, and it troubled her that they were as shocked as she had been. It meant they must not have seen Russell for some time. How long had he been alone like this?

211

She felt an old, infrequent, craving—for a cigarette, something to justify staying out here a bit longer—but stepped back inside, bracing herself against the odor. The smell reminded her of the recycling center, and of a man who once sat next to her on the bus wearing what looked to be the only clothes he owned, clearly not having bathed in a long while. The dirty-sweet scent of the destitute.

The thought that came to her next nearly caused her to phone Ted.

Her thought was of the homeless shelter on Dundas Street— that *that* must be the "inn" Russell kept mentioning. The place where he had been sleeping.

*

The year she turned fifteen (eighteen, according to the telephone company) was the year Uncle Wesley died. A heart attack. It happened soon after Russell moved out.

Because Russell moved out, if you asked Lucille.

Though Joan hadn't fully realized it then, it made sense that he and his father would clash. While Russell spent much of his final year of high school writing a musical adaptation of Rilke's *Sonnets to Orpheus*, Uncle Wesley was a man who, watching the *Ed Sullivan Show*, left the room whenever Jimmy Durante came on. That narrow a mind wouldn't have had space for the person Wesley must have sensed his son was turning out to be.

But now that Lucille was a widow, still her son did not move back home.

That autumn, when Russell started at the university, was also the first autumn that Joan was allowed to stay on at her job past summer, to work after-school hours. Her job now included further analysis of the repair index data after the cards had been needle sorted—fanning out each sorted stack like a deck of cards and ticking the corners by hand to count them. Though there was a calculator with numbered buttons and a big hand crank, it was on the desk of one of the full-time women, so she rarely used it.

Her favorite purchases that year were a pair of desert boots and a bottle of White Shoulders eau de cologne.

*

"Ah, a hoarder," was all Rena's brother said when they had to squeeze their way past the decrepit front door. "Pee-yew."

He wore a shearling jacket, khaki pants, and construction boots. As Joan walked him by the decaying walls to show him what was left of the house—while across the street Rena diverted Russell with a neighborly cup of tea—she realized that some part of her still hoped he might see the place as worth saving.

In the basement, he found a dead cat. "Must have starved. Hasn't been too long. He still has his fur."

Joan closed her eyes.

"House is too far gone, but the lot's valuable, of course." He named a price. It was enough money to keep Russell in that good nursing home for a long, long time.

Ted had taught Joan, over the years, how to behave in financial negotiations—not to show any emotion, not to make quick decisions. She gave what she hoped looked like a brisk nod, and said, "I'll consider it."

*

The following summer, a year after Uncle Wesley died, she was given a new position at the telephone company. One of the dispatchers had gone on maternity leave, and they needed someone responsible.

She had her own narrow desk, up on the mezzanine instead of down in the pit, and her own heavy black telephone, and she spent the day sending technicians to addresses all over the city. With her view of the main floor and the bustling pit, with her shiny new pocketbook resting by her feet and the new dress she had sewn radiating the scent of White Shoulders, she felt transformed into a new version of herself. She began smoking cigarettes and even developed a crush on Bob Buell, who treated her as a knowledge-able and efficient employee, not some kid he had to worry about.

When the school year started up again, and the dispatcher returned from maternity leave, Joan was given an after-school job back in the pit, taking calls for the technicians and once again tal-lying note cards. There was now a state-of-the-art machine that pushed the needles through the punch-holes mechanically instead of manually and even sorted the cards into categories—but Joan still had to add them up by hand and call in the final tally.

On a brisk bright day toward the end of spring, Bob Buell called her into his office. He did not smile when she took her seat across from him.

"You've been such a stellar young employee these past years," Buell said. "I wanted to give you a graduation gift. I called the high school, to confirm that your marks were sufficient to graduate. It turns out your marks are superb. It also turns out you're not graduating."

He watched her flinch. "What is your age, please?"

"Seventeen," she said in a whisper.

"In that case you've been seventeen for . . . how many years?"

She could not look him in the eye.

"Do you realize I could be fired for hiring someone underage? You must have been, my god—*twelve* when you started here?"

Joan wondered if it was worth mentioning that she had actually just turned thirteen.

In a quiet, shocked voice, Buell said, "They had you lie."

But if she had told the truth, she would still be shivering in the ugly rust-colored softball jacket.

Buell looked bewildered. "Who does such a thing? Who are your parents?"

Behind her eyes she saw the police officer at Eaton's pulling her mother aside, ushering them into the little back room. To Buell she said, "I'm sorry," so quietly, she sounded foreign to herself.

"And your aunt—I take it *she* knows your true age."

"She was trying to help me." Without Lucille, she would not have a bank account, and a pocketbook that matched her shoes. Would not know to float around in a cloud of White Shoulders.

Buell was shaking his head. In his expression Joan caught her first inkling of what Aunt Lucille had done, of what her mother had allowed—of what Joan herself had been. A child, in an adult's heavy wool coat.

Buell said, well, it was too late now, and in any case Joan was now of age. But in his eyes Joan saw herself shrink to the size of his pupils.

It was the moment she resolved never again to allow anyone, ever, to pity her.

It was the reason she never told anyone about being hired under-age, or the softball jacket worn all winter, or her mother sliding groceries up her sleeve. Well, she had told Ted—but even then she left out, for some reason, the part about the green coat.

*

Who does such a thing? Who are your parents?

Only later had she wondered if Lucille ever had Russell, too, lie. Some "small thing" he had been told was necessary, minor, that then embedded itself in his soul. A representational shame of which he, like Joan, could never rid himself. Or was it simply his mother's ease with deceit, like Joan's mother on her shopping expeditions, that had seeded an unbearable resentment? Was that why he hadn't moved back home until Lucille's dementia was already advanced?

Perhaps not . . .

She wondered this, vaguely, as she used the hotel's business service to print a photograph from her cellphone. Twenty minutes later, she taped the photograph to the wall in Russell's room at the nursing home—a private one, neat and bright, with two big windows facing south.

"See, Ted and I are right here, you can call us whenever you want. I've written our phone number on it, see? And you have my cell."

A framed photograph of Lucille and Wesley, from Russell's bedroom at home, now sat on his bedside table next to the telephone. Joan had placed others, of Russell, young and handsome, throughout the room, to let the staff see who he had been.

Still, she felt guilty; she was leaving him here. "I'll bring some ginger tea for you when I come back next month." The nurse had told her to be prepared for the dementia to have progressed—that Russell might not be the same when she next saw him.

"Thanks, Joanie. You're a doll."

"But no more hoarding." Already she noted that, after their lunch together in the cafeteria, he had taken two of the saltshakers back with him. Like her mother, with a tin of chestnut paste up her sleeve. "You have this nice, neat room here. Why not keep it that way."

Russell laughed, his same old beautiful laugh. If you watched him in that moment, you wouldn't think anything was wrong. But in other moments a flash in his eyes made it seem he had glimpsed what was to come.

She told him, "Toni and Jerome are coming to visit you this afternoon."

"Toni and Jerome."

"Your old friends from work. They live right nearby. You can take walks together. And I'll be back next month. Here, give me a hug."

A flicker of worry crossed his face. She wondered if he only now truly understood that he was to remain here.

"Look, I'll call you as soon as I get off the plane, okay? See, you have your own private line right here. I'll call you as soon as I land."

Guilt made her limbs heavy as she embraced him. Her wheelie suitcase felt heavy, too, as she dragged it out of the building to the waiting taxi. All she had wanted, for days, was to leave, to escape the assault of memory—yet it seemed incredible that she could leave Russell in this foreign land.

She told herself it wasn't such an enormous change; they were just ten minutes away from Clinton Street. With barely a detour, she could stop by for a final glimpse of the house.

But of course she couldn't. It was too painful. A cleaning crew was there right now, emptying the place out.

She shoved her wheelie bag up onto the seat of the taxi and slid in beside it. As the car pulled away from the curb and she took a last look at Russell's new home, she was seized with quiet panic, certain she had forgotten something.

A mere week ago she had known nothing of the grime-streaked walls, the crusty tin cans, the robust, happy ants. Russell's hand wrapped in dirty gauze.

That he could not explain it made the infected hand seem more than a mere accident. And though perhaps it did not even matter, though possibly there was no clear answer, it felt to her like a wound extending from the house itself. From whatever rift had caused him to move out and not return until it was too late. The more she considered it, the more it seemed Russell, too, must have a hidden archive of secret hurts. A deep pain pushed to some tight back corner of his mind.

Like *That* in the green coat.

Like her mother in the hospital bed, saying, "Forgive me, dear? Please?" And Joan letting go of her hand.

Joan had never told Ted about that, either.

*

From her bedroom window, Rena could see the cleaning crew across the street tromping in and out of Russell's house. Strapping young Ukrainian guys with paper masks covering their mouths and noses. Two large dumpsters occupied the entire snow-glazed lawn.

Her brother's truck was there, good. Rena had her tickets for him, to the game tomorrow, since she and Brendan had decided to take a last-minute jaunt to the Bahamas. Still in her exercise tights, she wrapped herself in her cardigan, stepped into her fuzzy boots, and, holding the tickets, hurried across the street.

One of the young men was heaving a near-bursting trash bag into one of the dumpsters. "I just have to drop something off," Rena told him, and headed inside, instinctively plugging her nose. They had opened all the windows, to air the place out.

It was cold in there with no heat. Bulging garbage bags slumped against the walls like carcasses. To Rena's surprise, a telephone was ringing. Not a cellphone with some electronic motif or pop song riff, but the loud, clattering *brrrrrring* of an old-fashioned landline. Rena asked if Mike was around.

"Mike!" one of the boys called toward the attic, as the ringing stopped.

"Sorry to miss your call—please leave me a message!" The warm, deep, confident voice seemed to come from the air.

A beep, and silence. From the attic came thudding footsteps, while from the corner of the living room a voice rose, slow and hoarse.

"Mum, it's me." The scratchy sound of someone clearing his throat. "So, I'm still here, they're taking a long time."

218

A sigh. A low cough.

Heavy footsteps, Mike coming down from the attic.

The corner of the room said, "I didn't mean to just leave like that. I . . . I never meant to hurt you."

There was the sound of labored breathing. "I'll be home late, I guess. They're taking really long. But I really want you to know how much I—"

The beep cut him off.

"Hey, Rena, what's up." Her brother was wearing a mask over his mouth and nose and protective goggles that made him look strange.

Rena meant to explain about the tickets. She heard herself say, "That was Russell. The man who lived here."

Mike said, "I guess we should disconnect the phone."

A whoosh of cold air came from the front door, ruffling the yellowed newspapers. The kid bagging trash was shaking his head. "That guy. He been calling all afternoon."

Acknowledgments

Judging a book contest takes time and energy and is no small task for an author trying to get her own work done. I'm forever grateful to Rebecca Makkai for selecting this book for publication. And I'm equally grateful to the stellar NUP team that has made TriQuarterly such an outstanding home for me.

My gratitude also to the editors of the following magazines for publishing these stories (in earlier versions):

Consequence and *Literary Hub*: "The Archivists"

Copper Nickel: "Three Times Two"

Five Chapters: "Oblivion"

The Florida Review and One City One Story Boston: "Relativity"

Harvard Review: "A Guide to Lesser Divinities"

Memorious: "Awake"

The Missouri Review: "Heart-Scalded"; "Providence"; "Seeing"

Subtropics: "Egg in Aspic" (as "Oeuf en Gelée")

My thanks also to the Somerville Arts Council, Princeton University's Lewis Center for the Arts, and Lighthouse Works.

Thank you to Kate Bergin for use of her fantastic painting—which touches on so many motifs in these stories—as the perfect cover for this book.

Endless thanks to my trusted friends and family who read the many drafts of these stories. I could not do this without you.

Thank you, Mom, and Mamuka, Aunt Magda, and Uncle George, for telling your stories.

This book is in memory of Judy Layzer.